# HEAVEN AND HELL FOR THE TOBACCO GIRLS

## THE TOBACCO GIRLS BOOK FOUR

### LIZZIE LANE

Boldwood

First published in Great Britain in 2022 by Boldwood Books Ltd.

Cover Design by The Brewster Project

Cover Photography: Colin Thomas

A CIP catalogue record for this book is available from the British Library.

Paperback ISBN 978-1-80048-517-4

Large Print ISBN 978-1-80048-516-7

Hardback ISBN 978-1-80415-776-3

Ebook ISBN 978-1-80048-518-1

Kindle ISBN 978-1-80048-519-8

Audio CD ISBN 978-1-80048-511-2

MP3 CD ISBN 978-1-80048-512-9

Digital audio download ISBN 978-1-80048-515-0

Boldwood Books Ltd
23 Bowerdean Street
London SW6 3TN
www.boldwoodbooks.com

*To all my Maltese friends and relatives on the island where I always had a warm welcome.*

# FOREWORD

*Ships of Steel for even keel*
*Need tons and tons of corset steel*

*Army trucks if they're to hurdle*
*Need the rubber of the girdle*

*The time has come, the gods have written,*
*Women now must bulge for Britain.*

— ANONYMOUS WORLD WAR 2
POEM.

# 1

## BRIDGET MILLIGAN, SPRING 1943

'Of all the shortages in this blessed war...'

Seething with annoyance, Bridget Milligan stepped out of her knickers and kicked them to one side. The next thing she did was to open a dressing-table drawer where she kept spare bits of elastic and a safety pin.

Her mother's voice sounded from the other bedroom. 'Are you ready yet?'

'I would have been, but my knicker elastic snapped.'

Her mother came dashing in. 'Give them here.'

Hands used to cutting down any item of clothing and making it into some very reasonable garments, she took the knickers, the safety pin and the length of second-hand elastic rescued from a pair of old-fashioned bloomers bought from a Salvation Army clothes auction. In normal times, nobody would have given such an outdated item a second glance, but these beauties boasted elastic round the waist and round the legs – nearly two yards in total. With a swift flick of her wrist, out came the poor-quality knicker elastic – poor quality because too little rubber was used in the making of it, thus it snapped easily. The bloomer elastic dated from earlier times when rubber had been plentiful enough. War made bigger demands on things that included rubber, vital for making tyres for road transport and aircraft.

'Won't be a minute. There,' Bridget's mother exclaimed as she snapped open the safety pin and tied the ends of the elastic together.

Bridget restrained herself from pointing out that they were leaving too early to meet the train from Devon. The air raids on Bristol had melted away, so Patrick and Mary Milligan had agreed it was safe to bring the younger members of the family, whose ages ranged from seven to twelve, back home. They'd been away on a farm in South Molton for some time and their return was long looked forward to.

'Michael will be almost a man and my girls too will have grown. Mind you, it's no surprise, our Katy always did like her food.'

Bridget's mother was all of a rush, barely brushing her hair, buttoning her coat up all wrong and not caring that she'd put her hat on back to front. She just couldn't leave the house quick enough, couldn't walk to the bus stop quick enough, and the bus wasn't going quick enough.

It was something of a relief for both Bridget and her father when they finally arrived at the handsome edifice of Temple Meads Station, a solid structure resembling both a church and a castle, built to replace Brunel's original, which was handsome but not nearly so grand in style. The Great Western Railway itself had been a marvel of its age, running as it did all the way from Paddington in London and down into Cornwall, crossing the majestic Saltash Bridge across the River Tamar. Isambard Kingdom Brunel, a man who just couldn't seem to stand still, was also responsible for the Clifton Suspension Bridge, which had a magnificent view of the city from three hundred feet above the Avon Gorge. Once inside the station, they checked with a guard where the train was coming in and made their way to the platform.

'Mother! Wait for us.'

Her mother was running ahead of Bridget and her father at breakneck speed.

'Rushing and tearing won't bring the train in any quicker,' called Bridget's father. His words having no effect, he shook his head and smiled. 'She can't wait.'

Her mother's desire to be reunited with her children was understandable after being so long separated, aside from the occasional visits to the farm.

Bridget noticed her father was limping. 'You all right, Dad?'

'Fine. I'll be fine.'

His response was predictable. Bridget balanced her speed between that of her mother and with a mind for her father. A wartime injury back in the Great War meant he wore a false leg so couldn't possibly break any speed record, much as he might try. Of late, people had begun referring to it as World War One, the present war they were living through being World War Two. She only hoped and prayed there would be no World War Three.

Slightly breathless, Bridget caught up with her mother, her father limping in behind.

'Well, that was a bit of a rush,' exclaimed Bridget.

'I didn't want to be late,' said her mother.

'We wouldn't have been.'

'We wouldn't have been if your elastic hadn't snapped. I told you those cami knickers needed more than a button to keep them up.'

Bridget caught the laughter in her father's eyes. 'Late for the train and all because of a pair of knickers,' she muttered.

Her mother wasn't listening. Her eyes were on the rails curving away from the platform and out of sight beyond the vast glass canopy and cast-iron rafters of Temple Meads Station.

Steam from other trains collected like great bundles of cotton wool into the high rafters. The smell of soot and cinders was strong.

Like many others waiting, her mother was a bundle of nerves, fidgeting from one foot to the other, waiting for husbands, brothers, sons or sweethearts, or, like Mary Milligan, the children she'd been forced to send to the country when the air raids had been at their worst.

Mary Milligan glanced back over her shoulder, her face wreathed in smiles, her eyes sparkling like a child in a sweetshop. 'No more bombs and safe for the family to come home. Isn't that wonderful?'

'It is indeed me dear, it is indeed,' Bridget's father shouted back.

Mary Milligan turned her gaze back to the shiny railway lines, unaware of the nervous guilt in Bridget's eyes that might betray that her daughter was about to drop her very own bombshell.

A train appeared on the rails beyond the tail ends of the platforms. Bridget's mother stood on tiptoe, craning her neck to help her see better.

'Is this their train? Surely it should be here by now?'

Apprehension caught at the nerves in her throat, giving her voice a higher pitch than was normal.

Other people surged between and around them. Her father stepped closer and Bridget followed suit, crushed in the crowd. He placed a reassuring hand on his wife's shoulder.

'Don't get yourself into such a tizz, Mary. It'll be here soon.'

Bridget glanced at her father and noticing he was limping more than usual asked if he wanted to find a seat and sit down.

He shook his head. 'I'm fine, my girl, I'm fine.' His smile was convincing enough, but she knew him better, knew he'd go through hell and high water as long as her mother was happy. His smile broadened when he said, 'We'll get a taxi back. The sooner we get your mother and kids home, the better.' He lowered his voice.' This is her day, Bridie. Something she's been looking forward to since the day she had to let them go.'

The train was bringing her four younger sisters and brother back from Devon. Sean, the eldest brother, had also been evacuated, but on becoming fourteen years of age had returned at the end of last year. Over the moon at first, her mother had been dismayed when he'd told her that he missed the countryside and would like to work on a farm. After a stiff talk from his father, he'd compromised and got an apprenticeship as a gardener with the local authority.

South Molton in North Devon had changed Sean. It remained to be seen whether it had also changed the younger children, but the decision had been made. There hadn't been any air raids for some time, so, at long last, and much to her mother's joy, it was deemed safe for them to leave the farm behind and come home.

Bridget eyed her parents with love and affection but also with guilt. They had regained their younger children, but were about to lose her. For some time she'd been manning the ambulances provided by the tobacco factory, but in the absence of air raids, this service was being stood down. No longer providing a support service in the war effort meant she was likely to be called up. In order to have a choice in where she served, she'd joined the Civil Nursing Auxiliary but as yet had told no one but her workmate Maisie Miles.

Maisie had been supportive. 'Oow, Bridget Milligan, you were born to look good in a nurse's uniform!'

It lightened her mood to think of Maisie's cheery words, but the butterflies in Bridget's stomach were still fluttering. She'd held off telling her parents until all her brothers and sisters were home to soften the blow.

As she stood there waiting for their train, she forced herself to think back, to go through all that had happened bit by bit, one step at a time, though what she had to do next – telling her own family – seemed the biggest step.

The interview had occurred only two weeks ago at the General Hospital in a room with coloured glass set into its imposing windows. Having received damage back in the blitz, some of its wards were still not operational, the smell of carbolic mixing with that of dust and cement.

To her dismay, she'd seen that one of the interviewees wore the uniform of Queen Alexandra's Imperial Military Nursing Corps. The service, founded by King Edward the Seventh's Danish queen, was known to favour girls from upper-class backgrounds. Eager to serve her country, Bridget had not considered that class would come into it, but suddenly her hopes were dashed.

A less autocratic presence was a matron in the territorial nurses and yet another had been a matron from a local hospital. The fourth member was a bald-headed man with sunken cheeks and eyes, his teeth flashing yellow between thin lips, a full ashtray in front of him.

Questions came at her at speed, voiced by plummy voices of the sort never heard on the factory floor.

They'd scrutinised her first aid and ambulance driving record, including her bravery assisting a pregnant woman to give birth in a bombed cellar.

'You were awarded a commendation ribbon,' said the man, his expression betraying no sign of being impressed.

'Yes,' she had replied quietly.

More questions were asked and her answers had seemed well

received. What did worry her was that she wasn't of the preferred class favoured by the QAs', as they were called, rather than their full and overlong title, and even the Territorial Nursing Corps might be a bit sniffy about somebody from a council housing estate who worked in a tobacco factory. The chain-smoking man might appreciate her though.

'You're a local girl, from the Bedminster area,' asked the QA matron, her tone as brisk and efficient as her military bearing.

Bridget had found herself wondering how much the matron had seen of Bedminster, its factories, its back-to-back houses and newly built council estates – everything that shouted lower classes, not the sort of people she would mix with.

'Yes.'

'And you're not married.'

'No.'

'Right.' A tick had been made.

Unmarried applicants were preferred. Bridget knew that much.

'I can't recall the city of Bristol or its immediate area having much to do with nursing or any outstanding research in the advancement of medical knowledge, but perhaps you might enlighten us of those you know of and admire.'

*This is it*, she'd thought. *I won't be accepted if this woman has her way and I so want to be part of the bigger picture.* She loved her workmates at the tobacco factory, but being apart from her darling Lyndon made Bridget think she should do more. Being a first aider and driving an ambulance had provided a foundation on which to progress but she found herself wanting to do and learn more, to go as far as she could.

A pair of unblinking grey eyes in a stone hard face had regarded her imperiously and silently waited for her to answer. All eyes were on her, in fact, and feeling the game was up and that she didn't have a chance, Bridget threw the dice. She'd show them that a girl from the tobacco factory who lived in a house rented from the local authority wasn't as dumb as they thought. Well-read and interested in history of any sort, Bridget delved into her knowledge of nursing and medicine and found a name.

'Edith Cavell, who tended to the injured on both sides during the Great War, besides helping over two hundred allied prisoners escape, lived for a while in Clevedon, which is about eighteen miles south of Bristol on the coast overlooking the Bristol Channel.'

It appeared they hadn't known. Taken by surprise, they all blinked but quickly recovered. How dare such a girl throw them off balance?

The thin-faced man found enough room in the overfull ashtray to stab out his cigarette stub. 'And medicine. How about medicine? Do you know of anyone locally who furthered human knowledge of disease and medicine?' His tone was brusque. It came to her he was a doctor.

Holding her panic in check, Bridget had turned her mind back to all the books she'd ever read. In her mind's eye, she saw rows of books with gold spines lined up in battalions on shelf after shelf after shelf. Which book had she read in which a pioneer of medicine had featured along with the city of Bristol? At first, she'd floundered. There were plenty of medical professionals she recalled, but it took a lot more thinking to recall one from Bristol. But he was there, a particular name that had made a big difference to the health of the city.

'William Budd was responsible for tracking down the origin and method of transmission of cholera from one person to another. He noted that in Bristol during a heavy downpour, the drains taking waste were overflowing into those carrying the water supply. He also noticed that ships in the city centre docks were supplied with water piped direct from a spring on St Michael's Hill, far away and uphill from the old drains and watercourses. Following observation and experiment, he noted that those who used the pure spring water did not suffer cholera. Those in the city dependent on the old medieval water supply, contaminated by overflowing drains, became very ill. It was on his recommendation that a new drainage system was installed. Unfortunately, he failed to publish his findings, so the breakthrough was attributed to a Doctor Snow in London, who—'

The QA matron, brass insignia blinking on her red cape, held up her hand. 'That's enough, Miss Milligan.' Her dour expression remained unchanged, leaving Bridget feeling like a fly about to be squashed.

The other members of the panel had asked her a few more questions, which she answered to the best of her knowledge, aware that her face was on fire, her head beginning to ache.

Once the last question had been answered, she was asked to wait outside whilst a decision was considered.

On being called back in, the QA matron was gone. The three remaining eyed her unsmiling and did not ask her to sit down. Her heart sank. They were going to fail her, to tell her to apply to where girls from her background were acceptable, not to a hospital. Girls like her didn't get to serve in hospitals because they were just...

'Miss Milligan.'

The clipped address of the Territorial Nursing matron had startled her from dwelling on the morose.

'This war is a time for all of us to pull together and that includes military nursing. The territorial nurses are being seconded into the QAs and both require nursing auxiliaries to take care of hygiene, sanitising, and other backup services that release fully qualified nurses to do what they do best – to tend to the sick and wounded. Congratulations. You'll receive your orders shortly. Good day.'

Her parting had been abrupt. Good day. Goodbye. Like another cigarette being packed away with many others.

Her mother's excited voice broke into her thoughts. 'Oh, Bridie, I'm so excited, I could burst. We'll all be together again. Isn't it wonderful?'

Bridget took a deep breath and said that it was. The day would remain wonderful until Bridget announced that they wouldn't all be together, that she was leaving. She only hoped her mother's spirits wouldn't be dashed too much or for too long. The return of the others should lessen the blow; that's what she had told herself from the moment she'd decided to do this.

Spring was chilly this year, the winds of March extending into April, yet she felt overheated in the dark green jumper and box pleated skirt she'd chosen to wear. Even her cheeks felt unduly warm. She unbuttoned her jacket.

'Are you all right, Bridie?'

Her brittle cheerfulness and hot face had drawn her father's attention.

'Excitement. I'm excited for Mum.'

His look lingered. Fearing he was reading her mind, Bridget placed an arm round her mother's shoulders.

'Won't be long now, Mum.'

It struck Bridget that Mary Milligan resembled a plaster saint when she looked up with frantic eyes at the station clock, a great big black thing with hands that jerked and fell back a bit each time it moved.

'Surely it should be here by now.'

Bridget offered to find a porter and ask if it was running late when in fact if it arrived right now it would be a bit early.

'If you could, Bridie.'

'After all, there is a war on,' Bridget whispered under her breath as she pushed her way through the crowds. It seemed as though everyone was either waiting at that station for somebody to return or waiting to wave them off. Soon she would be one of those leaving.

The porter she asked looked up at the station clock and checked its accuracy against the fob watch he took out from his waistcoat. 'Too early yet.'

'I realised that. It's just that my brothers and sisters were evacuated and are due back now. My mother can't wait to get her arms round them.'

His eyes twinkled behind wire glasses and he smiled in understanding. 'It might be a bit late, but not much. There's no military traffic until later. That's the way it goes when there's a war on.' He jerked his head at men and women in uniform, kitbags carried on their shoulders, the excitement and fear of the future blinking in their eyes.

She thanked him and returned to where her parents were standing next to a pile of brown sacks stacked high on a trolley.

'He said it's more or less on time, but that—'

'I know,' said her father, with a wry smile and slow nod, 'there's a war on.'

They chuckled a bit at the well-worn phrase uttered so often it had become a joke, a chance to lighten the moment.

Her mother seemed not to notice, her attention flashing between the gleaming and empty rails at the end of the platform and the slothful clock.

The clock ticked the minutes away. Her mother tapped an impatient foot. Bridget found herself counting, each tap as a second.

The loudspeaker system crackled into life and garbled something about a train coming. Necks stretched, eyes strained, hands shielding against the light at the far end of the station platform.

Her father nudged her arm. 'I expect it's the Plymouth Castle,' he pronounced with an air of pride in his knowledge. 'All these GWR trains are named after castles, Truro, Redruth, Exeter...' The look on his face as he said it gave away that he was recalling the bomb damage done to the Plymouth.

The train appeared with a clanging of metal and billowing steam. The clanging became a high-pitched screech as it came to a halt, the hiss of steam like the last wheezing of spent breath.

'Is this it? Is this the right one?' Bridget's mother bubbled with excitement.

Bridget's father laid an affectionate hand on his wife's shoulder. Bridget saw the moistness in his eyes.

'You all right, Dad?'

He swiped a work-worn hand at one eye. 'I'm fine. Just a bit of grit and soot.'

People in uniform outnumbered the civilians piling off the train. There were no children – not at first.

'Where are they?' Her mother sounded frantic as her eyes searched the seething crowd.

Suddenly, there they were. A shout rang out. 'Mum!' cried a childish voice.

Molly was running towards them, her pigtails flying out behind, until finally she threw herself into her mother's arms.

Tears flowed immediately. 'Oh, Katie my love.'

Molly bent her head back so she could better see into her mother's face and her mother could see her more clearly. 'I'm not Katie. I'm Molly.'

Her mother laughed as the other siblings came crashing in. 'Oh bless you, but who can blame me? You've all grown so much.'

Feeling this moment belonged most of all to her parents, Bridget stood back, blew her nose and wiped tears from her eyes. Her tears of joy were a trickle compared to the flood flowing down her mother's cheeks and she looked younger. She'd hated sending the children away but had been persuaded it was for their own good.

'My darlings, my darlings! You're home. You're home at last. This is a day I'll remember for the rest of my life.' Her mother's voice verged on the hysterical as she attempted to encircle all the children at once. 'My word. My arms aren't long enough.'

Bridget brushed the tears from her cheeks and caught the look in her father's eyes. He was standing slightly behind her mother, waiting for the children to leave her arms and fall into his. His face was a picture when it finally happened.

'Welcome home, my darlings. Welcome home.'

Much as he tried to stop it happening, a single tear escaped the corner of one eye and rolled down his cheek.

He hugged each of them, Katie, Molly, Mary, Michael and Ruby, in turn, then with an air of finality, said, 'Right. Let's get on home, shall we? Home is where the heart is.'

'Where's Sean?' asked Michael, their younger son, twelve years old now and the most senior of those who'd returned.

'At work. You'll see him when we get home. The house has been empty without you lot.'

Home. There was warmth in the way he said it, no other words needed. It was indeed true that the house had seemed empty without them. Her father fulfilled his promise and forked out for one of the blue taxicabs that waited outside on the station concourse. It was a tight squeeze, but they were happy so it didn't matter if the goodies they'd brought from the farm were bundled up on their laps on top of children who were already bundled one on top of the other. Never having been in a cab before, the children waved from the windows, bubbling with excitement all the way home.

'Everything is going to be wonderful,' said her mother as the children, food from the farm and suitcases tumbled like an avalanche from the taxi and onto the pavement outside the three-bedroom house in Marksbury Road. 'We're all back together again, just as it used to be. Isn't that right, Bridie?'

'Yes. All together again.'

*At least for now*, she thought. Soon, she would drop her bombshell and say that she would shortly be leaving.

## 2

If Mary Milligan had expected instant acceptance of their old life, she was sadly mistaken. The fact that the children paused at the garden gate and looked up at the house somewhat hesitantly touched Bridget's heart. They'd been over two years in the country, where they'd grown tanned and taller. The nearest house to the farm had been a mile away across green fields that turned gold in August when the harvest was gathered. The fields had seemed unending to children used only to the Novers, a hilly expanse behind the houses where brambles and nettles predominated. In Marksbury Road, the houses, which had only one living room, a kitchen and a bathroom on the ground floor, were set in blocks of four. Only the end two had a side entrance. The middle ones did not.

Only Michael, old enough to remember their home clearly, showed acceptance, or if he was disappointed didn't show it. The younger ones looked confused. Nothing much had changed since they'd left, but perhaps they couldn't really remember their old home or only viewed it as the place where their parents were, the basic details blurred by time.

Or perhaps, thought Bridget, they preferred the farm. After all, they'd got used to it over these past two years.

A smell reminiscent of rotten eggs came from the gasometer across the road. The youngest girls held their noses.

'What's that nasty pong?'

'It's from that big green thing over there.' Looking a little pensive, her father nodded at the gasometer. 'Don't you remember it?'

The youngsters shook their heads, confusion in their eyes.

'It warms our houses,' said their mother. 'They're making coke for the fire and it supplies us with gas.'

The process of turning coal into coke always stunk and would continue to do so for the foreseeable future.

The brightness in her mother's manner was undiminished. Nothing could dampen this moment. Dismissing her family's hesitancy, she chivvied them inside the gate and up the garden path.

'Let's get inside by the fire. Brrr,' Bridget said, shivering, though still feeling a little warm; anything to get everyone inside. 'It's so cold out here.'

Molly, the eldest girl, stopped to finger a strand of climbing rose as yet only in bud to one side of the front door. The rest of the front garden was grass. She glanced disdainfully at the garden. 'There's no flowers.'

Looking a little pained by the remark, Bridget's father unlocked the front door. 'In you go.'

They didn't move but stared into the small, dingy hallway.

'I've made suet pudding with treacle and custard,' Mary Milligan declared. 'It's your favourite... or was,' she added in a smaller voice, their manner finally beginning to register.

Bridget heard the first sign of disappointment in her mother's voice. She'd been so looking forward to this, had imagined them bounding up the steps back to the house in which each of them had been born.

'Hey, everybody. It's me! I've got a bit of compassionate, as they say in the army.'

Sean bounded up the garden path in his long, loping way, telling them all that the head gardener had given him permission to welcome his siblings home. The air of disappointment was suddenly abated.

Sean was instantly surrounded by his brother and sisters, all chattering at once. He asked how things were down on the farm and in the town, and they told him it all in fine detail.

Gertrude had given birth to a calf and they'd watched it being born. There was also a new cockerel and they'd named him Winston, and that Clarence, the cockerel who'd lived with the hens before that, had flown away around Christmastime.

Bridget hid a smile when she noticed Michael roll his eyes. 'And took the sage and onion with him.' She heard him mutter.

'I ain't saying no more until I'm warmed up,' said Sean, chivvying them into the living room. 'Now let's give this fire a poke.'

Coal glowed red and small flames erupted once he'd shoved the poker in deep.

The chatter continued, the kids tagging around behind Sean, telling him every bit of news that came into their heads – including some that shouldn't have.

'Beth left before we did, because she got very fat. Mrs Cottrell said it was lying in the long grass that did it,' proclaimed Molly.

Amusement shining in his eyes, Sean recalled that Beth was one of the land girls.

Bridget gulped and her father jammed his pipe in his mouth, both of them holding in an outburst of laughter.

Bridget's mother rolled her eyes. 'Mother of God. Now let's leave all this talk of the farm behind, shall we? Let's get your things up to your rooms. You're home now and I want things tidy, then you can have suet pudding. Bridget, put the kettle on, will you? I'll go upstairs and get everyone settled.'

With Sean's help, Mary Milligan shepherded her children single file up the narrow staircase to their beds. Chatter diminished only a little as their suitcases bumped against the walls, feet thudding up the flight of treads.

A lone voice drifted down from the top of the stairs. 'Are we all squashed in here together?'

Ah yes, thought Bridget. They've been used to having more room, two to a bed and not top and tailed as they were here. Five girls now in the biggest bedroom, her parents in the middle-size room and the two boys in the box room.

Their return aroused a memory of the time she'd stayed at the farm and a romantic moment with James Cottrell, son of the owners. He'd seemed nice at the time, but then any small escape from war seemed nice – until she'd known better. James had not been quite as nice as she'd first thought.

James had gone and although Lyndon, the wealthy son of the owner of a tobacco plantation, was far away, Bridget held onto the hope that they would eventually be reunited. They should not – would not – let differences in social standing come between them. In the meantime it was the war that had parted them, Lyndon returning to the United States where he had been employed to carry out a survey on the island of Hawaii. His plans had changed following the Japanese attack on Pearl Harbour. His letters had been sparse, but explicitly stated that he would get to England and her any way that he could.

The gas ring on the stove in the kitchen flamed at the touch of a match. Pipe in hand, her father went out the back door. Once the tea things were readied, Bridget followed him out and together they watched his pipe smoke rise up into the air.

The only heating in the house was the living-room fire. Bridget pulled a cardigan on over her knitted jumper and wound her arms more tightly round herself. This early in the year, there wasn't much in the way of sun and neither was there much growing in the garden.

The sudden deeper chill wasn't so much to do with the weather, but her gaze landing on the place where her father burned garden waste. Some time ago now, there had been more than twigs and leaves burning on that fire. Her mother had miscarried that morning. Too early in pregnancy to survive, the result had been wrapped up in newspaper and burned.

Turning her gaze away helped her forget, though not entirely. 'Mum's so happy to have the kids back,' she said, pushing away the upsetting memories.

Her father gripped the pipe with his teeth and nodded his agreement. 'Great that our Sean managed to get here too. The kids loved seeing him. I expect they've missed him down there.'

'Yes. Good timing.'

Her father nodded against his pipe smoke. 'It's going to take them some time to settle in.'

'It's been a long time.'

'Still,' he said, tapping his pipe against the wall to dislodge the small amount of tobacco he allowed himself. 'At least we're all still here, and that's what really matters.'

* * *

Belongings unpacked, and suet pudding demolished, it was Michael who started the questioning about air raids.

'We haven't had a raid for over a year,' their father informed them.

Michael's face dropped into disappointment. 'We ain't seen none of it down on the farm. I 'ope we 'ave another.'

'I don't, but there are bits of shells and stuff hanging around,' exclaimed Sean, who had been down on the farm himself during the air raids, but did have an unhealthy habit of exploring bomb sites.

Young Molly shivered and shook her head nervously. 'I don't want there to be any more air raids. I'm scared.'

Bridget hugged her. 'Mum and Dad wouldn't have brought you back if they'd thought you'd be in any danger.'

The girls were happy enough then, but Michael, his father's ARP hat perched on his head, maintained a disappointed expression. 'I've missed bloody everything.'

'Michael! Language!' His mother's rebuke was like water off a duck's back. It was left to his father to satisfy Michael's disappointment.

'Well, just in case they come back, you can come along to the air raid hut one night and wear my helmet.'

Bridget's mother frowned and hissed a warning. 'Patrick!'

Hearing her condemnation, he added, 'We're not expecting anything, but you might as well get the feel of the place, then you can work out how it was for us.'

Bridget hung around in the kitchen until the younger kids were in bed and her parents were alone in the living room. The time had come.

She stood like a statue in the doorway between the living room and kitchen, a silhouette against the feeble glow of the kitchen light.

She cleared her throat. 'I've got something to say.'

Her mother carried on knitting, unaware of the shattering news Bridget was about to announce.

'What is it, Bridie?'

There was a rustling as her father lowered his newspaper. He was out of tobacco but liked the feel of his unlit pipe at the corner of his mouth. His eyes fixed on the daughter he loved, the one who was there from the very first when he'd fallen in love with her mother. Bridget saw the concern in his eyes. Her father had a nose for whatever she did even before she did it.

She took a big breath, clenched her hands ever tighter, then let it out.

'I've given a week's notice at the factory and joined up. I'm leaving next week.'

At first, the silence was so total that the water dripping from the tap in the kitchen sounded like the banging of a drum.

Dismay had replaced the calm of her mother's face that had come on with the evening and the sense that all was as it used to be. She gasped. 'You're leaving home?'

There was a cryptic questioning look on her father's face.

Another big breath and Bridget said what she had to say. 'I've joined the Civil Auxiliary Nursing Corps. I've to report to the Royal Infirmary Hospital next week.'

'The Royal Infirmary?' The words that came from her mother's mouth sounded like a caught breath and there was horror in her eyes.

'Not the Bristol one. It's one in the Midlands.'

Before they fully had time to get over the shock, she told them hurriedly that in time she might enrol for four years of nurse's training.

'If it's what you want, Bridie, then, best of luck to you.' Her father's voice pierced the chill silence, not so much calm as measured.

Her mother slumped in her chair as though every bone in her body had broken before she looked up with a startled expression and said, 'Please tell me you won't be posted abroad.'

Bridget shook her head. 'I don't know about that just yet. Besides, I've got a lot of training to do first and that's in this country.'

Her mother stared wide-eyed as the details sank in. 'When do you go?'

'I told you. Next week.' The sudden impatience she felt was overridden by relief. She'd done it. She'd told her parents and the way was clear. She couldn't help adding that up until now she'd been lucky. 'I've held down a good job and although I love working at Wills, I feel it's time I contributed something to the war effort.'

'You did the first-aid course. You drove an ambulance. Wasn't that enough?' There was pleading in her mother's voice and on her face, though not an outright demand that she changed her mind.

'I want to do more. I'm sure I'll make a pretty good nurse – at least, I think I will.'

After methodically folding his paper, her father got to his feet and took the pipe from his mouth.

Her mother sat soundlessly, her face pale, her eyes round with shock.

She could tell her father was thinking deep thoughts as he tamped the last of the tobacco ration she'd brought him from Wills into the bowl of his pipe.

'Very commendable,' he said at last. 'I think you'll make a very good nurse.'

When he beamed at her, she knew everything would be all right.

What he said next was directed at her mother.

'Remember, Mary my love, it's thanks to the nurses back in the Great War, the QAs, that I'm still here,' he said softly, nostalgia softening his eyes. 'They helped me pull through.' He turned his gentle gaze on his daughter. 'You've my blessing, Bridie. I can tell you right now, my girl, that a pretty nurse in a uniform is better than any medicine.'

He looked at his wife, willing her to accept that their daughter was no longer a child. Bridget had turned twenty-one. It was her right to do whatever she wanted and to make her mark in the world.

Heart racing, Bridget turned to her mother. 'Mum? Do I have your blessing too?'

Her mother's mouth moved, but no words came out. Her whole body charged with emotion, Mary Milligan sprang to her feet. Bridget closed her eyes as the loving arms hugged her tightly.

'You do have my blessing, Bridie,' said her mother, her breath warm against Bridget's ear. 'You do.'

Glad the ordeal was over, Bridget declared her intention to go to bed. She paused with her hand on the doorknob. 'It's been quite a day.'

Her mother heaved a big sigh and agreed with her.

She met the gentle look in her father's eyes. 'Goodnight, dad.'

'Goodnight, Bridie. Sleep tight.'

\* \* \*

Bridget's parents, Patrick and Mary Milligan, did not meet each other's earnest gaze until they could no longer hear the soft thud of her footsteps going up to bed. Even then they didn't look up, both engrossed in their own thoughts, their own fears.

Mary's fingers trembled as she reached for another piece of old cardigan. She was using a large darning needle to pluck at a hole, searching for an end to begin unwinding. Ends and beginnings. That, it seemed, was happening a lot in this war and not confined to wool.

She became more agitated because the piece of wool she wanted was being elusive.

'This blasted war!' She threw the whole thing onto the chair arm, where it slipped like a living creature down into the big tapestry bag where she kept her wools and her knitting. When her eyes met those of her husband, they were full of tears. 'How many more will it take away from their families?'

Bridget's father shook his head at her. 'You can't stop her. She's not a girl any longer. She's a young woman and has made her choice.'

A fierce look mingled with the tears in Mary Milligan's eyes. 'Do you think I don't know that and why she's doing it? She's doing this for him, and don't tell me she isn't.'

Their eyes held in mutual understanding. Lyndon O'Neill, the man their daughter had no business loving, had been heading for Pearl Harbour immediately before the Japanese attack. Communications from him since had been sporadic and it was unclear where he was going next.

Patrick sighed. 'Of course she is. She's wondering where he is and whether he'll survive, and every young man she nurses will not be a stranger. It'll be her American she's tending.'

His beloved wife made disapproving shakes of her head. 'Have you seen them? These Americans? They're everywhere and the girls are throwing themselves at them, and as for the Yanks, they're chasing everything in a skirt. No respectable woman is safe from their attentions.'

To his ears, his wife sounded overly indignant and her cheeks were pink and he guessed the reason why.

'Mary, my love, are you saying they propositioned you?'

'One of them whistled and said I had nice legs.'

Patrick beamed. 'I would agree with him on that score.'

'It's not funny.'

Her indignation was still there, though it was difficult to maintain with Patrick being the way he was.

He shook his newspaper and tried not to chuckle. 'No. It's a compliment to you for still looking like a girl in her twenties and to me for having such good taste.'

She snorted. 'Really, Patrick.' Her face flushed redder, a flush of pleasure, thought Patrick.

He looked at her as she sat there, her right hand covering her left hand and her wedding ring. He knew where her mind was going.

'Despite everything, they're still in touch with each other... our Bridie and her man, Lyndon.'

'He'll let her down!' Mary's eyes blazed with anger, though that anger wasn't directed at him. It was for every man who'd told a woman he loved her, then let her down. 'She'll be left like I was...' Her hand flew to her forehead. She didn't want to cry and didn't want to remember, but the past had a way of creeping into the present.

Mary flexed her long fingers and didn't look up for some time. It wasn't often she thought of the first man she'd thought she'd loved. He too had come from a different background to herself. He was not an easy man to forget. She was reminded of him on a daily basis, each time she looked into her daughter's eyes. People remarked that Bridget's eyes were as blue as her mother's. Smiling, she always agreed that indeed they were. Deep inside, she knew it wasn't quite true. They were like his, the man whose name she tried not to remember.

Hoping to divert her thoughts, she picked up the pair of size nine needles and the few lines of plain and purl stitching. She'd found the silvery coloured jumper in the suitcase she kept on top of the wardrobe. It had once been hers. For a moment, she'd buried her nose in it and closed her eyes. There was no trace of that remembered scent of clover, lilac and a warm sunny day when she'd been young. What had once been could only be recalled behind her closed eyelids, along with another war and a man. His eyes had been the same colour as Bridie's and he'd been clever and well read. That's where she'd first met him in the library at the big house reading a book.

She'd been only a housemaid, barely seventeen and on the threshold of life. He'd been son of the master and from a different world to the one she'd inhabited. But it hadn't stopped them falling in love and believing it would last forever, just as it wasn't stopping Bridget from her own far-fetched dream. It wouldn't happen. It couldn't happen, and in time she would find that out. All she hoped was that it didn't break Bridget's heart as it had hers.

# 3

## MAISIE MILES

*Dear Tobacco Girls,*

*This is just a short letter of explanation. I had a bit of a mishap during a raid and was given the choice of coming home or staying where I feel a future unfolding. Surprise, surprise, I've met the man I consider to be the love of my life. Please believe me, this time it's for real. We've made plans for after the war and I intend sticking to them. Hope you are safe and well. Love to everyone at the factory. Yours sincerely, Phyllis.*

Standing on the factory steps in front of the main entrance, Maisie Miles, who had already read the letter, watched Bridget's reaction.

Bridget smiled sadly. 'I hope she really has this time.'

'You'll have to write to 'er and tell 'er your news. Bet she'll be surprised.' Maisie held back saying that she was going to miss Bridget as much as she missed Phyllis, perhaps even more.

'I will do...' Bridget's voice trailed away before Maisie glimpsed regret in her eyes. 'I feel guilty leaving you behind. The three M's will be down to one.' They had been Maisie Miles, Bridget Milligan and Phyllis Mason, before she married and became Harvey, when they'd first met, hence referring to themselves as the three Ms. Only two of them now, Phyllis serving overseas on the island of Malta. Once Bridget was gone only Maisie would remain working in the factory.

Maisie determined to put on a brave face and declared chirpily, 'No, they won't. They'll still be what they've always been, just not all together in the same place.'

Maisie had coped with the tearful moments the night before, determined she'd give Bridget a warm send-off without tears. Moping was something she could well do without if she was to face this new future she'd set herself. Still, a moment spent in the privacy of the ladies' cloakroom would sort out any stray sniffles.

As it was, she didn't get chance for privacy.

'How do I look?' Carole Thomas collared Maisie halfway along the corridor to the ladies' cloakroom, where she dragged her inside. Nobody else was in there.

With one eye on the mirrored walls and another on Maisie, Carole did a little pirouette. Her jacket and skirt were a shade of mid green – just a little darker than the overalls worn by the factory girls. Her blouse was crisply white and she wore a little cap set rather cockily on one side of her head.

Maisie assured her that she looked very smart, then added, doing her best to keep the envy from her voice, 'Are those *real* stockings you're wearing?'

Fists on hips, painted nails gleaming, Carole responded that they were. 'Two pairs once a month. A VIP escort has to look 'er... her... best.'

The VIP escorts, who had been brought in to improve factory relations with the outside world, were versed in production processes and knowledge of the general layout of the factory and offices so visitors didn't get lost. Thanks to the war, there should have been a diminishing demand, but it seemed that was not so.

Various groups came to visit, some of them foreign military personnel or local workers or women's groups. Theatre or cinema was the preferred entertainment, but a free tour of the factory – with a lunch thrown in – was hard to ignore.

Wills took pride in showing people round, even when it was only a contingent of the local WRVS or a battalion of Polish airmen in dire need of a day out. To this end, they employed the escort girls and Carole, who had the sort of looks that turned heads and the confidence to go with it, had been chosen.

Maisie felt a pang of déjà vu. In an attempt to improve her lot, her old mate Phyllis had made the effort to sound her aitches – just as Carole was doing now. If you wanted to get on you went to elocution lessons, and determined to give a good impression, the factory was paying for her to have them. Phyllis, one of the three Ms, had taught herself whilst awaiting the birth of a baby and living beneath her in-laws' roof whilst her husband was away at war. She'd miscarried the baby and Robert, her husband, had not returned following the retreat at Dunkirk. Once she'd received the message, missing, believed killed, she'd escaped the oppressive atmosphere of the semi-detached house in Bedminster and attempted to rebuild her life. In doing so, she'd finally ended up in the Women's Royal Air Force and found herself posted to a dangerous war zone.

Maisie only hoped that Carole wouldn't do the same. What with Bridget off to nurse wounded soldiers and Phyllis on the embattled island of Malta, her closest friends were getting a bit thin on the ground.

'So who are your first VIPs?' Maisie asked.

'Well,' said Carole, pursing her bright red lips. 'Americans. They're from the air base in Whitchurch.'

'Logistics,' Maisie stated.

Carole frowned. 'I wouldn't know about that. They're Americans. That's all I know.'

Maisie patiently explained that Whitchurch airfield, just a few miles from the factory, was a supply depot. The planes that flew in and out of there carried everything a military campaign might need. 'Everything from food to bullets.'

'Not fighter or bomber pilots then?' There was no doubting that Carole was disappointed.

'No, but you have to admit they're just as important. It's said that an army marches on its stomach.' She saw Carole's puzzled look. 'Someone 'as to make sure they're fed an' watered. Stands to reason.' She winked. 'Play yer cards right and you could end up with a steady supply of Spam and chocolate.'

Carole beamed. 'Oow, lovely. I'll bear that in mind.'

With a pronounced wiggle, she sauntered off to the handsome staircase that would take her up to the first floor. Portraits of both management and long-service employees hung from the walls. Maisie had only seen the upstairs corridor and board room once and that was when a woman who had worked at the factory for forty years had decided to retire. She'd been well thought of and the management had put on a celebration in her honour. It was even rumoured that her picture would join the ranks of those already there.

It wasn't that long ago that Maisie had begun working at W. D. &. H. O. Wills and far less time since Carole had started. Glamorous, sassy and having too much lip, Carole had been a right pain when she'd first arrived at the factory harbouring both wilfulness and arrogance in equal measure. Although only fourteen going on fifteen at the time, even teaching her the ropes of the job had met with sniffy contempt.

Maisie had coped with the disgruntled repartee and the barely controlled temper. It had struck her that there was a different Carole beneath the surface and she'd gone out of her way to find out more. It turned out that Carole's mother was a tart and that the kid had had more uncles than hot dinners.

At one time, she was being pursued by Eddie Bridgeman, a local gangster with a penchant for young girls, but that no longer seemed to be happening.

Carole had shrugged when she'd asked her about it.

'He does not bother me any longer,' Carole had declared, her words pronounced without a hint of accent.

Maisie was puzzled but wouldn't be looking a gift horse in the mouth. Eddie hadn't been bothering her either as he had in the past when he'd been overly familiar, his intentions far from honourable and encouraged by her stepfather, Frank Miles who was now a guest in His Majesty's Prison, Horfield.

Carole was different now. Just like Maisie, she had reaped the benefit of factory camaraderie and had bloomed. Her being promoted to a VIP escort had been a big surprise. Those favoured were normally in their twenties, but the war had changed all that.

It was no secret that good-looking and well-groomed girls were considered ideal for the job. Clear pronunciation was also a great asset. Carole was well qualified on the first two counts and was working on the second. Maisie did all she could to encourage her, recognising something of the girl in herself, both coming from a rough background and neglected at home.

Young Eric, one of the lads who pushed a trolley that collected the leaves, passed Maisie on her way back to the stripping room. At sight of his astounded expression, she guessed immediately what he was about to say.

'Have you seen Carole? She looks like a film star.' Amazement was quickly replaced with a worried frown. 'Ain't likely to look at me any more. Goin' up in the world. Wish I could join up right now,' he said, a firm set to his jaw. 'I reckon I'd look like James Stewart once I'm in uniform. She'd fancy me then I reckon.'

Maisie assured him that he was probably right, though the truth was she could see no resemblance at all between him and James Stewart, but it would be nigh on cruel to burst his bubble. Instead she mentioned hearing that James Stewart had joined the struggle against the Nazis even before the United States had entered the war.

'Who knows, you might bump into 'im when you do finally get into uniform – if you go into the RAF that is. I heard that's what he joined before America came in on our side.'

It was a forlorn hope that James Stewart would be that accessible to the likes of Eric, but worth mentioning just to see his face light up.

His cheerful whistling followed her all the way along the corridor to the doors of the canteen. Neither he nor Carole had seen any trace that she might have her own worries. She'd kept a half-baked smile on her face when speaking to each of them. No trace of that smile now remained. The corners of her mouth were downturned and a single furrow creased her brow.

Light glimpsed through the oval portholes of the canteen doors did nothing to alleviate the sense that the world was turning colder and she was beginning to feel very alone.

Learning that Bridget had joined the military nursing corps was bad enough, but not entirely unforeseen. That morning, though, she had received a Red Cross postcard from Sid.

*Dear Maisie. I'm a prisoner of war, but I'm all right. Thought I might send you a little poem. Hope you don't mind. It takes my mind off things.*
*Faggots, mash and mushy peas,*
*Somerset cider and strong Cheddar cheese,*
*Wiltshire bacon and soft white bread.*
*Can't get any of this out of me head.*

She'd felt numb as she'd read it. Bridget had remarked that Sid had a way with words and she had to agree. To get round the censor striking out sentences in his letters home, he'd done little drawings hinting at where he was, but of late his words had changed. He was a prisoner in a Japanese camp following his capture at Singapore. Maisie had clung onto the belief that he was capable of looking after himself, but the poem was telling her in no uncertain terms that he was yearning for food. All the food mentioned related to home, some of it in very typically West Country terms. She presumed the Japanese didn't understand what these things were and that his poem wasn't really a poem, but a shopping list of everything he was missing, that he was hungry, perhaps even starving.

Forcing her worried thoughts aside, she threw a beaming smile at her dear friend. Bridget looked flushed and excited sitting there in the canteen telling everyone who would listen about joining up. Congratulations came thick and fast, one person after another coming up to pat her on the shoulder or shake her hand.

'Is there anyone you ain't told?' asked Maisie. 'Better make a list.' Maisie pretended to fetch a pencil and notebook from her pocket as Bridget bubbled with laughter.

'Stop making fun,' said Bridget. 'I've told everyone who matters.'

They settled down with their cups of tea.

'How were the kids?'

Another heaved breath. 'Not too bad.'

'I bet yer mum's over the moon – like a dog with two tails that can't stop wagging.'

Still flushed with happiness, Bridget said that she was.

'It made me telling them I was off a bit easier.'

'Good.' Maisie dipped her hand into her overall pocket. 'I've got news too.'

'You're joining up?'

Maisie shook her head. 'No.' She passed over the postcard she'd received from Sid.

As she took it, Bridget frowned. The card was dirty and the words were smudged, but she read every word.

'Food,' said Maisie, looking dejectedly at the one and only biscuit she was likely to get that morning thinking she should be grateful. Sid would gobble it down 'All he talks about is food. He's telling me he's starving, Bridget. I'm sure of it.'

Bridget sucked at the biscuit she'd dunked into her tea. Her eyes fluttered as she returned the card to Maisie. Sid had been a well-built young chap, and although Maisie had insisted they were only friends, their relationship had been going on for some time.

'Poor Sid. I can still see 'im on the pier at Wesson, eating a bag of chips even though 'e'd already scoffed 'is sandwiches.' Maisie looked down into her empty cup. 'I wonder 'ow many of the people we knew when war broke out will be there when it ends.' Wesson was Weston-Super-Mare to posh folks, but that wasn't Maisie. She wasn't posh and never would be.

Bridget cradled her cup with both hands. 'I'm hoping to still be around.'

Maisie met her eyes over the tops of their respective tea cups. 'And you 'ope Lyndon will be too. 'Eard anything?'

'Just the odd letter. It's been so long and he's so far away. I wish...' She stopped what she was going to say.

Maisie, always instinctive about such things, filled in the words for her. 'You hope and pray that Lyndon stays alive and that you see 'im again.'

Bridget pulled a face. 'I wish I'd married him and gone back to the States with him. He did ask, but...' She shrugged. 'That was then and this is now.'

Maisie chewed at her bottom lip. She hated seeing the wisely serene Bridget looking so down. She decided it best to keep to the positives. 'Still, at least you've broke the news to your mum and dad.'

'Yes. They're OK.' She smiled. 'Funny how common it is, saying OK. Everyone's saying it.'

'All these Americans we've got 'ere,' commented Maisie and suddenly forgot not to mention Lyndon. 'Shame yours ain't 'ere.'

Bridget's forehead flopped onto her hand, hiding her face. There were no tears as yet, but they weren't far off.

'Sorry, Bridge.'

Looking down into her teacup, Bridget shook her head. 'I keep thinking that we'll never see each other again. This war rumbles on, lurching from one disappointment to another.'

'At least he didn't get hurt at Pearl Harbour. That was lucky.'

Bridget conceded that it was. Lyndon O'Neill had been sent to Pearl Harbour just prior to it being attacked by the Japanese. He'd been supposed to go on from there to Manila in the Philippines but instead had been recalled to Washington. Only the military were being allowed to venture into the Pacific. Lyndon had been seconded to report on civilian morale and the US government knew the inhabitants of the Philippines were under attack. Their survival was presently more important than their morale.

'It's been a while since I heard anything much. He said his aim was to join any arm of the military bound for Europe.' She shrugged. 'He's untrained. It could take some time. Scares me to think of him joining up. I would hate it if he ended up like...'

'Like Sid.'

'I'm sorry, Maisie. I didn't mean...'

Maisie tossed her head. 'That's OK, Bridget. I wish he wasn't a POW, but there, that's Sid, getting 'imself into the thick of it. What with 'im and Phyllis.' She tutted in an amusing manner, sounding more like his mother than a sweetheart – which she insisted she wasn't. It was noticeable that she no longer denied it.

Bridget smiled wanly and fingered the handle of her cup, turning it on her saucer like some kind of direction finder – though it seemed she'd found her direction.

'My parents have accepted that it's what I want to do. Anyway,' she finally exclaimed, pushing the cup and saucer away, 'I'm planning a night out before I go. Just a few of us.'

'Count me in.'

'Miss Cayford and Aggie too if I can get them to come. I thought we could go to the Services Club again in Little Paradise and have a dance and a singsong.' She smiled whilst swiping a tear from her eye.

'Wouldn't miss it for the world. I 'ave 'eard that girls in uniform 'ave a rare old time, that's why so many have joined up. They get to see a bit of life and a lot more romance than at 'ome.'

Bridget smiled

'I will miss you all, but I feel it's something I have to do.'

'Of course you do,' Maisie responded, with due seriousness before she said, 'We're going to launch you on your way like they do a ship. May God bless her and all that...'

It gladdened Maisie that her exuberance finally brought a smile to Bridget's face. At the same time, she envied her but also feared for her. Who knows where she might end up? There was no need to mention anything more about Lyndon. Neither of them could be sure that Bridget would ever see him again. Nothing was certain in this topsy-turvy world.

**4**

## PHYLLIS HARVEY (NEE MASON)

The breeze coming in from the Sicilian Channel, the most fought-over part of the Mediterranean Sea, sent silky strands of hair across her face, which Phyllis brushed aside, unwilling to have anything impair the serenity, the sheer beauty, of the sun slowly setting into the sea.

She sighed and rested her head on Mick's shoulder. 'It's so peaceful here. Hard to believe that this is Malta and there's a war going on.'

Mick jerked his head in the direction of the most important radar station on the island. 'Difficult to ignore with that thing just over the brow there.'

They couldn't see the radar mast from where they were sitting on a rocky promontory at Dingli Cliffs, but they knew it was there, the soft hum of its searching eyes scanning the distant horizon for enemy planes.

'I'm trying to ignore it,' she said, nestling more tightly into Mick's protective arm.

His lips brushed the top of her head. 'That's fine. Just so long as you never ignore me.'

Perhaps it was the glow of the sunlight that made her feel as though she were floating above the ground. Everything was just so wonderful. She was in love. She was sure of it this time and prayed they would get through this war and plan a future together – no matter where it was – England or on the other side of the world in Australia.

Mick Fairbrother had taken the news that she was married surprisingly well. He'd remarked that she'd been young and had never strayed far from home. He added that the only casualties in war weren't only physical and mental. There would also be emotional casualties, long absences opening cracks in stumbling relationships.

'You know what I think?'

'No. What?'

'That we'll come back here in years to come for a holiday. It's bound to be different in peacetime.'

'All the way from Australia?'

'All the way.'

His hug squeezed the breath out of her, but was nothing compared with when he kissed her. Closing her eyes seemed to intensify the other sensations she felt and when his hand caressed her breast, she felt as though she were melting from heat, from the rush of blood, from the need to have him all to herself forever.

'You know,' he said, his lips leaving hers. 'I'm grateful for this war.'

She looked at him in surprise. 'How could anyone be grateful for war?'

Creases fanned at the corners of his eyes as he smiled down into her face.

'I wouldn't have met you if things had stayed the same.'

His words sent a shiver down her spine as though a ghost had suddenly tapped her shoulder or a shadow had passed between them and the sparkling sea.

She knew without needing to dig deep that the Harvey house was the ghost tapping at her shoulder, along with Robert and his ghastly mother. Nothing could persuade Phyllis to go back there, even though she was still married to Robert. Immediately following Dunkirk she'd received news that he was missing presumed dead. Her mother in law had refused to believe her precious son was dead and wouldn't allow her to believe it too. For a while she'd been a virtual prisoner in that house, but with the help of her friends, Bridget and Maisie, had escaped. Having lost the baby and feeling her life aimless, she'd joined up. It was sometime later that she'd learned of Robert's return – not that he'd gone out of his way to pursue her which was strange. She could imagine his mother fussing over him and spitting blood that she, Phyllis, had dared to leave.

She and Mick had discussed her getting a divorce, hopefully with the help of his uncle who was a solicitor in London – if that was what she wanted. Of course it was what she wanted. Thanks to injuries sustained during a bombing raid, she'd spent some time in hospital and was given the option of returning to England. Even though it meant leaving behind the intense bombing Malta was enduring, she decided that despite the danger she would stay. She wanted to be with Mick and nothing, not even a war would prevent her from doing that. 'You're right, Mick. This war is a good thing – for us at least.'

'We're the lucky ones. Not everyone's been so lucky,' said Mick, his hands kneading her shoulders, fingers caressing her face, her neck and her body, the gleam of sunset setting his hair on fire.

His arms were hard and strong as he held her, their chests tight against each other. His breath warm against her ear.

'Neither of us would have ventured far from home if it hadn't happened. I would still have been working the sheep station and not flying reconnaissance missions over enemy territory. On the other hand, I might never have got ideas about growing grape vines and making wine. But we have the sunshine in Australia and I do believe certain areas of New South Wales and Victoria have the right soil. It's something to check out.'

She wanted him to say that she would be coming with him, but didn't want to push her luck. They both had to feel the same and stare into the same future – just as they were staring into this wonderful sunset.

'I'll remember this moment for the rest of my life,' she said wistfully, wisps of auburn hair floating like spiders' webs in the warm air.

Stroking her hair away from her face, he said, 'So will I.' After kissing the top of her head again, he broke off and took out a packet of cigarettes from his breast pocket. 'I need a smoke.'

She studied his profile, the slope of his forehead, the straight nose and the sensuous strength of his lips as he pursed them round the tip of the cigarette. He breathed in, then exhaled smoke into the air, where it lingered a while. The smoke was like her, she thought, disinclined to venture far from him.

'I've told my friends in the tobacco factory about you. I know it might sound silly, but I told them that I thought you were the one.'

He turned and looked at her, smiling and frowning all at the same time. 'Silly? I don't think it's silly, and in case you've got any doubts, I think you're the right Sheila for me,' he said suddenly. 'Now there's a bit of clichéd Australian – Sheila's an OK name, but I've a preference for Phyllis Harvey.'

'Not Harvey,' she said, shaking the thought of her married name away. 'I don't want to keep that particular name.'

His whole face when he turned to her seemed brighter than the sun. He gave her hand a reassuring squeeze. 'It won't be Harvey. You'll be Mrs Fairbrother. You just wait and see.'

* * *

A few days later after that wonderful moment on Dingli Cliffs, Phyllis reported for duty as an operator for Command Radio Telephony. Her job in what was termed the Filter Room was to receive and write down information coming in from one of a number of radar stations located round the island, not just from the one at Dingli. It was then forwarded to the Plotting Room in the war rooms at Lascaris, a fortified provision situated above the Grand Harbour.

Back in October and needing their few personnel to have as many skills as possible, the High Command had decided to train more people in radio telephony. Phyllis had applied and completed the shortened course before she was injured. Some of the more seasoned operators resented the fact that she and a couple of others could wear a 'sparks' badge, whereas they had had to train for far longer to gain one.

Normally there were enough operators without the need to bring anyone in who hadn't been formally trained, but an outbreak of illness, plus the lack of replacements being sent from Britain, meant it was a case of needs must.

The German Luftwaffe had taken over the bombing from the Italians in its entirety and were proving their usual efficient selves. Air raids had increased, the screaming of Stuka dive bombers or the throb of Heinkels which carried a heavier bomb load sounding day and night.

Despite fatigue and hurrying for the shelters, both men and women managed to grab a few precious hours in good company and in a place as far away from an RAF station or plotting room as possible.

Phyllis and Mick weren't the only ones to sit staring at the setting sun or moonlight on water. To get any kind of solitude away from the main conurbations such as Valletta meant walking, cycling or, depending on the lucky chance of getting hold of petrol, travelling by car to the more out of the way places.

Days and nights continued to be demanding. The moment Phyllis went on duty, mooning over precious moments spent with Mick inevitably took a back seat. Enemy planes were yet again howling overhead and doing their damnedest to knock out the hard-pressed defences of the island.

Sweating beneath her hard hat, Phyllis concentrated on the figures being passed to her, listening to what the pilot or radar station were saying, speaking back, asking for confirmation of details and informing the appropriate runway when a fighter pilot was running out of fuel or weapons and had requested permission to come in. Her job was then to log in those returning, her heart lurching in her chest when some didn't. It was also her job to find out which runway was still able to take a returning plane, that is which ones were under attack or had so many bomb craters that landing anything was quite impossible.

It was a long shift. Her eyes ached, her ears ached and her tin hat was beginning to feel as though she had a ton weight on her head.

'Tea, Harvey?'

She took the mug gratefully, commenting that her mouth was as dry as a bone.

Audrey was her running mate for today, a pert blonde from Ipswich who knew how to sail and did so quite often with her Royal Navy boyfriend who worked in the wages department on Cottonera Creek, situated in what was termed The Three Cities. She had a jovial sense of humour and so, it seemed, did her boyfriend, Matthew. 'He said to me, the wages department is in a smallish building next door to the Navy bakery which is huge. Reckons the sailors say that they get more bread than they do bread. Get it? Get it?'

Audrey laughed loudly at the punch line all by herself; she had repeated the same joke a few times already. But that was the way it was; Audrey was doing her best to keep up spirits, to inject some humour, however trivial, whenever she could.

Phyllis always made a point of laughing as though hearing it for the first time. Audrey was doing her best and needed reassurance.

The enemy never left them at peace for long. The heads, as the naval types insisted on calling them, were down the end of a long concrete passageway and had a view of the sea. The window's panes had long been shattered by the blasts from explosions so there was plenty of fresh air. no matter the weather. and seeing it was set high above a pile of rocks, privacy was not an issue. All in all, it was rather pleasant to gaze out and feel the fresh air blowing in before going back on duty.

As usual the fighters had been sent up to apprehend the incoming raiders. Sometimes the radar station to the north on the smaller island of Gozo would report the sighting; sometimes Dingli or one of the others on the main island passed on direction, height and numbers of aircraft.

'Raiders at two three degrees. Ten thousand feet. Approximately forty. Stukas and Heinkels.' Phyllis spoke the details in addition to the written report. Recording information helped assess and improve efficiency. It was also useful in case short-wave radio signals proved weak.

With a sick feeling in the pit of her stomach, fearing for every fighter pilot up there, Phyllis read what each radar station was saying and passed it on.

Tea was consistently being brewed but often left to go cold.

*Needs must.*

Those two words again. Tea was much needed to moisten their dry throats so they could keep talking and passing on information as and when it was received.

She coughed as a bomb landed close by, dislodging a cloud of dust from the stone walls. Sometimes her eyes were stinging at the end of a shift – a twelve-hour shift that sometimes felt like twenty-four.

By eight that evening, the shift was over and in dribs and drabs those who'd given their all were venturing into the outside world. As they walked away, they passed those going on shift.

Even Audrey was silent before seeming to jerk into action on remembering that she was meeting her beau, Matthew. 'He's got a couple of hours off. Just enough, eh?' With a casual wave and a saucy wink, she was off.

'Cigarette?'

The girl asking was Mariana, a Maltese plotter whose face was turned rosy by the dying rays of the setting sun.

Hands shaking, Phyllis cupped her hand round a cigarette Mariana was lighting for her. She hadn't been much of a smoker, but that had changed since coming here. Smoking helped their nerves, gave something for their hands to do when they no longer had dials and switches to play with. Hardly play. The defence of this island depended on every little thing they did. It seemed also to depend on the cigarettes she'd once had a hand in making; Woodbines. What else?

Each breath was one of relief; magically flying away in a wreath of smoke. The relief was that they'd done their bit despite the casualties incurred and the new piles of honey blonde stone that had once been buildings. Malta had many such piles of stone their honey hue turned pink by the setting sun.

She thanked Mariana for the cigarette. 'I needed that.'

'Are you off back to your billet?'

Phyllis said that she was. 'A cup of tea and a slice of toast. How about you?'

She'd asked the question she most dreaded asking of a Maltese person; they had big families, everyone related to everyone and all needed to be fed. They were hard hit by rationing, but then wasn't everybody?

'I'm off to hear a mass. You can come if you like.'

Phyllis's first inclination was to decline. Her mother had attended church on occasion, sometimes Methodist and sometimes Church of England. Her allegiance varied, but she'd never forced Phyllis to do so. God always seemed so far off back in the red-brick church with the green copper spire that her mother had gone to or the equally red-brick Methodist church. But here, with stars beginning to prick the sky and the incoming surf whispering onto the rocky coast, it was different. It seemed to her that talking to God was more relevant when living into tomorrow was not such a certainty.

And so it was that, arm in arm – so they wouldn't lose each other once darkness fell or could catch one another if they stumbled – they made their way to one of the many churches on the island.

The interior of the church was bright with gold and coloured glass, the smell of incense, old wood and effigies and statues of saints dating back to the beginning of Christianity.

Phyllis did as Mariana did and lit a small candle that she knew should accompany her prayer.

Mariana explained that it didn't need to be voiced out loud. 'Just in your heart.'

Tears came as Phyllis wiped at the grit she felt in her eyes. The dusty air following the latest air raid had a lot to do with it, but there were other things too.

Words did indeed pour from her heart. She had thought she was going to pray just for Mick and everyone she knew back home. Perhaps it was fatigue that made her change her mind, or perhaps that the whole world needed her prayers. She'd seen so much death and misery since coming here but also resilience. 'Life is for living,' she whispered softly, staring up at a cold-eyed plaster saint, and knew she would never again take life for granted. As far as possible, she would live each day as if it were her last. The words of the wedding hymn Love Divine came to mind and so did Mick. He was where she prayed her future lay. Nothing would dissuade her from that, but a little divine help wouldn't come amiss.

# 5

## BRIDGET

The news from the Far East had not been good following the attack on Pearl Harbour nearly eighteen months ago and the subsequent fall of Hong Kong and Singapore. Like winter, the darkest hours seemed to go on interminably, but just as with winter, spring and summer followed. Even so, Bridget was thankful that Lyndon was back in the USA.

He'd written that things were beginning to go in the right direction, but it seemed that direction – for him at least – was not towards England and her.

*But honey, it's not for the want of trying. I'll be back. You wait and see.*

It was the waiting that was hard. Beating back the fear that she might never see him again, Bridget carried his last letter everywhere with her – this one she'd received just this morning. Tonight she'd tucked it into a silk pocket in a quilted shoulder bag her mother had made her. Regardless of which way the battles went, making something new from something old was as challenging as making a bread pudding from brick-hard bread and a roast dinner with only a sliver of meat and a generous helping of Pete the Potato.

The shoulder bag matched the hat she was wearing, both made by her mother from a Victorian gentleman's smoking jacket bought at the church jumble sale. The black quilting of the hat and bag had been the main body of the garment. Her mother had trimmed the hat with the contrasting gold of its wide lapels and used the silk cord waist tie as the strap for the shoulder bag. Bridget had pronounced it lovely and meant it.

It was still light when she left the house and made her way across the tip, past the gasometer and towards Sheene Road. Engrossed in thoughts of what tomorrow would bring, she was only vaguely aware of a figure lurking in the shadow of the huge iron beast which continuously leaked a little of the gas everyone relied on to cook their food.

'Got a light, babe?'

Startled from her thoughts, she blurted a swift, 'No. Sorry.'

'How about coming over here. It's nice and dark. I could make you happy. I have chocolate. I have stockings.'

She didn't answer, but shook her head and hurried on, her speed curtailed by the uneven ground, the scattered stones, brambles and weeds.

'Hey, babe?'

American. There were so many over here now, but not like Lyndon, she thought. Not at all like Lyndon.

Once she was on the main road, she slowed her pace, but no matter how much she told her racing heart all was well, it kept racing and she dared not look over her shoulder to see if she was being followed.

She saw a group of older women that she knew who were on their way home from a whist drive. They'd had the same habit before the war and it was well known that they'd carried on regardless of Herr Hitler and his plans. She waved at them, asked if they were doing all right and they asked the same of her. Her heart rate slowed and she managed to laugh it off.

'I'm fine. Just some bloke down the cut getting a bit fresh.'

'One of them Yanks?'

'I think so.'

She felt oddly guilty saying that, because it was a bit like betraying Lyndon, though goodness knows he was a world away – in location as well as in manners.

One of the women, the mother of a girl she knew, leaned in and whispered close to her ear, 'You've 'eard about them utility knickers, 'aven't you? One Yank and they're off!'

There was laughter, though Bridget only managed a smile, her cheeks colouring profusely. Lyndon was a Yank. She told herself he wasn't like that.

\* \* \*

Relief swept over her once she'd got to her destination, where Maisie, Carole, Aggie and a few others awaited her.

'You look smashin',' said Maisie as they swung into the Services Canteen and Dance Hall in Little Paradise. Even Carole, who preferred praise to fly in her direction, agreed that she did.

A party atmosphere ensued as their heels clattered over the wooden floor, smiling, laughing whilst declaring what goodies they'd each brought to make the evening a success.

Carole had brought doughnuts.

'Oh yeah. Got a Yank in yer pocket,' ave you?' said Maisie teasingly.

Carole shook her pretty little head. 'No, but me mum does. He works in the kitchens at that camp up at Whitchurch Airport.'

Maisie looked at her pointedly. 'Does yer mum know you pinched them?'

Carole's blonde curls bobbed round her face as she shook her head. 'Nah! She won't notice they're gone. She would have noticed the stockings though. Made sure she hid them away out of my reach.'

The last words were delivered in a very deliberate fashion and without dropping her aitches. Like everyone else, the war was challenging Carole to become better than she was. In the meantime, she was out to have fun.

'Raise your drinks and your doughnuts. Here's to Nurse Bridget Milligan, the Florence Nightingale of Marksbury Road.'

Bridget only managed to eat one doughnut. Everyone else was eating them as fast as they could, the alluring fattiness and sweetness sorely missed in the last few years.

Carole was grabbed by a hunk in a uniform and whirled onto the dance floor. Maisie was too, and even Aggie, their supervisor at the factory and old enough to be their mother, was giving it her best, kicking out her legs and showing the elasticised legs of her knee-length bloomers.

Bridget refused a few soldiers who asked, preferring for now just to watch until she had some control over her nerves. *What have I done*, she thought to herself. *I'm saying goodbye to all my friends and my family.*

A sense of impending doom came upon her. Joining up had been done with her eyes wide open – or so she had thought. Only now did it hit how much her life was about to change, along with the world and everything else in it.

'You daydreaming, honey?'

The voice surprised her, but not as much as the fact that she was in a man's arms and being whisked onto the dance floor without being given chance to refuse.

She looked up into his features which hadn't registered at first.

'I'm not sure I want to dance. You didn't ask, did you?'

'I did and you didn't say yes, and you didn't say no.'

'I didn't hear you.' It occurred to her that he might have been the same GI – general infantryman, as they were called – who had accosted her back in the shadow of the gasometer.

'You don't mind dancing with me, do you, honey?'

His voice was as deep as the sea, dark as molasses. There was kindness in his eyes.

'No. Of course not. Why should I?'

He laughed gently. Despite his size, everything about him seemed gentle. 'Because I'm black.'

She tilted her head back slightly. The lighting in the club was far from bright, but she could now see the colour of his skin clearly enough and she thought black wasn't quite the right word.

'You don't look black. You look brown. Like a conker.'

He pulled in his chin and said with some surprise, 'What's a conker?'

She laughed and went on to explain. 'The fruit of the horse chestnut tree. It's shiny brown, like a mahogany sideboard. Yes,' she said after some thought. 'A similar colour to a mahogany sideboard.'

He laughed and shook his head. 'Well, that's two new descriptions applied to me that I ain't come across before.'

'I suppose we're all going to learn from each other,' said Bridget. 'Different words and different people from all over.'

'You could say that,' he responded. 'Ain't this war all about people not being cruel and being nice to each other?'

Bridget agreed that it was. 'It takes all sorts to make a world. We're like an Irish stew – I'm of Irish blood, you know – loads of meat and vegetables all thrown into the pot together.'

He laughed at that. 'That's a pretty good way of putting it. My name's Jonah.'

'Mine's Bridget. Pleased to meet you, Jonah.'

'Pleased to meet you, Bridget. You speak with some intelligence. Do you think I can see you again?'

She shook her head, a sad smile on her face. 'I'm afraid not. I'm off to my posting tomorrow and I don't know when I'm likely to get leave – not for six months at least.'

'That's a shame. God knows where I'm likely to be in six months, though as long as I stay alive, that'll suit me fine.'

She let him whirl her round for a bit longer, his proximity making her ponder on whether Lyndon too was dancing with a stranger, someone with whom he might escape for a while and pretend there was no war, no fighting, no shortages and only fun.

'You've got that faraway look again. Is he serving too, your man?'

She nodded. 'He's American.'

His eyebrows rose. 'Really?'

'He was at Pearl Harbour, then the Philippines, but now he's back in the States.'

'He a military man?'

She pulled a face. 'Not really. He gathers information, gives pep talks and things like that.'

'Good job he didn't stay in the Pacific theatre. Things are pretty scary out there.'

She suppressed a shiver, recalling the letter she received this morning:

*My darling,*

*I'm pushing the fact that my knowledge of Europe – vis a vis Great Britain – is greater than my knowledge of the Pacific or of military strategy. Seems I'm destined to fly a desk not a fighter.*

*Watch this space, honey. Fingers crossed.*

*Love Lyndon.*

'How did you meet?'

Because Jonah was interested, yet also polite and genuine, she decided he was certainly not the man from earlier in the evening. She went on to tell him how she'd met Lyndon, where he came from and what he did.

There was sadness in his eyes when he looked at her and said, 'I hope you see him again, Bridget.'

'And you?'

He threw back his head and laughed. 'I'm married with two kids and another on the way. I joined up because I had no permanent job, none that paid very well. My family needs the money and I...' He paused as he sorted out his reasons. 'I want to prove to myself that I can be more than what some folk think I should be – especially white folk. I'm aiming to learn a trade whilst I'm here. Might even stay in the army for the long haul and get a decent pension. My family need that. I need that.'

'What did you do when you did have work?'

His mouth set in a straight line. His soft brown eyes regarded her as though considering the right words and whether she could take what he was about to say.

'I didn't work on a tobacco plantation, but it was something similar, where the work was seasonal, but there was nothing else around. Not where I lived. Not for the likes of me.'

She continued to look up at him even after the dance was over. 'I hope you get all you want and all you deserve.' With a quiet smile, she stood on tiptoe and kissed his cheek. 'Be lucky, Jonah.'

'Thank you.'

Waving her hand in front of her face, she declined dancing the jitterbug in favour of sitting a while with a cold drink and her thoughts for company.

Hot and breathless from some pretty frantic dancing with both white and black men, Carole, Maisie and her other friends from the factory slumped into their chairs and cooled their faces with pieces of newspaper folded into fans.

Bridget's mind was consumed with thoughts of what would happen tomorrow. Temple Meads Station at 9.30 sharp and a train to Crossborough, a town she'd never heard of in the Midlands, hardly a danger zone like Malta where Phyllis was stationed.

'I smells trouble.'

Deep in thought, she hadn't really noticed the frown that crumpled Aggie's brow but did hear her remark. Her fierce gaze was fixed on a crowd of American white soldiers, who were glaring daggers at Jonah, the guy Bridget had been dancing with. Jonah was drinking, laughing and joking with soldiers whose complexions ranged from coffee with milk to dark molasses.

Bridget turned to Aggie. 'Is something wrong?'

The big woman who called the younger factory girls her 'chicks' jerked her chin at the group of white soldiers. 'You know, chick, I've 'ad all sorts in my pub over the years. From all over the world. Well we would, wouldn't we? Bristol is a sea port. Bound to get all sorts, but I ain't never seen two lots of blokes from the same country so divided. The gap between them is as big as the Avon Gorge. It's as though they ain't fightin' on the same side at all.'

With mounting concern, they watched as a couple of the white Americans accosted the club stewards, Sergeant Fred Downton and Polly, his wife. There was nodding, strained conversations and pointing fingers, first at the black guys and then at them – Bridget and her friends, the women who had dared dance with men of a different colour.

Aggie got to her feet. 'I don't like this. Best if we leave.'

'No.'

It was Maisie who protested. Although small in stature, she had the heart of a lion.

Looking determined to act, she got to her feet. 'Bridget is off tomorrow. It's 'er last night, this is the big send-off and I ain't 'avin' them spoiling things.'

Everyone regarded Maisie, unsure of what she might have in mind. Bridget feared the worst. Maisie had long had the habit of sticking up for the underdog, and in this bar there were plenty of those tonight.

Like a bantam cockerel looking for a fight, she strode across the dance floor with fists clenched. Voices were raised and although the Downtons were doing their best to calm things down, it wasn't working.

Maisie heard what the Downtons said. 'Look, this club is for all services personnel, no matter their...'

'If you ain't goin' to throw them out, then we will. Dancing with white women! We don't like that.'

An infuriated Maisie stabbed her finger into the back of the soldier. He spun round his fist raised ready to lash out. His fingers unclenched, his arm fell to his side. The surprise on his face was a joy to behold. There was Maisie Miles, a foot shorter than him, dark curls framing her face, brown eyes glaring and the finger that had stabbed him now in line with his nose.

'That's up to us, mister, not you!' snarled Maisie. 'Now look yer, soldier. My mate Bridget is off to 'er posting tomorrow. Off to nurse blokes like you that might get injured in this lot. So I'm telling you now, we ain't 'avin' any nonsense from somebody who don't seem to know what this war is all about. It's about all races being equal, though I would 'ave thought you Yanks would know that.'

'All men are created—' he sputtered.

Maisie interrupted. 'Not women? Well, don't say that too loudly around yer, Yank. The women of this country ain't been winning ribbons for knitting bloody socks. We've been ambulance drivers, pilots, radar operators and God only knows what else. You're insulting us and you're insulting yer own country. Carry on as you are and I swear that every woman in this place will walk out. Think of that soldier. A dance 'all and no women. Unless you like dancing with each other? Is that yer bag?'

There were dropped jaws and some sniggering. One of them remarked, 'Hey, little lady, you've got a lot to say for yourself. Where did you spring from?'

Maisie pushed her face forwards so that her eyes glared up close to his. 'A bleedin' tough place where even the women would make mincemeat of the likes of you, soldier boy. Save yer energy for fighting the Nazis not yer own blokes.'

The face of the one whose back she had poked turned red, his jaw set square. Her insinuation about preferring blokes to girls had also hit home.

One of the others stepped forward to press his point. 'Well, you look a bit dark yourself, honey, a bit Italian, so I think…'

One of his pals laid a firm hand on his arm. 'Let it go, Chuck. We've insulted their pride and we sure as hell don't want to be stuck here with no broads, do we?'

Bridget read Maisie's mind. These were young guys away from home and on the biggest adventure of their lives and girls were a big part of that adventure. There was always a leader in a group out to cause trouble; the kind of bully who led when in the company of his mates, but kept his head down when all by himself. Maisie had picked him out.

She stood like a rock, a very big rock, not the small person she was physically.

'Your choice.' She directed her statement at the bully and saw the consternation in his eyes, knew he wanted to hit her but was also aware it wouldn't look good; brave men didn't hit girls – at least not in company. There was also Jonah and his friends paying attention to what was happening and unlikely to stand back and do nothing if things got nasty.

Nobody moved.

'Right,' said Maisie, turning her back. 'Let's 'ave a bit of music then, shall we?'

Before the altercation, the music had been from a wind-up radiogram, a larger appliance than a straightforward gramophone, though not that much louder. The gramophone where the records were played sat on top; the rest of the cabinet was taken up with a wireless. Mrs Downton turned it on and they were listening to Ambrose playing band music from a hotel in London. On seeing the impact the music was making, one of the soldiers whisked Maisie onto the dance floor. Mrs Downton exchanged a look of satisfaction with her husband and turned the music up louder.

Other soldiers, both black and white, followed suit, grabbing a partner, their former antagonism drowned by music.

Only the ringleader didn't join in but left in a bad temper, causing the club's double doors to crash behind him.

The tinkling notes of a piano began playing, along with the music from the wireless, though more up tempo. It was Jonah, the guy Bridget had been dancing with. He began to sing, his voice so rich and vibrant that it even had Aggie tapping her feet before she, too, was again throwing herself about on the dance floor to music that owed more to jazz than to swing.

The music and words of 'Chattanooga Choo-Choo' was not only irresistible to feet longing to dance, it took over the very atmosphere, infusing it with warmth and vitality. Everything else that had happened was buried in outright joy. Even when the music on the wireless changed, Jonah was still at it, belting the piano and singing loud for the fast numbers, more gently for the slower numbers, his voice caressing the lyrics of 'The Way You Look Tonight'.

Bridget barely noticed when someone else asked her to dance. Tears stung her eyes as she listened to the words she'd last heard sung by Fred Astaire. Lyndon had sung them to her – or at least she thought he had. Perhaps he hadn't, perhaps it was just that she felt it was the kind of song he would have sung to her. It felt as though he was here, sitting in the empty chair opposite, singing or saying them to her. She didn't mind which. All she wished was that he was here or that she could turn back time and they were lying in bed together on that single night away, the only time she'd ever felt his naked body against hers.

When Bridget didn't respond, the young man took Carole away and swung her round the floor instead.

\* \* \*

Absorbed in having a good time, nobody noticed the return of the bully, except for Maisie. He lurched in staggering and it didn't take a genius to realise he was drunk and, it appeared, not alone. Or at least, that's how it seemed until she realised that the two dark-clad figures standing behind him were not American. Neither were they soldiers or returning to support their mate. One of them was Alf, her half-brother.

This, she decided, was turning into a most wonderful night indeed!

Excusing herself from her dancing partner, she headed towards the two darkly clad figures but found herself face to face with the bully's wide chest.

'You little slut,' he muttered, his eyes small and piggy in his bright red face. 'I'm gonna take you outside and teach you a lesson.'

He lurched forward, his hands forming two massive claws. If

he'd managed to grab her with those big, rough hands, there would have been nothing she could do, but his grip fell short. Suddenly, his arms were flailing like windmills, his feet sliding from beneath him as he was jerked backwards.

'Hey, Yank. That's my sister you're threatening.'

Too drunk to find his feet, the bully was turned onto his front by two pairs of calloused hands and propelled head-first into the pair of double doors. He went through them like a battering ram, the doors closing with a clatter behind him.

Alf picked her up and swung her round, both laughing with glee as Maisie bombarded him with questions about where he had been, when he had got back and how long before he went off to sea again.

'Whoa, whoa! Too many questions. Can a man get a drink here?'

There was a smile on Maisie's face. Alf was the apple of her eye, but in her enthusiasm to greet him, she'd failed to acknowledge the man he was with. On first sight, she saw he was built like a bull, big and solid. Like Alf, he was dressed in the dark navy of a merchant seaman.

She smiled up at him. 'Hello, mister. Do you want a drink too?'

She barely heard him respond that he did, his white teeth flashing in brown skin patterned with indigo-coloured whirls on his cheeks, forehead, nose and chin.

'OK, Alf, so who's your friend?'

'Kauri my shipmate. Kauri, my sister Maisie. He's Maori, the native people of New Zealand. Right. Now about that drink...'

'Pleased to meet you,' said Maisie once she'd recovered. Her friends also acknowledged the new arrivals, eyeing Kauri with undisguised curiosity.

Over a drink, Alf told her that serving on a merchant ship had become downright dangerous. 'It's the U-boats. I've had two ships torpedoed from under me.'

Maisie stared at him in horror. Her half-brother had never been one for letter writing. She'd told herself that no news was good news, but now it seemed she'd been kidding herself.

'I didn't want to worry you. Anyway, got picked up quick the first time,' said Alf, 'but the second time took a bit longer. Drifted for miles we did, but got picked up eventually. Had to spend a bit of time in hospital.'

'And you never thought to tell me?'

He shrugged casually in the way she remembered. 'Anyway, all's well that ends well. Kauri was a big help. He knows a bit about the ocean, more than most blokes. Knows how to gather rainwater and fish with nothing much more than a piece of string.'

Maisie looked round to ask more about it of Alf's friend, but he'd gone. Jonah was belting out another number on the piano and Kauri was singing along with great gusto.

Aggie waved and shouted across the room.

'Nice to see you again, Alf. Ain't seen you for ages. Is that yer mate over there singing a bit off-key?'

'He thinks he can sing.'

Aggie laughed. 'I knows what you mean. My old man tells me I sing like an earwig.'

Alf frowned. 'I didn't know earwigs could sing.'

'They don't. What 'e meant was that neither should I.'

Aggie nudged Bridget, who was sitting beside her looking pleased for Maisie but half wishing it had been Lyndon who'd come through that door.

'He ain't the first Kiwi I've seen. You get all sorts in a sea port and our pub's 'ad its share.' Besides working at the factory, Aggie ran a quayside pub with her husband who was called Curly though he didn't have a single hair on his head. She reckoned going out to work kept her sane and she might commit murder if she had to be with her old man day and night.'

Bridget gazed around the room. 'What gets me is that we've seen more people from other countries in one year than we ever did all our lives.'

'You're right there. I know some people who barely know their neighbours in the next street, let alone people from another country.'

Alf greeted Bridget and Carole; the latter staring at him as though inclined to eat him for supper. Maisie smiled. Alf was a good-looking bloke, more so now that the sea had hardened him up, but Carole wouldn't stand a chance. Alf wasn't female-inclined.

Towels were being placed over the beer pumps. The last glasses were being gathered for washing. The lilting melody 'Goodnight Sweetheart', sung soft and low, signalled that the fun was over.

As the last notes drifted away, Alf told Maisie that he and Kauri were staying at the Seamen's Mission. 'I'll be there a few days.' There was something about the look in his eyes that told her she wasn't being told everything.

'I'm glad about that. Couldn't see you stayin' with me and me gran seeing as...' Her words trailed off. Their eyes met. That's when she knew that whatever he was holding back had to do with her stepfather, Frank Miles. 'What is it, Alf? What ain't you tellin' me?'

Alf hesitated before answering. 'Me dad's in the prison hospital. He ain't expected to last long, so...' That casual shrug again. 'I'm 'ere to do the right thing. Visit the old bugger before he kicks the bucket.' Another pause. 'I don't suppose...'

Immediately guessing what he was about to say, Maisie shook her head vigorously. 'No. I don't want to see 'im.'

'I can't blame you fer wishin' 'im dead.'

'I don't say that I wish the old sod dead, but I owe 'im nothing.

He never did right by me and can't expect something returned that was never given. No, Alf. He's your dad, not mine.'

'You're right. We shared a mother. That's all.' There was regret in his voice coupled with sadness. 'I wish things 'ad been different. Wish I could 'ave done more for both of you.'

'You were only a kid, but you looked out for me, Alf. I don't know what would 'ave 'appened if you 'adn't.'

The thought of those days sent a shiver down her spine and further strengthened her resolve not to visit her stepfather. The bitter memories came flooding back at just the thought of him. Her mother had given birth to Alf some time before she'd fallen for a dark-eyed handsome man, left Frank for him and given birth to Maisie. Frank Miles had never forgiven her mother. Her natural father had been found dead. The finger was pointed at Frank, but nothing was proved. So her mother had gone back to Frank, who had lost no time in taking his revenge on her with his fists and on the daughter. It wasn't ideal, in fact far from it.

As a kid, she'd been half starved, dressed in rags and witness to his flailing fists connecting with her mother's body. It hadn't been until Alf was big enough to defend their mother that things had improved. It still didn't excuse Frank's treatment of Maisie, the threat to sell her off to Eddie Bridgeman, the local gangster who liked young girls too much. Then there was Frank's dealing in rotten meat on the black market, that had caused the death of two children. No. She hoped he rotted in prison. It was a case of just desserts.

'I can't, Alf. I just can't.'

'I understand.'

* * *

They all left in a crowd, Carole living closest being the first to peel off into her house.

'Glad of the blackout,' she murmured into Maisie's ear before setting off down the garden path. 'Me mum can't see that big New Zealander. She'd drag 'im in without a second thought, all services free of charge!'

There was laughter and the realisation on Maisie's part that she'd come to like Carole a lot.

Bridget and Maisie hugged before splitting up to make for their appropriate bus stops. Aggie headed for home down on the Welsh Back and Maisie peeled off to join Alf and his friend, Kauri.

Alf shouted his good wishes. 'All the best, Bridge. Sorry I can't be there to see you off.'

'A working girl has to work,' Bridget returned laughingly, though her stomach churned with a mix of apprehension and fear.

'Make sure you write.'

'You mean like you do, Alf Miles!' Maisie exclaimed.

Bridget laughed. 'I will.'

It was hard to let go. Their tears had mingled by the time they did.

'Be happy,' Alf shouted as she disappeared into the darkness.

Bridget pretended she didn't hear. The tears were streaming down her face. Just for once in this blasted war she was glad of the blackout so nobody could see them and it wasn't just because she was leaving her family and friends at the factory behind. Overcome with nervous fear, she was grieving for Lyndon and a past that might or might not catch up with them.

# 6

## MAISIE

Alf and his New Zealand friend had waited with her for the bus to Totterdown, though Kauri had offered to walk Aggie home, an offer that had led to a bray of derisive laughter.

'As if I need that,' Aggie declared. 'Nobody would dare.'

They had to concede that she was probably right.

And so it was that they saw Maisie get on the bus before winding their way back to the city centre and the Seamen's Mission in Anchor Road.

Spotlighting the pavement ahead of her with her trusty torch, Maisie made her way from the bus stop on Wells Road down to where she lived. Everything was in darkness, of course, though there were faint outlines she could just about recognise in the city panorama spread out like an army blanket beyond the wall at the end of the road.

After almost bumping into the street lamp outside her grandmother's house, she swung into the short path, got out her key, unlocked and went in, expecting light and finding only darkness. She paused and not just because she could barely see where she was going. On nights when she was likely to be home late, her grandmother left on the hall gas light and the one further down the passage. Tonight all she could see was the glimmer of the tiny pilot lights, like white pinpricks in the darkness.

Shutting the door softly behind her, Maisie stood and listened but heard nothing, just the slight click of a warm house settling down for a cold night.

'Gran?'

Her voice bounced back at her from the empty passageway.

Once she'd flicked the pilot light onto the gas mantel, she hung up her coat and headed for the kitchen. Those lights too were unlit. A saucepan containing the last of the evening meal they'd shared was still on the stove. The gas was out and the dishes they'd used were unwashed. Gran had insisted she would do them. They never left dishes unwashed.

'Gran?'

Maisie turned to the living-room door which was back along the passageway at the front of the house. Just for once it was closed. Maisie frowned. It was rarely closed. It was where her grandmother listened to the wireless and shouted a greeting the moment Maisie was in from work.

Her sense of panic grew.

'Gran?'

She grabbed the big round ivory doorknob, gave it a twist and when that didn't work, heaved her shoulder into the door. A gap opened, just enough to allow her to squeeze through.

A faint light glowed from within so that she could see that her grandmother was lying on the floor behind the door, her body preventing it opening.

\* \* \*

There was blood on one side of her gran's head which was what had decided Maisie to get a neighbour to find the local bobby. He'd been only two streets away so hadn't took long getting there.

Once he'd had time to assess the situation she made him a cup of tea, plus one for herself. He supped his back appreciatively. Hers was still cooling on the sideboard as a wave of emotions struck her. She hadn't long moved in with Grace Wells, her grandmother, and had grown rapidly fond of her.

The police constable sat down beside her on the settee and patted her knee. Maisie moved away from him, a clear signal his intimacy was unwelcome.

It was unclear whether he noticed or not, though his tone did become more officious.

'There was nothin' you could 'ave done, me love. The doctor reckons she 'ad a funny turn – probably her 'eart. She'd put on the light in this room and drawn the blackout curtains and then was 'eadin' off to light up the gas, I expect. That was when it 'appened.'

'She left the lights on for me when I came home, but they weren't on when I got in.'

She looked down at the floor, the brown and green of the highly polished linoleum, the aspidistra plant growing in a dark blue bowl set on a dark blue pillar. She'd remember all of it for the wrong reasons. Grace Wells, her grandmother, was dead, and that toerag Frank Miles was still alive – though only just by the sounds of it. In her estimation, he deserved to die; her grandmother did not.

The pounding of the front door echoed along the passageway.

'Ah. That should be Mr Flower,' said the constable, resigned that the welcome respite from pounding the sloping streets of Totterdown and the Wells Road had ended.

Mr Flower, the undertaker, had the look of a man well suited to his profession having gaunt features and eyes that, although deep-set, seemed too big for his face. His whiskers were profuse, resembling those seen on old Victorian photographs. A silver watch chain glimmered from his waistcoat, which was black, as were the rest of his clothes.

The constable introduced them. 'Miss Miles is the deceased's granddaughter. It was she who found the body.'

He stood with his helmet tucked under his arm.

'Thank you and goodbye,' said Maisie, indicating the narrow passage and the front door.

'Right,' said the constable, setting his helmet back on his head and looking disappointed that he wasn't being asked to stay.

'Commiserations, my dear,' said Mr Flower, bony white hands clasping his top hat at loin level. A bald spot gleamed with reflected light as he bent from the waist in a deep bow, his voice a respectful hush. He told her all the formalities that had to be adhered to, the choice of casket, method of burial, church arrangements. 'The latter dependent on your grandmother's last wishes. I understand she was a woman of property and of a prudent disposition.'

Maisie's gaze fell to his overly long fingers, their whiteness grimly stark against the dark serge of his trousers.

'In which case,' the undertaker went on in a controlled, monotone manner, 'she may have instructed a solicitor as to her final wishes. As a woman of property,' he added again, just in case she hadn't heard the first time. 'Do you happen to know any details?'

Her mind went to the roll-top bureau in a dark corner of her grandmother's bedroom. Even when her eyesight was deteriorating, she'd sometimes spent time up there, her perusal of paperwork reliant on a pair of spectacles and a magnifying glass. Any time Maisie had chanced to enter the room, the roll-top of the old desk, the wooden slats dry and split in places, rumbled shut.

Her chin jerked in a sharp nod. 'I know where to look.'

He wasn't to know that she referred to money as much as to

paperwork. The old desk also held a small metal box, its contents referred to as petty cash. Money for paying for what needed paying; her grandmother had informed her of its existence. 'In case of unforeseen circumstances,' Grace Wells had told her.

Maisie was no fool. She'd understood what her grandmother meant. This, she decided, was the one and only unforeseen circumstance she'd been referring to.

'My grandmother left me enough in cash to pay for her funeral.'

'Ah!' said Mr Flower, his grim expression suddenly lifted at the thought of cash on the nail; the funeral costs paid up front before a sod of earth had been turned in the cemetery. 'Then leave it with me, my dear Miss Miles, to take care of everything. My bill will be with you by tomorrow at the end of the day – seeing as it's cash – unless, of course, you'd first like to peruse any documents Mrs Wells left behind?' He looked hopeful that she wasn't going to do that. Perusing legal documents could take time, and besides, she might be one of those who wanted a cremation – a modern idiosyncrasy in his view, and costing far less than a dug grave, a fine oak coffin and a marble gravestone.

Maisie was resolute. 'No. The money was left for this. Bring me the bill.'

'I will indeed,' he said, his elongated frame unbending in a series of three portions, upper body, upper legs, then lower from the knees. He towered over her, so tall that he was forced to hold his top hat in his hands, his scalp collecting a white film of lime wash from the ceiling. 'I'll get my assistant in from outside. One at a time to discuss arrangements you see, but I'll need his help to lay her out in the front room.'

She nodded, unwilling to help, devastated by the suddenness of what had happened. Her grandmother deserved respect and she would get it.

'The gas bag is being filled. As soon as it's done, we'll be round to collect her – unless you'd prefer to wait until tomorrow along with the bill?'

'No. That's fine.'

It wasn't really fine but not due to the bill but to something that struck her as slightly disrespectful. She would have preferred the vehicle to run on petrol not dependant on gas from a huge bag fixed to its roof. It didn't seem right somehow, but then, there's a war on! God, how she was beginning to hate that sentence.

After closing the door behind him, she made her way up the stairs to her grandmother's bedroom at the front of the house and stood eyeing the sturdy furniture, the lace cloth covering the tallboy, the cast-iron bed with its shiny brass knobs.

The room still smelt of her, a mixture of lavender and mothballs but equally of crisp linen laundered weekly and smelling of fresh air. Maisie smiled. Her grandmother did like a good drying day. Memories of her wisdom and sayings crowded into her mind and brought tears to her eyes. She'd only made Grace Wells' acquaintance on finding out that Frank Miles was not her father – a fact Maisie was rather grateful for. As she had lay dying, her mother had told her the truth about her parentage and that she should look up Grace Wells, mother of her real father and therefore her grandmother. Initially, their introduction had not been promising, but after only a little time, Maisie had found herself valuing their relationship, had moved in with her and had come to love her.

There was a numbness in her fingers, her feet and an odd constriction in her throat. She told herself that she wasn't going to cry. She clasped her hands tightly together as though that would stop her feeling the pain of loss. Not just the loss of her grandmother, but that of her friends and her brother no longer being here. She would be all alone in the world, but she wouldn't cry!

Grief took hold of her. At first her shoulders hunched then

heaved with sobs. Her face swiftly became wet with tears and for some reason she thought of Sid.

\* \* \*

It was the next day when Maisie finally felt up to opening the roll-top desk. Dust motes moved in the air in front of the light streaming in from the window as she passed through them and stood before what her grandmother had referred to as her office.

It was a big old thing, but despite scratches and damaged slats, it was well polished. The brass handle at its curved base was warm in her palm. For a moment, Maisie hesitated before turning the key and tugging it upwards.

Items of paperwork were secreted in pigeonholes of varying sizes built into the structure. A fountain pen and three pencils were arranged neatly, alongside a bottle of ink above a blotting pad.

Everything was as her grandmother had left it and to disturb it in any way seemed disrespectful, but it was something she had to do.

She took a deep breath, pulled the old piano stool from beneath it and sat down.

The paperwork mostly consisted of paid bills and a book recording sums paid in respect of loans made at substantial interest. There were not so many as there used to be, her grandmother fully accepting that her faculties were failing her. Common sense dictated she curtail her business to a size she could cope with. All of the properties she'd owned had been sold – except for the one they lived in. From what she could see, it was owned outright. But what now? Maisie thought. She must have left it to someone and that someone would be mentioned in the will.

Secreted between the pigeonholes was a letter-size drawer with a small brass knob. One look and Maisie knew this was a secret place, out of sight of prying eyes.

First, she brought out a small pile of letters tied with a black ribbon. Someone had died. She presumed her grandfather, Grace Wells' husband. Below that was a leather photograph folder. Setting both aside, she took out the very last item, a dark brown envelope of what Maisie guessed was the correct size to contain a will. Not that she'd ever come across one. Her mother had owned nothing.

Maisie's heart skipped a beat. The feeling was so strong that she clapped a hand on her chest. 'Oh my,' she said softly.

Not having been in this situation before, she wondered whether it was for her to open the envelope or whether she should take it to a solicitor.

For now unable to bear opening it, she set it to one side. Tomorrow would be soon enough.

Tomorrow came and she found herself unable to face breakfast and it was after midday when she plucked up the courage to go back to the bureau.

Yet again she weighed what she presumed to be the will but paused, still undecided, still half afraid of what was inside.

Suddenly an impatient rapping on the front door reverberated through the house.

It seemed too early for it to be the bill from the funeral directors, but she wasn't expecting anyone else, unless a neighbour was calling to offer condolences. That's what people usually did.

Daylight fell into the hallway as Maisie pulled open the front door and there was Alf, cap in hand, looking aggrieved.

'I went to the factory to tell you I'll be off soon. They told me you weren't in today. I'm sorry about your grandmother.'

Her head fell heavily against her brother's chest. 'Alf, you cannot believe how glad I am to see you. Mind,' she said as she straightened and wiped at her eyes, 'you did give me a fright. I thought it was a bomb going off the way you hammered at that door.'

He laughed as she let him in. 'You ain't usually so nervous.'

She glanced at the front windows of the tiny, terraced houses that made up the street. All of them had their blackout curtains closed and a card of condolence stuck up in the window. Even if some might not have liked her grandmother, they certainly respected her.

On closing the door, Maisie took a deep breath. 'It's being alone in this house with only a corpse in the front room. The funeral directors laid 'er out in there. I could 'ave 'ad them take 'er to the funeral parlour, but she took me in. Don't seem right to chuck 'er out now. Want to see 'er?'

Alf was about to shake his head and say no, but reconsidered. 'It won't 'urt to pay me respects. I didn't know 'er, but she looked after you so that's a good enough reason for me.'

The front room was cold and dark. Like the rest of the street, Maisie had drawn the blackout curtains.

'The funeral directors are taking her later this afternoon. I couldn't bear to rush it. I needed time to say goodbye. She didn't chuck me out and I can't chuck 'er out either.'

Hat in hand, Alf moved to where Grace Wells lay on the special table Mr Flower had brought with him. It was a fold-up type so easy to get through the passageways of awkward houses – or anywhere else for that matter. Not that she'd needed it explained to her, but she'd let him carry on anyway.

She told Alf all about it as he bent his head over her grandmother. It was impossible to see much of her features, of course, but from the expression on Alf's face, Maisie found herself wondering if Alf had ever seen Grace Wells before.

Once he'd finished, she shut the door behind them and led him through to the kitchen.

'Cup of tea?'

She detected a frown on his face.

'I seen 'er before.'

It was odd that what she had been thinking had come out without her encouragement.

She looked over her shoulder as she put the kettle on the gas. 'Where?'

He shrugged. 'I think it was a funeral. Don't know whose funeral it was, but I remember it being a big turnout. One thing though, I remember the horses. Big black horses with plumes on their heads.'

Arms folded and her curiosity aroused, Maisie asked him when it was.

He shrugged again, threw his hat onto the table and pulled up a chair. 'I was only a nipper. I remember our Ma holding onto me hand.' He shook his head. 'That's about it. Just those great big black horses.'

'Never mind. It was all a long time ago. I'm going through her paperwork. There's a will. I haven't opened it yet.'

'Well, p'raps she's leaving you a fortune.'

'I don't know about that,' said Maisie as she poured the tea. She didn't mention that the envelope looked new and that it was possible that her grandmother might have drafted a new will. In a way, she didn't want to open it and find out, not so much because she'd be disappointed if she hadn't left her anything, but because she wasn't around to be thanked if she had.

Alf took an appreciative gulp of tea. 'Strikes me you're the only living relative. Then whatever she left is yours.'

Maisie sipped at her tea. 'I don't want to talk about it, Alf. Not with 'er lying dead in the next room.'

He nodded his approval over his cup. 'Course you don't. I can understand that.' He set his cup back into the saucer. 'I'd better be off.'

Maisie looked at him with worried eyes. 'You've only got two days.'

Using both hands, he set his cap back on his head. 'That's the way it is. Me and Kauri are booked to leave Avonmouth on the ten o'clock tide.'

'Will it be a long trip?'

Alf patted the side of his nose with one finger. 'That's not for me to say or you to know. Careless talk costs lives.'

She smiled through the tears that threatened. He was only her half-brother, but no one had ever been closer.

Suddenly her hand flew to her mouth. 'Alf. I forgot to ask about Frank. Is he...'

'Gone?' He shook his head. 'No. He's hanging in there. That old sod's too mean to die and give us all a break.' He paused and there was concern in his eyes when he looked at her. 'He asked after you.'

'Me?'

Alf nodded. 'He told me he was sorry fer treating you and our Ma how he did. He hopes you'll forgive 'im and...' Alf looked sheepish.

Maisie instantly knew what Frank Miles, her evil old stepfather, had said. 'He asked if I could visit 'im.'

'Yep,' said Alf, taking a firmer hold on his cap as he kissed her on the cheek. 'That's what 'e said. Now you take no note of it. Just take care of yerself. I'll see you whenever.'

'Yeah. Whenever.'

As she waved him off, she couldn't help old memories crowding into her mind. Some of them made her feel sick and some just sad. One thing she was certain of was that she wouldn't be visiting Frank Miles in prison even if he was at death's door.

After Alf had gone, she leant against the front door, steeling herself for what was to come: opening that envelope.

A few words of encouragement first. 'Get on with it, you lily-livered chump.'

She clomped back upstairs with dogged determination, plonked herself down on the stool and dragged the envelope and the other stuff towards her.

'Here goes...'

The letters she put to one side, the photograph folder to another, the envelope right in front of her. As she did so, something slid out of the photograph folder. Nothing was holding them in except for the fastening. Meaning to slip them all back inside, Maisie picked up both folder and photos and glanced at the latter before putting them back – then paused.

The photo was of a funeral cortège – a set of coal-black horses and an ornate hearse with etched glass windows. Three people stood in front of the hearse, their expressions glum, eyes fixed on the camera. One of them was a younger version of her mother. Her belly was big. A small boy was holding onto her hand. Alf, she thought sadly and thought how much she would miss him.

The third person, a man, had his arm round her mother. He had an open, honest face and despite his sombre dress, there was only what she could describe as liveliness in his eyes. His eyes were what she fixed on. They were as dark as her own, his skin a shade darker and reminding her of the Italians, who'd ran the ice cream parlour, interned at the beginning of the war.

Suddenly the ticking of the clockwork alarm on her grandmother's bedside table seemed louder than it had been as her breath caught in her throat. After slamming her hand down on the alarm, Maisie turned back to the photos of people she assumed were her relatives..

Placing that photo right in front of her, she picked out another.

This one was of another man in old-fashioned clothes and skin much darker than the man with his arm round her mother's shoulders. He was also older, with a few white streaks in glossy black curls that looked clamped to his skull. There was a young woman next to him with a strong face and a forthright look in her eyes. Her heart almost stopped.

Maisie turned the photo over and read what was written on the back: Mr Clive Wells and his new wife, Grace, 1888. These, she realised, were her grandparents, her father's parents: her grandmother fair, her grandfather a coffee brown – like some of Jonah's friends.

She shuffled the photos back and forth, Alf as a small boy standing at the side of the woman she knew to be her mother, the glimpse of a horse's head wearing a black plume. Her breath caught in her throat. Alf had described the funeral extremely well.

She found her father's birth certificate, but not her grandfather's. A little more searching and she found a postcard from somebody called Octavia. The postmark was Jamaica.

> *Dear Clive,*
>
> *I hope you have settled in the mother country. I saw our father in town driving his new motorcar with his wife and children. I waited until he was alone before I told him that you had married an Englishwoman. He sends you his best wishes and also promises to pay money into a bank account. It is to be used to set yourself up in business. You are only half British, but he says that should not deter you.*
>
> *Perhaps we will meet again, but perhaps not. Whatever God decides for you, I wish you and your new wife well.*
>
> *Your loving sister, Octavia.*

Dealing with her grandmother's death had been difficult, yet somehow there was a kind of relief, a calming, in reading the card and seeing the old photographs. So many things had become clear to Maisie.

She'd never been quite certain that her stepfather had killed her real father. Knowing him and now knowing of her father's antecedents, she totally believed it. As good as her real father might have been, Frank would have felt insulted that his wife had found a man of foreign extraction more attractive than him. Nothing could detract from the fact that he'd been a bully, a drunk and a thief. Her wish that Frank Miles would rot in hell was keenly felt.

And was it really possible that her grandfather was from Jamaica?

In an effort to believe, she regarded her reflection, saw the dark eyes, the springy curls and a complexion that bordered on olive – certainly not black. But Grandfather Wells didn't look that dark, her father lighter. And did she care? She decided she did not. This was the way things were and if she had known them, she was sure they'd have been better people than Frank Miles.

She opened the envelope she'd assumed contained the will and was only partially disappointed. It contained a letter referring to the will from a solicitor's address in Bristol centre.

Her grandmother's life was over and, in a strange way, it seemed hers was about to begin.

# 7

## BRIDGET

There had been tears at Temple Meads Station from Bridget's parents mostly, her siblings' interest vying between her and the trains.

'We'll miss you,' they'd finally called out as a sea of family waves had seen her off.

Through the train window, she stared at fields, towns and villages, church steeples showing above huddled houses and girdled with trees. In the past, she would have enjoyed such scenes, but there was a dullness and slowness to everything, including the tedious train journey.

The Midlands. A town called Crossborough. She really didn't know what to expect.

The carriage compartment was stuffed with a mix of people that changed every time they stopped at a main station. Everyone seemed to be in uniform. Everything smelt of damp wool and tobacco smoke and those who weren't in uniform seemed like islands, unwilling to smile, let alone speak. Some huddled behind newspapers, the headlines shouting at her in large black letters.

ALLIED GAINS IN NORTH AFRICA – END IN SIGHT
GRAIN SHIPS SUNK IN NORTH ATLANTIC
UTILITY FURTHER REDUCES CLOTH FOR
WOMEN'S SKIRTS

Bridget closed her eyes. None of the news was very uplifting and she was very much looking forward to the journey's end, despite its distance from everything and everyone she knew. An adventure, she thought to herself. Just like Phyllis, though closer to home.

\* \* \*

A bus ride and a lengthy walk later, Bridget arrived at Crossborough infirmary, its edifice of grey stone with ramparts supposedly resembling a castle, but to her mind more of a prison.

Dour expressions on old paintings looked down from the walls of the reception hall, a place of high ceilings and marble floors. She shivered, at the same time thinking a nice red rug and less dark old oil paintings might make the place look warmer.

A matronly woman with a clipboard asked her name, looked her up and down and, apparently satisfied at what she saw, ticked acceptance on the clipboard.

'Along that corridor to the waiting area at the end. You'll be called when they're ready.'

There were two other girls. One looked as though she'd stepped out of a fashion magazine. She didn't so much walk as glide; her clothes looked expensive, she was tall and slim with blonde hair resting in a victory roll at the nape of her neck. The other girl was very dark with big brown eyes and full lips. Overall, she looked ill at ease with her surroundings. Bridget smiled at her and whispered hello. The girl nodded back but didn't smile.

'My ma scoured Selfridges for the requisite black stockings and shoes. Found them eventually. My name's Mathilda by the way. Mathilda Fortescue. You can call me Tilly. I'm from London.'

Everything about the statuesque blonde named Tilly shouted class. Her clothes were of a quality that only smart London shops could supply – at a huge price. She was smoking a cigarette through a pink and silver holder. It looked as expensive as she did.

Each to their own, thought Bridget and smiled anyway. 'Well, that was lucky for you. My name's Bridget. Bridget Milligan.'

'Irish?' she asked with a slight arching of her eyebrows.

'A long way back.'

'Ah!' she responded with an air of finality. 'We all go back some-where, I suppose. How did you fare with trawling the shops for the clothes requirement?'

'We managed,' Bridget replied. 'I've got everything. I think the black stockings were the most difficult to get hold of.'

The fact was that they were the only things she'd been required to bring with her that weren't second-hand. The black duty shoes and slippers were from one of the many clothes exchanges that had sprung up in church halls and community centres. She'd never had use for a dressing gown, but her mother, being handy with a needle, had applied herself to Bridget's needs and made one from a pale green silk bedspread dotted with appliqué flowers.

It was noticeable that Tilly didn't ask the other girl whether she'd had trouble finding the desired items of clothing. Her profile incredibly classic and strikingly beautiful, looked isolated and thoughtful. Bridget determined to reach out to her.

'How did you get on finding stockings and things,' she asked. 'My name's Bridget by the way – just in case you missed it.' She smiled in a way that invited an exchange of names; a smile at least.

The girl looked a bit surprised to be asked and her hesitance proved her undoing. Just as she opened her mouth to respond, a woman in a white coat approached. Her hair was iron grey and set in a rigid style. Her jaw and lips were rigid too without the slightest hint of a smile.

'I'm Sister Jackson, the assistant matron. This way please. One at a time to see matron. You first.'

She pointed at Bridget, who smiled nervously at her companions and followed the stalwart figure along to a dark green door.

Matron was as unsmiling as her assistant. Bridget was not invited to sit down but was asked about her standard of education, did she read a lot and how about writing? She said that she did read a lot.

'Good. You will be taking exams and although you are only a nursing auxiliary, a decent command of reading and writing is required. This is not a place for silly girls who can barely write their name. I will also stress right here and now that cleanliness must be of the highest standard. We cannot allow for cross-contamination occurring. In that regard, you must not under any circumstances wear your vest to bed or your bra on top of your vest. Day clothes must be left off at night. Bathing is an absolute; once a week at least if water rationing allows. Two inches the government ordain and two inches it must be. Right!' She nodded at the assistant matron before her stern features returned to Bridget. 'Wait outside whilst I interview the other girls. Sister Jackson will then take all three of you over to the nurses' home where you will find a freshly laundered and ironed uniform awaiting you on the bed. Ensure you keep it that way. Slovenly habits will not be tolerated. Put it on immediately, and be warned, you are not allowed to wear it outside the hospital grounds. You are not allowed to wear your apron outside the ward. Is all that clear?'

'Yes, matron.'

Outside the interview room, Sister Jackson pointed in the direction of the hard wooden chair that she'd sat on earlier. 'Wait there.'

Tilly was already on her feet. 'Mathilda Fortescue. I presume I'm next.'

Perhaps it was the fact that she was a foot taller than Sister Jackson along with her upper-crust name delivered in a cut-glass accent, but she was not contradicted.

'Well,' said Bridget as she sat back down, 'for a moment there, I thought I was up before a sergeant major, not a hospital matron.'

The girl with the big dark eyes and warm brown skin looked at her. 'Matrons are all like that. My name's Christina Reyanne by the way.' She offered her hand to be shaken. Bridget noticed her pale pink palms and felt their silky softness as they shook hands.

'Have you worked in a hospital before?'

'Yes. I have. I'm a qualified nurse. I tried to get into the QAs, but there were so many applicants, they could pick and choose as they liked. I even tried the Territorial Nursing Corps, but that was pretty much the same, though they did put me on their waiting list.'

For some reason, Bridget had expected Christina to have a regional accent, but she didn't. In fact, her voice was almost as refined and clear cut as that of Mathilda Fortescue.

She eyed her dark good looks, the glossy brown skin combined with black hair tucked away into the open fretwork of a navy blue snood. She reminded her of the Italians who had run an ice cream parlour in East Street. They weren't there now, taken away by the police and incarcerated simply for being Italian.

'My word. You're going to know so much more than the likes of me and her ladyship.'

'Ladyship?'

Bridget jerked her chin in the direction of matron's office. 'Matilda Fortescue.'

'Ah yes.' Christina smiled. 'She will no doubt do very well and join the QAs.'

'Oh my. I suppose that means she's qualified.'

Christina's smile widened in a knowing but slightly contemptuous way. 'She's from the right background. That's qualification enough.'

'So why did you come here?'

Along with a heartfelt sigh, Christina's demeanour changed. 'I come from London. Nurses, no matter your race, are in big demand there. But my fiancé is interned not far from here at a village called Pucklechurch. Do you know it?'

'I've never been there, but I've heard the name.' Respecting her privacy, she waited for Christina to explain why he'd been interned.

'He's a German He has a German father and a French mother'

'I see.' Bridget felt instantly sorry for her and glad she'd left her to explain. 'Will he be interned for long?'

Christina shook her head. 'It could be only temporary. There's a bigger camp on the Isle of Man and if he doesn't get sent there, he might get sent to Canada.'

The velvet brown eyes filled with unshed tears. Bridget could see there was more but left Christina to tell her in her own good time.

Another heartfelt sigh. 'I wanted to be near him.. My mother was French, born in France, but my father hailed from Martinique. I don't know whether you know where that is...'

'It's a French island. In the Caribbean.'

Christina nodded and looked surprised that Bridget knew of it. 'My fiancé worked for the French embassy here in London – not an important position. If he had, he might not have been interned.

'I hope it all works out for you,' said Bridget. She reached out and gave Christina's hand a squeeze.

\* \* \*

Throughout the country, even before war was declared, initial training had been introduced in a military medical section annexed to a main hospital. Some were privately funded hospitals, some not. Crossborough was an infirmary, the third category and the least well funded. Built in Victorian times, it had an air of poverty about it and had been created for patients the least able to pay for their treatment. The sight of the adjacent cemetery viewed through a ward window sent a shiver down Bridget's spine. Past patients must have had the same reaction. Gradually, over a period of weeks, things began to improve. Better equipment began to arrive and a laboratory was created in a series of red-brick huts with green tin roofs.

Despite being away from home, Bridget began to enjoy her work, though the hours were long and her feet ached like mad by the end of the day.

'Oh no,' she exclaimed as she eased off a shoe. 'Another hole.' She wriggled her big toe. No matter what she did her big toe always managed to push its way through her stocking.

Christina passed her the needle and thread. 'Keep it. You need it more than me.'

Bridget accepted it gratefully. Out of the corner of her eye, she saw Christina looking at Tilly's suitcase, which was stored on top of their one and only wardrobe – shared between three.

'Miss Mathilda's got a load of stockings in that case. I can't believe she got them all from shopping in London.'

Bridget glanced at the suitcase, then tellingly at Christina. 'What are you saying?'

A wicked smile upturned the corners of Christina's dark pink lips. 'I would say she has connections with the management of Selfridges, Harrods, or some overly generous American friends.'

'Now, now, Christina,' Bridget responded laughingly. Either suggestion could be true. A woman wanted to look her best. Just because women were donning uniforms didn't mean to say they stopped being feminine. Mr Churchill himself had stated that women looking their best lifted the spirits of fighting men.

\* \* \*

The next day, Bridget was back on duty, trailing along behind a surgeon who wanted to appraise their capabilities before the ward they were in was taken over by casualties arriving from North Africa. Great battles had been sweeping backwards and forwards across the Sahara Desert and the talk was that the campaign there was almost over. The nearest hospitals in Malta were being overwhelmed and although journeying through the Mediterranean and up the Western Approaches to England still carried some danger, hospital ships were getting through.

Shortly it would no longer be just a case of administering to civilians, the military was taking over and that included the nurses of Queen Alexandra's Imperial Military Nursing Corps.

No matter how hard she concentrated, Bridget prayed that nobody she knew would come through here; that everyone would get home safely.

'Milligan! Stop gazing out of the window and repeat what I've just said.'

The piercing eyes of the surgeon, Mr Gillespie, glared at her from beneath beetled brows of black hair.

He reined in a look of surprise when she repeated what he'd said word for word, then glanced out of the window thinking that perhaps there was something out there that shouldn't be missed. All he saw were leaves glittering against the startling white of silvered tree trunks swaying like lithesome dancers amongst the tombstones.

Tilly gave her a nudge as they left the ward and headed for the canteen. 'Darling, I fancy you have a photographic memory. I would never have been able to recall as you did, almost word for word. That dirge of a voice is even duller than that of my father, and that's saying something.'

They laughed then, glad to find something funny amongst all the doom and gloom that surrounded them. Bridget found herself warming to her new friends and, although they were a mixed bunch, finding comparisons with the girls at the tobacco factory. There was the same chumminess, the loyalty and feeling that they all had to pull together.

The military medical staff took their breaks in a hastily erected Nissen hut, a continual curve of corrugated tin painted in dark green much the same as the new dispensary/laboratory. Red crosses against white backgrounds picked all the huts out as hospital buildings though Crossborough was not heavily bombed as some of its larger and more industrialised neighbours.

Having had the chance to see her fiancé, Christina was a little happier at lunch. 'The camp is surrounded by trees. He's been doing work on a nearby farm and catching rabbits. No one is going hungry and the guards aren't too bad.'

'Will he be moved on from there?'

Christina shrugged. 'We can't say for sure, but if the farmer insists he's a hard worker, then there's more chance he can stay put.'

On hearing about this, Tilly promised her that she would write to someone important so he wouldn't be moved on. 'Anyway,' she added, 'as a former employee of the French Embassy and his mother being French, he shouldn't be there at all. Surely the Free French and General de Gaulle could make good use of him?'

'I doubt she can do anything,' Christina confided to Bridget when it was just the two of them.

'We can but hope and pray that he stays close.' She shrugged. 'Who knows? She might be able to do something.'

It always amazed both Christina and Bridget how many products Tilly kept in her suitcase, a whole drawer on the dressing table and along the cast-iron mantelpiece. Equally they enjoyed watching her brush her hair, spit into a block of mascara and brush it lavishly onto her copious eyelashes. Lipstick too was not a problem. It seemed she had three tubes, each of a slightly different shade of red. Tilly firmly believed in painting her face before painting the town.

Bridget felt obliged to make comment one evening. 'How do you manage to get hold of such wonderful make-up.'

Tilly laughed. 'I have a pre-war drawer full, darling. Would you like some?'

Bridget turned down her invitation to share the mascara. 'Actually I don't wear make-up.'

The classy beauty's jaw dropped. 'You mean those eyelashes are natural? And that skin is natural?'

There was something very satisfying about confirming that indeed her looks were all down to nature. 'My mother's the same. She doesn't look much more than late twenties, and that's after seven children.'

'Good grief,' Tilly muttered. 'I'm sure I'd look a fright after one!'

Despite their differing backgrounds, all three auxiliary nurses got on well. To Bridget's mind, it was the war that had broken down barriers and brought them together. She wondered whether they would still be friends after the war was over or part and go their separate ways. One thing both she and Tilly had in common was that Bridget's father had served and been injured during the Great War and Tilly's father had been a brigadier who had lost one eye due to shrapnel. 'Went to work in the War Office after that. Got himself a desk instead of a field gun,' Tilly had quipped.

Over late-night tea and toast, she had gone on to relate something of her home life. 'He uses one eye and a magnifying glass to read in the library at home. Books are his passion.' She had gone on to describe walls lined with shelving crammed with books. 'My mother continually nags him to get rid of some; he'd need a dozen lifetimes to get through them all.'

Bridget's eyes had sparkled as she remarked that it sounded wonderful. 'I've only got a small shelf of books.'

'All you need,' Tilly had declared as she took her ivory cigarette holder from the voluptuous cleavage straining against her buttons. 'Fancy a cigarette, darling?'

Together they had smoked, drank tea and ate a delicious slice of carrot cake, a popular recipe that did indeed use carrots to give the cake sweetness, plus just a teaspoonful of saccharine. Cakes, people had come to realise, were a good use for dried egg.

Bridget got out one of the textbooks they used for their studies. She so wanted to pass the first exam, both the practical and the theory, the details of which were mostly to be found in this book.

She looked up to find Tilly with her head held to one side, regarding her as though trying to see all the personal history she hadn't yet mentioned.

'What,' said Bridget, a warm smile flickering round her lips.

Tilly took a good long draw on her cigarette and leaned against the back of the chair, one hand tucked under her opposite arm. She looked about to say something, when her attention was diverted to the window. Doctors and laboratory people walked backwards and forwards across the grass.

'I say. That's a dish. Bags me. I saw him first.'

Bridget saw a blonde Adonis of a man wearing a white lab coat, a stethoscope resting like a medal of merit against his chest.

'Then he's all yours,' returned Bridget. 'I'm spoken for.'

Her smile vanished; Lyndon had been a subject of discussion.

'I know what you're going to say. I don't know when we'll meet again, but there is a war on.'

The clichéd line was overused, but nobody was in any doubt that the war had disrupted lives as no war in history had done before. To Bridget, it had become a mantra, something to fall back on when there was nothing else to be said.

Tilly blew a ring of smoke into the air and sighed. 'Ah. Your American. We all dream of the man we want to wake up with.'

'Is that so bad?'

'Desire is never bad in my book, though I do favour a man who is rich as well as handsome. I can't help myself.'

'I don't care about money. I just care about him.'

Bridget went back to a bit more cribbing for the exam. It mattered a lot to her that she passed with flying colours. Although her parents had voiced reluctant approval at her leaving home, she was twenty-one and had volunteered though in time would have been called up anyway. Becoming a nursing auxiliary had seemed a natural progression from doing first aid then driving an ambulance as she had done back at the factory. It was early days, but injured men were being brought in from all over the world.

The door to their room suddenly burst open and Christina came running in, face flushed. 'My fiancé is being set free. They want him in London.' Her excitement bubbling, she looked directly at Tilly. 'Whoever you wrote to did this for him – for us.' In seconds, she'd wrapped her arms round Tilly, who looked jolly pleased with herself.

'Not a problem, darling. As they say, it's not what you know, it's who you know.' Tilly smiled and winked.

\* \* \*

Inevitably, it was left to the auxiliaries to carry out the most menial jobs on a day-to-day basis alongside learning the more intense procedures that would take them through their examination. Once they'd passed auxiliary, they could, if they so desired, apply to join the Territorial Nursing Corps, which entailed yet more examinations, but at the end of it lay the prospect of becoming a fully qualified nurse. Those from the right background had the option to apply for a post in the QAs, but only after spending some time as a fully-fledged nurse.

Their first job of the afternoon was to wash out the glass syringes used for injections and it was a job Tilly hated. There were far more of them today than there usually was, some of them brand new and still in their wrapping. New they might be, but matron still insisted on them being washed.

'You do it,' Tilly said to Bridget, shoving the bundle of cloth containing one fragile syringe to Bridget. 'Please,' she begged. 'Do this and I'll get my dad to send me down a few books – which I won't read, unless they're fruity romances. I do love a fruity romance.'

They exchanged smiles but curbed their laughter. The QA matron was on the prowl, a stout woman of formidable height, her grey and red uniform big enough to power a decent sailing yacht.

Tilly wrinkled her nose whilst washing kidney dishes, some still stained with blood residual from a recent operation.

Bridget carefully unwound the gauze with which each syringe was protected and immersed them in the sluice, a contraption as big as a bath which produced a constant stream of hot water. Sometimes they discussed having a bath in the sluice, the only place hot water was guaranteed to flow. Government guidelines still ordered no more than two inches of water in a bath – hardly worth bothering with and never warm enough.

The glass of the syringes was extremely fragile, but regardless of its fragility every bit had to be washed, the metal plungers meticulously cleaned. As she set to washing the third syringe, Bridget felt the matron's beady eyes peering over her shoulder, so close she could feel her breath upon her neck.

Even though matron's attention was somewhat nerve-wracking, she took her time. Not one little bit of the device was ignored.

'Absolute cleanliness, Milligan. You know why don't you?'

Of course she knew why. 'Somebody's life might depend on it being clean.'

'Hmm,' muttered Matron. 'More than ever before very long.'

Bridget didn't really understand the cryptic comment. Getting things scrupulously clean was what she did day in and day out.

Finally, confident the job had been done to the standard required – not just her best but as per the strict instructions – she wrapped the final syringe in a cocoon of clean white gauze.

The wordless grunt Matron uttered sounded appreciative. What she said next confirmed it.

'These syringes have and will save many lives,' said Matron. 'It's imperative that none are broken. Take note, Fortescue.'

'Yes, Matron,' Tilly responded.

Bridget knew Tilly had damaged a few. All it took was for the thin glass to clink against the sink and it was gone, smashed to smithereens.

She felt Matron move away to stand over Tilly. Bridget's attention remained fixed on the gauze bundles.

Matron moved back to her. She fingered the gauze-wrapped syringes, then another of her approving grunts. 'You're to have the job permanently,' she said at last.

Though unsure why, Bridget thanked her.

'The syringes are part of the wider picture. There are three aspects to this procedure, Milligan. Each one contributes to the injection of something quite special into an injured man. I've been told by your tutors that you study hard and retain the information you're told. Come to the pharmacy when you've finished.'

'Goodness me,' exclaimed Tilly after she'd gone. 'My dear, you must have impressed Mr Gillespie big time.'

Bridget piled the bundles into her arms. 'I wonder what she wants me to do.'

Tilly giggled. 'Say nothing, my dear. Just wait with an open expression for her to tell you.'

* * *

The military nurses and medical staff had their own pharmacy centre, which was situated in what had once been the stables for the horses that had drawn ambulances back in the days when King Edward the Seventh had been king and the infirmary newly built 'for the benefit of the poor and destitute.'

Varnished wooden rafters open to the roof held apart white distempered walls along which were ranged rack upon rack of shelving of various sizes and glazed cupboards. A huge oak refectory table dominated the centre of the room. Pestles and mortars, three microscopes, banks of glass phials and tubes took up most of the room on the table.

The man in the white coat, who she recognised as the one Tilly was taken with, placed a large tin on the table. It resembled a paint tin, but Bridget knew there was no requirement for something like that in here.

'I've brought you a nurse, Doctor Khan. The one I told you about.'

'Good,' he said without looking up from what he was doing. 'Brian. Show her what to do.'

The pharmacist called Brian flashed a swift smile and, after a profuse goodbye to Matron, showed Bridget how to mix yellow powder as finely as possible so it could be stored as a liquid in a series of small glass containers.

'We keep it in here,' he said.

Everything seemed simple enough.

'Do you understand, nurse?'

She said that she did. Being just as careful as she had been with washing the syringes, she now measured out the yellow powder, fascinated as to what it might be.

Once she'd finished, Brian came over to collect it.

'Great. Another batch.' A fatherly figure of portly proportions, he beamed at her as though she'd just accomplished the most precious thing in the world.

'Is it that important?'

She had the instant impression of tears coming to his eyes. 'We think it's a lifesaver. It's called penicillin.'

* * *

It was the following day when Bridget got the chance to see just how lifesaving it was. A young man who'd injured his leg in North Africa was brought home on one of the latest hospital ships. His wounded leg had been immersed in plaster of Paris for the journey. Arriving at the hospital in Crossborough, it was her task to remove it. The stench cutting it off was terrible and hours later she could still smell it.

The corporal, a young man in his early twenties, was already in a bad way with a high temperature and soaked in sweat that smelt rancid, lacking both freshness and even masculinity.

Peering studiously at the wound, Mr Gillespie asked the young man, whose name was Arthur Crown, how he'd got it and, despite his usual dour manner, seemed to take a genuine interest in what the young man told him.

'Piece of shrapnel pinged against a tank, then rebounded and hit me. Weren't expecting it...'

Although he tried to sound casual, Bridget noted that the young man's voice shook as he told his tale and so did his bottom lip. His face had a sweaty gleam about it and every so often he trembled as he attempted to swallow a sudden stab of pain. There was also a haunted look in his eyes and in the way he kept asking the medical staff what his chances were. There was one question above all others.

'Am I going to lose my leg, Doc?'

Gillespie took a closer look at his injury and sniffed. 'It smells bad, but...' Bridget was startled when suddenly his hand landed on her shoulder. 'This young lady is going to inject you every four hours and I'll eat my stethoscope if we don't see a marked improvement by tomorrow morning. She'll administer the first one right away. You've got the best of both worlds, corporal, a magic bullet and a pretty nurse. What more could a man want?'

Bridget had only recently learned how to give an injection. Everyone was taught how to do it, but this was her first time with a real patient, a flesh and blood arm.

Gillespie patted the corporal's shoulder and smiled in a fatherly way Bridget had never seen before. 'We'll get you better, corporal. Trust to modern medicine. We now have a wonder drug.'

Bridget leaned in to fluff up his pillow. 'Despite the stupid old war, we're living in a time of wonder. Have you ever heard of William Budd?'

On hearing her mentioning the name to the corporal, Mr Gillespie paused and eyed her quizzically. 'You've heard of William Budd?'

She nodded. 'Yes sir. I'm from Bristol. He did a lot of his research there.'

Gillespie seemed to descend into deep thought before he scribbled on the medical notes clipped at the foot of the bed.

'An injection every four hours, nurse. Let me see you give the first one so I know for certain that you've got it right.'

Bridget gasped.

He pointed at the suffusion of yellow fluid Matron had had her prepare earlier.

'Yes, doctor.'

With great care, she suffused the correct measure of the yellow stuff she'd pounded into liquid into the syringe. Despite the doctor's presence, she kept her nerve, determined not to have her hand shake as she plunged the syringe into Corporal Crown's thigh. The poor man deserved better than that.

The needle went in. She did everything as she'd been trained to do.

'Good,' said Mr Gillespie and left.

She felt the corporal eyeing her. 'Did he mean it? Will that injection save my leg or will he be back later to have it off?'

News of the new wonder medicine had been mentioned in the newspapers and she felt confident enough to tell him that he was in with a very good chance indeed. She added her own brand of encouragement.

'Do you like dancing, corporal?'

He nodded. 'Yeah. Matter of fact I do.'

'So do I. It's a date. Once you're up and about, you can take me dancing – unless you have prior engagements. A good-looking chap like you must have a whole army of girls to choose from.'

Hope and belief in what she'd said brought a new brightness to his face. 'That's a date all right. Blimey, I'm almost glad I got injured if it means I get to go dancing with a good-looking girl like you.'

She laughed and told him she'd be back later to give him his second injection. There were two more after that before the night duty nurse took over. As it worked out, Bridget's replacement took sick and rather than someone else step in, she offered to carry on.

'I want to see this through,' she told Matron.

Matron Elizabeth Bentley, unmarried, an officer in the QAs and totally devoted to her profession, smiled in an understanding manner. 'I had a feeling you might say that. It gets you, doesn't it; a yearning to save lives. Once it does, it'll be with you for the rest of your life.'

Bridget thought of what Matron had said in the early hours of the morning when she was giving the corporal his fourth injection. The sweating had ceased and a calmer, healthier look had come to his face. He looked at her bleary-eyed as she injected his thigh.

'I was dreaming about you,' he said in a lazy, sleep-filled voice. 'But having you here is better.'

'Even though I'm sticking another needle in your leg?' Her perfectly arched eyebrows, dark enough without the need of an eyebrow pencil, were coupled with an amused smile.

He groaned before saying, 'You can stick a needle in me any time you like. Forever, if my luck's in.'

The corporal was a likeable young man, but he wasn't Lyndon.

'Just concentrate on getting well.'

'I will if it means going dancing with you. What's your name?'

She tapped her badge. 'Milligan. I'm only an auxiliary, but one day I might be a real nurse.'

'You are a real nurse to me. As good as any.'

His words were worth a king's ransom. She was so far below the famous nurses of Queen Alexandra's with their smart red and grey uniforms. Her uniform was ordinary and she was of the lowest rank possible.

'I mean your Christian name. What's your Christian name?'

Having patients being party to first names wasn't exactly frowned on, but it was considered more professional not to. After all, the nurses were here to help make men well so they could be sent back into battle, not to encourage romance. Fighting men were merely another weapon along the path to victory.

It was gone two in the morning and she was tired. 'Bridget, though my family call me Bridie.'

'Bridget. Bridie.' He rolled each version of the name over his tongue. 'I like the name Bridie. It's like a bird on one hand and like a bride on the other. My name's Philip, but you can call me Phil – but only if you let me call you Bridie.'

'I'm OK with that.' She leaned in closer and whispered, 'Just don't let the doctor or Matron hear you.'

She placed the syringe back in the kidney dish, along with the piece of gauze for the needle to rest on, and for a moment eyed the droplet of yellowish liquid that dropped like a tear from the needle. A wonder drug, they were calling it. The magic bullet.

'You're not engaged then,' he said suddenly as she pulled the bedclothes back over him and folded them beneath the mattress as she'd been trained to do.

The question took her by surprise, but she answered evenly. 'No. I'm not.'

'Bet you've got a boyfriend though.'

She hesitated for only seconds before replying. 'No. I haven't.'

Later on, as she sank into her bed, she cursed herself for not mentioning Lyndon but counselled that she'd done it for a good reason. Phil Crown had suffered a serious injury and he needed encouragement, as well as penicillin, and for now at least she would give him that. And who knows when she was likely to hear from Lyndon again? His last letter had arrived some time ago and since then there'd been silence.

Bridget's eyelids began to flutter as the same old words echoed in her head: the world was at war and nothing would ever be the same again.

**8**

## LYNDON

It had finally happened. It was the merry month of May and here he was back in England. All of a rush, but he'd got what he wanted, though so far hadn't had chance to contact Bridget. Getting back to the States from the battle-torn islands of the Pacific hadn't been a picnic, and running around trying to get training – any kind of training – that would get him back to England had been something of a task. Eventually, his old man had got hold of the right head of department and stressed that his son knew Europe and specifically Britain.

'He'd choose to be English if he wasn't an American. He knows the differences in culture, embraces them in fact...'

Over the years, his father had socialised with people who could swing decisions. Without any military training, there was no swift way to get back to Britain, but Lyndon's knowledge of the country and people swung the issue. They called it cultural education, which meant imparting information about the country in which they were guests to the young servicemen, some of whom were no more than eighteen years of age.

First off was the air force.

The venue was a hangar in a US air station in Lincolnshire. A hastily erected stage occupied one end in front of a wall-sized map of the world. Lyndon blinked as an arc light lit up first the station commander who introduced him. Then he was in the spotlight, the main event for the forest of young men's faces all waiting intently to hear him tell them of what he knew of Great Britain and what to expect.

All the movie stars he'd ever watched flashed into Lyndon's mind. If they could stand up in front of an audience, then so could he. Unlike them, however, he received no appreciative clapping or words of encouragement. He was on his own and faced with hundreds of young, intense expressions.

Setting the groundwork, he went through the history of the country they had come to in order to be mainline warriors in a softening-up exercise from the air, part of the plan for the invasion of Europe. Before they asked, he informed them that he didn't know when that was likely to be.

'I'm sorry to say that General Eisenhower and Churchill have kept me out of the loop on that one.'

There were smiles and some laughter, just as he'd known there would be. He went on to advise on other things – about loose talk and loose trousers.

'As regards the last, the Chief Medical Officer can advise better how to avoid ending up with more than a brief and casual liaison.'

Sniggers this time. Thank goodness it wasn't him that had to tell them about sexually transmitted diseases; best left to the professionals. It wasn't his area of expertise anyway.

Having spent time in Britain and taking part in the mass observation exercise, he was considered the right man to enlighten these guys that the language was English and although some words and spellings might be different, it was their language before America had taken it on. He had every intention of expanding that expertise in his chosen line of work, but more than anything else, he was desperate to see Bridget again. For now, he pushed the matter to the back of his mind and went on with his well-rehearsed set piece designed to give US nationals some idea of the country they now found themselves in.

'I've spent some time here before and after the outbreak of war. I know these people and I'd like to get a few things straight so you don't go blundering into situations likely to alienate the local populace. So get this, guys. Hitler's Germany has held a knife to Britain's throat since 1939, so don't take it too badly if they regard our country as Johnnie Come Lately in response to one of you guys spouting off that you're knights in shining armour. Despite being the only country in Europe to hold out against the Nazi regime, they've had a few years of bombing and privations. So some of the dames here might be bare-legged because they lack a decent pair of nylons – though no doubt some of you might generously oblige by standing them a pair – in the interest of international cooperation of course...'

There were more sniggers, more grinning glances between one man and another – even the station commander grinned.

Lyndon carried on, 'As for the women in uniform, especially those sporting ribbons of citation, they didn't get them for knitting. So show them respect. They've been brave because they had to be.' He exchanged a nod with the commanding officer before turning back to the lively faces, all full of confidence but about to discover the true horrors of all-out war. 'I'm proud to have stood here in front of you.' He nodded again. 'That is all.'

He turned away and stepped aside, glad of the shadow beyond the light that hid his expression and the pain in his eyes. All those young men, many of whom would never see their home again.

\* \* \*

Three days' leave, not much time for him to travel cross-country from the flat lands of East Anglia to the more variable terrain of the West Country. Bridget had informed him that she was becoming a nursing auxiliary, but at that point wasn't sure where in the British Isles she might end up. Unfortunately, he'd left in too much of a hurry to learn where. But one way or another he'd find her.

Bristol was first on his hit list. Somebody there, her parents or friends, would fill him in on the details.

With this in mind, he phoned ahead to one of the board members of W. D. & H. O. Wills to see about some accommodation and learned the hotels round and about were pretty full.

'My house is large. I'm sure we can fit you in.'

He accepted the invitation to Mr Albert Shellard's substantial home in Leigh Woods, just a stone's throw from the Clifton Suspension Bridge spanning the gorge and the River Avon.

The train was slow and the compartments crammed with soldiers, sailors and airmen going home on leave. Lyndon had brought food and drink for the journey, plus a few extras like chocolate, tins of meat, Bourbon and cigarettes. The latter certainly helped oil the engine of allied bonhomie.

The patchwork of fields, grazing animals and church spires, surrounded by ancient trees, became shrouded in darkness. He came to believe that they'd stopped at every station, every inconsequential halt in England, before finally they slid into the muted light that was Temple Meads Station, Bristol.

Where once the light was given by large lamps, some dating from the Victorian period and converted to electricity, some still gas, these had been replaced by blue shrouded bulbs, less likely to be seen by enemy aircraft.

A taxi took Lyndon to Shellard's home, Goram House. Goram, he recalled Bridget saying, was said to be one of the giants who had hacked out the Avon Gorge. Pure fantasy, of course, but he never tired of listening to Bridget's tales, and not just because of the story. He liked the sound of her voice, the dancing look in her eyes as she imparted stories of Bristol, the city she'd grown up in.

Shellard answered the door himself. 'My boy. Sorry about this, but my butler had to retire, so I'm it. Impossible to get a younger replacement. Never mind. We just remind ourselves that there's a war on and carry on. I was unsure of your ETA, but Geraldine, my daughter, has cobbled together a bit of supper for you. Vegetable soup and some kind of rhubarb cake. It's jolly good.'

Lyndon pulled out the bottle of real Scotch untouched by his travelling companions on the train. 'A little nightcap, sir?'

Shellard's eyes lit up. 'I wouldn't say no. Fancy a cigar?'

So together they drank and smoked until the door crashed open and in came a young woman wearing the green sweater and jodhpurs of a Land Girl, one of many who had replaced farm labourers called up to do their duty. A halo of rich brown curls surrounded her face. He guessed her pink cheeks meant she wasn't well pleased.

'Well, that's typical of men! Have a drink, a smoke and a chinwag before bothering to tell me! I've brought the stink of the farm with me and am more than ready to have a bath and get to bed.'

Shellard leaned forward. 'Sorry, my dear. May I introduce—'

'I know who he is.' Her mouth snapped shut. 'I'll bring the food in and that's it.'

She marched out of the room with as much gusto as a trooper going into battle and came back in precisely the same manner.

'There,' she said, placing a silver tray on the nearby table. She looked pointedly at Lyndon. 'We're on lesser rations in this country than you well-fed Yanks, so it's a case of what you see is what you get. There's nothing more.'

He thought of the items in his kitbag, the tins of meat, bars of chocolate plus yet another bottle of whisky. By the time he'd fetched them out, she had already taken a few strides to the door. 'Then you might be able to make use of these.'

The change in her manner was minimal, but better than nothing.

'Ta.' She grabbed the lot.

Once she'd gone, Shellard talked business and readily accepted another few drams of whisky, whilst Lyndon ate everything put in front of him.

What with the journey and the drinks, it wasn't difficult to fall asleep that night, though at one point he did open his eyes and found himself looking at a photograph of a smiling Geraldine Shellard. 'She's smiling,' he murmured. 'Well, that's something.'

\* \* \*

Breakfast the next morning was placed under his nose in the same take-it-or-leave-it style as the day before, this time by an overweight woman who introduced herself as the cleaner and sometime cook. She informed him that both Shellard and his daughter were not around. Mr Shellard had gone to the factory and Miss Geraldine was looking up an old friend.

Lyndon used the phone to get a taxi, which took him away from the leafy avenues around Leigh Woods, down into the valley and across the river to Bedminster, where he asked the taxi to wait.

Mary Milligan's face dropped at sight of him. 'Oh. It's you.'

Not a good start, but he pulled himself together and asked if Bridget was at home.

Her mother told him the news that she'd joined up and was serving as a nursing auxiliary in another part of the country.

'Do you have her address?' he asked.

The same soft brown hair as her daughter flicked round her

mother's face as she shook her head. 'It's a secret location, so I can't tell you.'

He held his smile, though knew she was lying. Reluctantly he swallowed the urge to say so. 'Thank you, ma'am. If I could just give you my address in London and phone number...'

She took the piece of paper he handed her and might have slammed the door in his face then and there, but didn't get the chance.

As she took the piece of paper a gang of kids shouted from across the road.

'Got any gum, chum?'

Two small girls broke away from the group, running across the road, eyes shining with expectation.

'We likes chocolate, Mister,' said one of them. Both were smiling. Their likeness to Bridget was indisputable.

'You're Bridget's sisters, I guess.'

They nodded.

The sound of their mother's voice came from the front door. 'Molly. Mary. Leave the man alone and get in here.'

He felt a stab of pain in his chest to know that his instinct had hit pay dirt. Bridget's mother wanted him gone and he couldn't understand why. His love for Bridget was genuine, yet her mother continued to view him with hostility.

He met the look in her eyes with defiance, delved into his pockets and handed chocolate to Bridget's sisters and chewing gum to the rest of the kids as they fenced him in with a sea of outstretched hands.

Bridget's mother was still at the front door, a strained expression on her face.

*I'm not leaving things like this*, he said to himself.

'That's the lot,' he said. He pulled out the linings of his pockets. 'Empty!'

'Thanks, Mister.'

They ran off including the two little girls who'd been ordered to come indoors.

Well, he too was about to disobey orders. He headed back up the garden path to where Mary Milligan stood like a sentinel in her front door looking warily at this American who wasn't easily dismissed.

'Mrs Milligan, my intentions towards your daughter are honourable. I want to marry her, but this war has got in the way. That's the only thing stopping us for now, but it will happen, with or without your consent. Thank you for listening.'

He turned to leave.

'It won't work you know.'

Her tone was sharp and made him turn round.

He shook his head. 'How can you know that? Times are changing. Nothing is the same as it was and once this war's finished, things will be even more changed.' He shook his head again as he turned away and headed for the garden gate and the waiting taxi.

His mood was morose as he considered if he could ever convince Mrs Milligan that Bridget and he did have a future together. His priority for now was finding out where Bridget was stationed and if Mrs Milligan was reticent, there was one other person at least who might enlighten him on that score.

'Driver. Drop me off in East Street by the factory entrance.'

9

MAISIE

The funeral had been a small affair and Maisie had preferred it that way. The sky had been overcast and the grass at the graveside whipped wetly round her legs.

She knew nobody there and didn't want to. She kept her eyes down, fearful of meeting the gaze of anyone who might mention her grandmother's stock in trade. As it was all the people there were too old to have once needed her services. They were more likely people who had borrowed money from her – possibly glad at her passing and the probability that they wouldn't be paying it back.

Shortly afterwards a letter came from her grandmother's solicitors asking her to attend.

It was a warm day, but Maisie felt none of its warmth. She was nervous. The truth was that she had never had occasion to enter a solicitor's office ever before and the prospect was slightly nerve-wracking. Even the name, Ernest Peregrine Pomeroy, followed by some letters of qualification engraved into a shiny brass plaque at the entrance, she found intimidating.

Inside wasn't much better. A painting of a woman wearing old-fashioned widows' weeds hung above a marble fireplace and an unlit gas fire.

Maisie shivered. Heat would have helped lighten the gloom and lift the sullen chill. The chair she sat on had a hard seat and the arms had long lost their varnished shine. How many hands had done that, she wondered.

The fingers of Mr Pomeroy's secretary pounded the typewriter keys. Her tight expression showed no sign of a willingness to talk. Like the room, she seemed unduly cold, the drabness of her dress matching that of the dull bronze walls.

A door to her left creaked stiffly open and a man entered. He was stooped, wore a dark, old-fashioned suit and had a head of pure white hair. Judging by the size of his whiskers and creased face, he was of the same vintage as the painting above the fireplace. Watery blue eyes regarded her from behind a pair of wire-framed spectacles.

'Miss Miles. Sorry to have kept you waiting. Do come through.'

Hoping that Mr Pomeroy's office was warmer than the waiting room, Maisie sprang from her chair and followed. The brown lino of the waiting room also covered the floor of the passageway to his office, shiny in places and cracked in others. The room his bowed legs led her to might have been just as gloomy and lacking in interest if it hadn't been for the books. They were everywhere: on shelves, on his desk and piled like stepping stones round it. Light fell from a single window and a Turkish rug, though threadbare, added colour.

He sat down behind the desk and began shuffling papers, muttering to himself as he did so.

Not knowing what else to do, Maisie continued to stand, unsure whether it would be impolite to sit down in this alien environment that smelled strongly of old age and lavender polish.

Mr Pomeroy continued to talk to himself as though she wasn't there. 'Now where did I put that... if only Claude was here...'

The floorboards beneath her feet creaked as she adjusted her stance, putting pressure on her right foot to ease the weight on her left.

Mr Pomeroy looked up, an expression of surprise on his care-worn face. 'Oh, Miss...' he glanced down at the file in front of him. 'Miss Miles.' He gestured to one of the two chairs in front of his desk. 'Do take a seat, Miss...' Another glance at the file.

'Miles. Miss Maisie Miles, regarding my grandmother's will. You asked me to come in.'

She chose the most well upholstered of the two chairs, even though a spring was leaving a forceful mark in the tapestry covering.

'Ah yes. Didn't we meet at her funeral?'

'No. I believe it was your nephew, Mr Claude Pomeroy. He told me he'd been called up, so all matters had been passed to you.'

'Ah yes. I had retired, you know, and was spending time culti-vating my roses.' For a moment, the thought of roses seemed to add brightness to his eyes and a slight smile creased his papery cheeks. His sigh was heavy with regret. 'There you are. There's a war on and needs must.'

Maisie sat patiently, but couldn't wait to be out of there. So many thoughts careered around her mind. Could she continue to live in her grandmother's house? Was it hers? She had little knowl-edge of the law and wished with all her heart that Bridget was still close at hand. Bridget knew everything.

At last, he looked up. 'Grace Wells has left the house and just about everything else to you. The only exception is the old garage along Coronation Road. She's left that to a Mister George Barton in appreciation for all he did for her late husband.'

Maisie shrugged. 'I don't know the bloke, but if that's what she wanted it's OK by me.' She took a deep breath as she took it all in. It seemed like a dream, going from nothing to owning a house. She needed to hear it again. 'I've got the 'ouse in Totterdown. Are you sure I 'ave?'

The pale eyes peered at her as he nodded. 'Plus some shares and bank savings.'

'I know what a bank account is, but shares? What are they?'

Laying one piece of stiff paper aside, he took up another piece. 'The shares are in a piece of land in Avonmouth close to the docks. Just a field. It's owned in partnership with said beneficiary George Barton. The bank account is in the sum of two hundred and thirty pounds.'

Maisie's jaw dropped. 'Does this mean I'm rich?'

'Not so rich as comfortably off. You have a house, a considerable amount of cash and a share in a piece of land.'

She knew she must look like a fish out of water, but hearing all this was jaw-dropping. What struck her more so was suddenly realising that her grandmother had become as fond of her as Maisie had of her.

'I will get all the papers in order stating your ownership and rights as beneficiary.'

'What about this George Barton? Does he know about me and owning that bit of land with 'im?'

'Yes. I have written to him as I did to you and asked him to come in and see me – straight after you, as a matter of fact.'

Mr Pomeroy rubbed at his forehead as though the mere thought of having yet another appointment this morning was too much to bear. Roses, she thought. He'd prefer to be back with his roses.

Sensing the appointment was over, Maisie got to her feet. 'The sooner this war's over, the better, eh? Let's 'ope it won't be too long and you can go back to your roses. Please, don't bother to get up. I can find me own way out.'

He gave her a wan smile and there was sadness in his eyes before he bent back to his paperwork. No doubt he was worrying about 'Claude' coming back. She sincerely hoped it would happen.

The man sitting in the waiting room looked up as Maisie entered. He had the black hair of a gypsy and the pallor of a man who spent most of his time indoors. His shirt was white and his dark grey suit was matched with a navy-blue tie and shiny black shoes. His mouth was set in a straight line and, for whatever reason, there was no friendliness in his eyes and he did not return her smile.

She could handle that and it didn't hurt to build bridges and find out more about the other beneficiary to her grandmother's will.

On a whim, she offered a hand. 'I take it you're George Barton. I'm Maisie Miles. Grace Wells was my grandmother.'

For a moment, he looked at her hand as though she was offering him a bunch of nettles. Finally, he shook it reluctantly, more of a fleeting touch than a firm shake. Their eyes met. The warmth in her eyes was not reflected in his. In his there was only distrust born of surprise.

'I didn't know Grace had a granddaughter.'

She smiled. 'Well. You do now.'

Mouth still a grim line, she felt his eyes following her to the door and knew he was wondering what she'd inherited from her grandmother and what was left for him. She could have lingered and asked him questions, but this ordeal had been difficult enough. She was still raw and enclosed in her own world. She didn't want complications though had a sneaking feeling she would get some.

The blossom was out on the lime trees in Queen Square. Maisie breathed in the freshness of the air.

As usual, there was a mix of military personnel, laughing and joking their way across the square and enjoying the freedom of fresh air, temporarily at least. It felt as though Maisie was walking on air. Getting used to being a woman of means was going to take time. In her mind, she detailed a party at which she would tell everyone her good fortune. They would probably expect her to leave the job. Well, that was something she just could not do. Her friends at work meant everything to her. Even though Bridget had left to become a nurse and Phyllis was serving abroad, their replacements had become friends. Even Carole Thomas, who had been a right little cow at first, had mellowed into a nice person. They went out together to the old haunts she'd once patronised with Bridget and Phyllis. It made her feel young to be with Carole and hear about the many dates she went on.

Jonah, the black American took her out on occasion. He described his job with US Army logistics as counting boxes, anything from ammunition to tins of beans.

'I'm basically a storeman. Even when the big battle comes, that's all I'll be doing,' he told her. 'Only the white boys fight.'

They were just friends. He was married with children and in her book that meant the relationship would never go anywhere.

As for Sid, well, he was far away incarcerated in a Japanese POW camp. She wrote to him and he wrote back. The cards he sent came through the Red Cross, sometimes six or even ten at a time. From this, she'd deduced that the Japanese allowed only infrequent access to Red Cross visits. Hopefully Sid would come home again. He was her only remaining link to the past when she'd first begun work at the factory. Everything was changing and her longing to see him again surprised her. The death of her grandmother, Grace Wells, had completely changed her life. She was rich – comparatively so. What would her friends say?

'*Well what a stroke of luck!*'

'*There's no stopping you now.*'

'*You'll be too posh to speak to the rest of us.*'

Happy thoughts popped like party balloons and her smile became a frown. The last thing she wanted was to be considered posh, as if being better off than most of them would change her. Maisie shook her head at the thought. No. She wouldn't change. In fact, she didn't want anyone to change, least of all the attitude of her workmates.

She'd taken a day off work for this morning. Her head reeling with what had transpired, her intention now was to catch the bus back up to Totterdown where she would sit down with a cup of tea as she thought things through. A day alone. She could certainly do with that.

Unusually, the bus was on time and, at this time of day, not absolutely choked with passengers. Women with shopping bags jostled with men in uniform, the latter doing their best to peer through the wire window screens at the passing scene, a wartime safety measure against flying glass. Not that there was that much to see. The whole city had a drab look about it, even the grander buildings in the city centre. The air smelt dirty, rank with the fallout of dust from bomb sites and the mildewed stink of mud from the river.

Once she'd stepped off onto the pavement, the conductor on the bus rang the bell to tell the driver to proceed.

That cup of tea was calling her. So was the need to think. The sooner she got there, the better.

It was wise to walk carefully down the steepest street in Totterdown. Any attempt to hurry and Maisie would find herself gathering speed and shooting off like a human cannonball over the wall and into the tangle of thickets and brambles stretching all the way down to the main road to the city of Bath, some eight miles or so distant.

Walking slower was always difficult on the knees and it was sometimes necessary to grab one of the cast-iron bollards and railings placed there specifically for that purpose. The residual excitement transferred to her feet. Even with the help of the bollards, it was difficult not to hurry.

'Looks like you got a visitor, love,' shouted a woman, one of two chatting on the doorstep of a house close to hers. Her house. It hadn't yet quite struck home. Hers. All hers.

Absorbed in her own world, she didn't take much notice of the comment, though felt eyes following her all the way down the street.

Her gaze followed the same direction to where a lone figure waited for her outside the front door of Gran's house.

*My house*, she corrected herself.

Her first impression was that he was wearing a uniform. Her second was that the tall, broad-shouldered figure was very familiar.

The clip-clop of her heels echoed between the sweep of flat-fronted houses, most of which dated from early Victorian times. White paint striped the lamp posts, in this street more so for the benefit of pedestrians than cars. Even horse-drawn transport had difficulty coming down here. For safety's sake done with the brakes on. Going back up took a lot of effort from the horse, straining into the harness, the milkman or baker walking alongside to help lighten the load.

At the sound of her heels, the figure looked straight at her and swept his cap from his head. A warm smile spread across his face.

'Maisie?'

Maisie's foothold on the cobbles and flagstones faltered. Her speed increased and she cried out.

'Whoa!'

Slamming into his chest was like hitting a brick wall. His arms round her, she looked up at him in amazement, one hand holding onto her hat.

'Lyndon! What brings you here?'

'Good job I was. Looked as though your brakes failed.'

She laughed and told him how good it was to see him. He filled her eyes, though not enough for her not to notice that the two gossips down the road were no longer talking. Their eyes were on her and Lyndon.

'We'd better go inside. I'll make you a cup of tea.'

'As long as it's no trouble.'

She grinned and jerked her head to where the neighbours had been joined by a third woman. 'None at all. Anyway, we don't want to disappoint that lot. They need something to gossip about.'

All of them were looking, surmising and making their own opinions of what a pretty dark-haired girl and a tall handsome man, obviously a Yank judging by his uniform, were up to.

Sunlight streamed through the kitchen window. Maisie insisted Lyndon take a seat whilst she put the kettle on and got out her grandmother's best blue and white willow-pattern china.

As she set out the milk and sugar and poured the hot water into the pot, he told her about going round to Bridget's house.

'Her mother told me her address is top-secret.' He shook his head. 'I don't believe that.' He shook his head again. 'I thought she'd warmed to me walking out with Bridget. Seems I was wrong.'

He sipped at his tea.

'I can give you the address.' She wrote it down. 'You won't have too far to go.'

'You mean she's close?'

'She was supposed to be at the local infirmary at first, but you know how it is. Plans changed at the last minute. She's in some place called Crossborough. You can either write or go there. I would suggest you go there. It's quicker, the postal service being what it is these days.'

It thrilled her to see a renewed brightness in his face, though not nearly as much as how thrilled she'd been to tumble into his arms. In a way, she agreed with Bridget's mother that they were from two different worlds and it just couldn't last. On the other hand, she could understand Bridget's feelings for him. Reminding herself that this was Bridget's fellah, she pushed back the envy.

'Another cup of tea?'

He shook his head. 'No. You're a swell friend to both me and Bridget. Thank the Lord I found you in. I went to the factory first. They told me you had the morning off. That bubbly blonde gave me your address.'

'Carole Thompson?'

'That's the girl,' he said, getting up.

Maisie had been careful not to disclose to too wide an audience where she'd gone this morning. They'd known it was something to do with her grandmother's death, but that was all. 'I think she's left me her old armchair and I'm thinking I might shove me 'and down and see if there's a few shillings got lost down there,' she'd quipped on telling them about her appointment.

'Might even be 'alf a crown,' laughed Aggie Hill.

But it was more than that – much more. What would they think now, Maisie wondered. And was she up to handling that much money, that much property and the possibilities it might bring? She needed advice from someone that she trusted.

It occurred to her that as a well-educated man used to dealing with business matters, Lyndon might be a good sounding board for what had passed that morning.

'Please,' she said, grabbing hold of his hand. 'I'd like it if you stayed a little longer. It's important.'

He looked warily down at her hand lying on his. 'Umm...'

'I'm not after me mate's bloke. It's business. Stuff I don't know too much about.'

'You need some kind of advice?'

'Yes. I want to tell you something and I want to ask you something. Will you sit back down – just for a minute? It won't take long.'

Looking curious as to what he might hear, he sat down on the chair.

'Carole probably told you that my grandmother died.'

'Yes. I'm sorry. I should have mentioned that I knew. Sorry again.'

His words were as disarming as the genuine sympathy written on his face.

'Thankfully, it was quick.' She took a deep breath. 'I'm going to tell you something in confidence; I don't want anyone else knowing, not even Bridget.'

'You must have good reason, especially for not telling Bridget. So why tell me?'

Why tell him and nobody else? Because she considered that he was in a similar position and would understand, or she hoped he would.

So that's what she put to him. 'I've come into this house, some cash and even some land. My grandmother left it to me in her will. It was very good of 'er, but on the other 'and I'm not sure I want any of it.'

'Your grandmother obviously thought a lot of you. Be grateful for what she's given, it was probably her way of saying that she loved you.'

'I don't doubt that, but the problem is...' She looked down into her cup and gripped it tightly. 'I'm worried that me workmates won't think I'm one of them any more. They'll think that I'm rich and posh. I couldn't bear that. They're my mates.' She looked up at him, her big brown eyes owning a startled look. 'I think I'd sooner give it all away.'

He looked at her for what seemed many minutes before a slow smile of realisation lit his face. 'You're telling me because I'm a rich guy who's fallen in love with a factory girl. You're counting on me to understand.'

There was kindness in his expression.

'Yes.'

'It's a wide chasm to cross. Don't I just know it! That doesn't mean you shouldn't attempt to cross it. Thing to do is to start thinking of building a bridge, something that won't force you apart, but bring you together. Keep schtum for now by all means, but if they're real friends – or really love you – then in time it should all fall together.'

Bridget loving him was understandable.

*I could love him too*, thought Maisie but blinked the thought away.

'You won't tell anyone.'

'Of course not.'

'Promise?'

'Cross my heart and hope to die.'

Maisie had no doubt his heart was there; a big heart, full of love for Bridget. She found herself wishing all would be well for the two of them. 'I wouldn't want me mates thinking I'm gone all stuck up.'

Lyndon smiled. 'You could never be that, Maisie. You're a great girl and always will be.'

# 10

## CAROLE

The tobacco girls were pouring out of the factory at five fifteen on the dot, all rushing to get a bus, to get home to family or a stint doing fire watch or some other war-driven work, though it seemed air raids were a thing of the past.

Carole was in the habit of walking home with Pat Wooster who lived just beyond Little Paradise in Mill Lane. The houses in Mill Lane overlooked a round green metal construction dating from the last century in which men could relieve themselves.

'Strange that there ain't one for women,' remarked Carole.

'Nah,' returned Pat. 'They leave us to do it in our knickers.'

Carole frowned. 'You know, Pat, if things don't change for women after this lot is over, there'll be riots.'

'You think so?'

'I know so, and I'll be in the front line, just like them that went after votes fer women years ago. This time we'll be wantin' more than votes. You just see if we don't.'

Being a down-to-earth, uncomplicated sort, Pat was a bit neither here nor there on the subject, but she did admire Carole's rebellious attitude. Like Carole, she was one of the VIP escorts employed by the factory to take people round and show them what was what. Nowadays, it was mostly service personnel or ladies' groups who knitted, cooked or ran outside tea stations for those who needed it.

During working hours, they spoke clearly and carefully, as though they were well-educated girls and not locals who casually dropped their aitches the moment they'd left work.

'Gotta fag?'

Carole stopped to give Pat a fag and lit one herself. She didn't know quite what made her do it, but she turned right round to look behind her. As she did so, a faceless man in dark clothing leapt into a doorway. Thinking him one of Pat's admirers, she blew smoke in the direction of the rank of shops they'd just passed. 'Who's that then?'

Pat asked her what she was on about.

'A bloke. The minute I turned round, he disappeared into a shop doorway. Thought he might be your boyfriend.'

'Don't think so. P'raps he suddenly forgot something.'

'Well 'e won't get anything in that shop. It's been boarded up for months. Got no back on it if I remember rightly. It got blasted to kingdom come.'

Pat turned to peer in the same direction. 'Can't see anyone there now.'

'Hmm.' Carole wasn't convinced. The fact was it wasn't the first time she'd had the feeling she was being followed. Now when had it begun? She cast her mind back but couldn't pick out any particular time. She slipped her arm into Pat's, clutching it tightly to her side. 'Come on. Let's get on 'ome.'

The man forgotten, they carried on talking about shoes, dresses and the prospect of getting their hands on a new pair of stockings.

'I saw you talking to a real good-looking Yank today. Is that your date for tonight?'

Carole's eyes sparkled. 'Wish he was. What a dish!'

She went on to tell Pat that Lyndon O'Neill was the son of a plantation owner and was enamoured of Bridget Milligan.

'He was looking for Bridget. They're sweethearts. She's gone doing nursing and he wanted to know her address. I told him I didn't know.'

Pat looked at her askance. 'Do you?'

'Yeah.' Carole drew out the word slowly. 'I pretended not to know and that I was free if he fancied a bit of company. I was wearing me best uniform so didn't look like a common factory girl. Wouldn't have none of it though. Seemed to go deaf. Went on to ask if Maisie was in. I told 'im she had the day off on account of her grandmother dying.'

'But she already 'ad the funeral, ain't she?'

'Yeah. I didn't mention any of that though. I gave him her address. Thought the business about her grandmother might put him off. Anyway, I knew she wouldn't be home. She had some legal stuff to sort out at her grandmother's solicitors. Reckoned it would take her a while.'

'So he might not have caught up with her.'

Carole's bright blonde curls bounced round her face as she shook her head and grinned. 'I hope not. I could do wonders with that man given half the chance.'

They both laughed before Carole sprang off from Pat, waved goodbye to her friend and entered Little Paradise.

Before putting her key in the lock, Carole glanced back to the end of the street where she'd parted from Pat. A man was leaning against a low stone wall reading the paper. He didn't act furtive or look in her direction and she couldn't say for sure whether he was the one she'd seen earlier.

Just your imagination, she told herself. Not so long ago her mother had still been here – no chance of any peace when she was around making a living from lying on her back. Carole hated those times, but now since her mother had scarpered up north with some rich old bloke – good luck and good riddance, she'd thought at the time – living alone could be scary.

Shaking the worries from her head, she told herself to go and put the kettle on.

'And at the same time do yerself two slices of toast.'

\* \* \*

Gerald Crozier was careful not to glance in Carole's direction as she let herself into the house she shared with her mother. It beat him that he'd been given the task of shadowing her, but as long as Eddie Bridgeman was paying him, it didn't matter much.

'Just make sure she don't see you and she don't come to any harm. That's yer job, you muttonhead!'

Well, the making sure she didn't see him had gone a bit wrong. He suspected she had clocked him but the shop doorway had been handy, though a bit dangerous. The slats of a wooden barrier, hammered in place for safety's sake, had been torn away. There were looters who didn't have a brain, who reckoned it was worth the risk to enter a bombed-out shop. He'd done his bit of looting bombsites, but not when the back of the building had been blown off and the contents blasted to kingdom come.

Raindrops as big as pennies began to fall onto the piece he was reading about a request for families to invite American soldiers to tea or some other social event. It was an effort to get them acclimatised to the British way of life. 'Bloody cheek,' he muttered. a lot of British families wouldn't have enough tea for themselves, let alone for entertaining Yanks. Yanks earned more than their British counterparts anyway and because of that, plus their smarter uniforms, were much preferred by the girls.

No, he thought, screwing the paper into quarters. He for one would not be inviting any Yanks round for tea – unless they came bearing gifts. Fags, booze and nylons. Then he might consider it.

He turned his collar up against the impending downpour and pulled the brim of his hat down so that the rain dripped off without him getting soaked.

A quick glance at his watch told him it was six thirty. Judging by past experience, the little cutie would be dolled up and ready to have fun by seven thirty, eight at the latest. He just hoped she wouldn't be staying out too late.

'I want you to follow her the minute the factory closes to the minute she gets home and stay around in case she goes out again.' Eddie had wagged a finger in his face. 'Don't let anyone get fresh with 'er. Got it?'

'Got it, Eddie.'

Once out of sight of Eddie Bridgeman, he'd grinned and shook his head. Truth was he'd seen Eddie hot for other bits of skirt in the past, but never as bad as this. He wanted her watched all the time and any bloke who showed too much interest was to be warned off.

Gerald sniggered. 'Must be love.'

* * *

Later that week, Carole and Pat had a date with a couple of Polish chaps who they found wandering along East Street hemmed in against a shop doorway. Only a few English words had got through their native tongue and the crowd, for some obscure reason, had decided they were German.

'Polski,' one of them had shouted. 'Polski. Warsaw. Poland!'

A good job, a smart uniform and a more careful pronunciation had given Carole confidence.

'Right,' she'd said, wading into the crowd, Pat just behind her. 'What may I ask is going on here?'

Added to her voice and attitude, her confidence had given her an air of good education and almost a right to give orders.

A bloke of rotund proportions who looked like he might be a bank clerk had adjusted his spectacles. 'It's best you keep away, little lady. These men sound like Germans and could be dangerous.'

Taking umbrage at being patronised, Carole had barrelled her way forward until her nose was just a bit higher than his. 'They're Polish, not German. Look at their uniforms. Do you see a swastika on their shoulders?'

The man, who wasn't the only one in the gang who smelt of brown ale, had turned condescending. 'An' what would a young tart like you...?'

'I'm not a tart, and they're not German. Didn't you hear what he said? Polski. It means Polish. Poland. Warsaw. That's what they were saying if you'd had the gumption to listen instead of falling out of the pub and shouting your head off with the rest of this rabble.'

He couldn't have looked more deflated if she'd punched him in the stomach.

As for the rest of the crowd she'd labelled rabble, they grumbled a bit but took it on the chin that she was posh and so was bound to know better than they did.

'We didn't mean nothing by it,' said a rough-looking woman with a thin face, no teeth and a battalion of steel curlers covering her head. 'I don't speak foreign. Just wondered that was all.'

'Never you mind, Fanny,' said one of the blokes, his big hand clutching at her wrist. 'Let me buy you 'alf a brown ale down at the White 'Orse.'

'Ooow, ta! Don't mind if I do.'

Carole, feeling more than a little full of herself, had smiled at her new friends. 'Come along, chaps. Sorry about this happening. We'll take you for a cup of tea.'

The young men did not refuse.

Over tea, they had told them they were based out at Filton Aerodrome. 'We do not fly,' they'd said, one of them spreading his arms like wings and at the same time shaking his head. 'We guard factory.'

Carole had been hoping that they were pilots – the glamour boys of the services, but she wouldn't let it show.

'For now,' said Benjamin, the second of the two, who spoke the best English – not as though the mob had given him chance to be heard. 'We fly soon.'

So here they were waiting outside the picture house for their dates. The nights were lighter and the summer breeze carried the smell of flowers as well as bombsites.

'You wouldn't think it was June, would you,' Pat commented. 'This old coat of mine could do with a revamp. I might have to make a blanket coat for next winter if I don't do something with this.'

Carole muttered a wordless response. The two Poles should be here by now, but there was no sign of them. A small frown puckered her forehead as she looked round, not so much for them, but for that shadowy figure she'd thought was following her.

Pat threw down her cigarette end and ground it out with her shoe. 'They're late.'

'Hmmm.' Carole was thinking the same thing. It wasn't as though she was dead keen on either of them, though Benjamin had had the most melting brown eyes. But who knew what might have transpired?

The light was fading fast. The yellowish gleam of early evening hung like a faded net curtain over the city. Slate roofs and tiles shone wet and shiny. There were no lights of course. The blackout was still in operation even though they'd had no air raids for quite a while now.

'I'm going in without them if they don't get a move on,' muttered Carole, then brightened on spotting them.

'We got the wrong bus,' said Benjamin.

'Never mind,' said Pat. 'We'll forgive you.'

* * *

Gerald Crozier hated light nights. That was what was so good about the blackout: nobody could see him hanging around. Summer nights were a bit of a bind, staying light until nearly ten o'clock. Harder to hide.

He toyed with the fact that Eddie had specifically told him to keep an eye on the blonde bird and whether he should follow them inside with two blokes. It was a hard choice. He didn't like the pictures. That darkness and all them people watching the film and smoking made him feel claustrophobic. All the same, he had to report back to Eddie and, with that in mind, he went to the phone box up on the corner and phoned him.

'She's with a bloke?'

Eddie was angry. Gerald could imagine his eyes getting blacker, his face redder.

'I didn't know what to do, Eddie? I could 'ave a word with 'em I s'pose.'

'A word!' It sounded as though Eddie was about to explode. 'You'll 'ave a word alright. I want whoever's with Carole to be warned off.'

Gerald gulped. 'I can do that if you like, Eddie, but there is two of them...'

'For God's sake man. Take Roy and 'Arry with you. They'll give you a 'and.'

* * *

Jan and Benjamin turned out to be the perfect gentlemen. They paid for everything and Carole was impressed. Pat said the same, whispering in Carole's ear on the way out, 'And that Jan didn't try it on. That's a change!'

'I'll take advantage of your arm,' said Carole, when they offered to escort them home. 'Can't see a thing in the dark and that rain's made the pavements wet.'

She glanced over her shoulder then smiled. 'Your mate and mine have found a cosy shop doorway.'

'Don't worry. He can look after himself. And so can I.'

During the short walk, Benjamin told her that he came from Warsaw and had only just managed to get out before the Germans had marched in. She asked him if he had any brothers and sisters. He shrugged. 'I used to.'

Carole frowned. 'That's a funny answer. Do you or don't you?'

The sound of their footsteps echoed off the flat-fronted houses of Little Paradise as Benjamin took his time answering. 'It's a funny time – no – that is not the right word. Strange. Strange?'

'Strange. Yes. That is the right word.'

'I don't know if I still have a family. I am Jewish. The Germans do not like the Jews.' She sensed rather than saw him shake his head in a disconsolate manner. 'You have heard the rumours?' They'd come to a stop outside the house she lived in.

She'd heard of the creation of death camps, of people being told they were places of work when in fact the real work was to kill people.

He faced her, the warmth of his breath on her face. 'They are not rumours. They are true. My family...' The helpless shrug of his shoulders was matched by that in his voice. 'I do not expect to ever see them again.'

Carole felt gutted for him. It was small recompense for his loss, but she stood up on tiptoes and kissed him.

\* \* \*

Benjamin touched his lips after she'd kissed him. He was still relishing the feel of Carole's lips on his as he made his way to meet up with Jan, who had taken Pat home in the next street. At the end of the street, he detected the glow of a cigarette and heard girlish laughter. Jan, he thought, and smiled to himself. Jan was still having fun and Pat had seemed like a nice girl.

Benjamin prepared to wait on the corner, pulled out a cigarette and lit up. Just for a second, he saw something – someone – move. It was fast and he was unprepared. He had the impression of an arm raised to strike him. He countered the blow, but too late to avoid it. The cobbles were lumpy against his back and he fell awkwardly, felt his leg crook at an awkward angle.

Breath stinking of whisky and cheap cigarettes fell over him. A voice rasped onto his face. 'Stay away from that girl or you'll be sorry. Eddie Bridgeman says so.'

One more blow and he was out cold.

* * *

# 11

## PHYLLIS

In April of that year, the island of Malta had been awarded the George Cross for outstanding bravery in resisting the Axis powers. The King himself had sent a personal message saying how grateful he was and how proud as a nation the Maltese should be. The award was normally only awarded to individuals. This was the first time the George Cross had been awarded to a whole population. Perhaps it was the official recognition for steadfast defiance that made them regard the current bombing and privations as less intense that they had been. Fuelled perhaps by less air raids and ships getting through with food, people began talking about the future once the war was finally over.

During yet another brief respite from duty, Phyllis, Vera, Mariana and a steward named Nancy from Bolton were drinking what passed as gin in a local bar carved into the bare rock. The rock lent coolness to the bar without the need of an overhead fan. The place was small, no more than five tables and some rickety chairs, but to them it was heaven.

'All I've ever wanted to do is get married and keep house.' Vera blew a puff of smoke into the air. 'I want a bloke to keep me. That's what I want.'

A faint blush coloured Nancy's cheeks, the fingers of her right hand twisting the engagement ring on her left. 'Pete said I don't need to work after we get married, but I can if I want to. Only until we have children, that is.' Dark eyelashes swept over her cheeks as her blush intensified.

Mariana patted Nancy's hand. 'You're a very lucky girl. Just as I am.' The slender but stalwart Maltese plotter was engaged to a pilot stationed at Saafi, an airfield on the centre of the island. The wedding was planned for the autumn, on the assumption that things would be less frantic than they had been. Everyone was invited, including Phyllis and Mick.

Pete, Nancy's beau, was a gunner who gave the enemy hell from the fort of St Angelo overlooking the Grand Harbour.

'So what will you and Mick do when this is all over?' asked Vera.

Phyllis felt a strange reluctance to say anything. For a start, she had no wish to detail her efforts to get a divorce from Robert. Stating what she wanted to happen might bring bad luck, though she couldn't for the life of her think why. She put down her drink, raised her eyebrows and laughed. 'Mick lives on the other side of the world.'

'So what's to stop you going there?'

For somebody who had very definite views on what a marriage should be, Vera could be very broad-minded, one of the few who took on board that what might suit her might not suit everyone else.

Phyllis pulled a face and out popped the truth. 'I've got to get divorced first.'

'Why?'

'Vera, honestly.'

Nancy exchanged a look of embarrassment with Mariana. 'Oh

dear.'

Mariana looked amused. 'Yes, I am Catholic. We do not divorce. We marry for life. But my beliefs are not necessarily yours. They are what I was brought up with. But you must choose for yourself.' She cocked her pretty head sideways. The incisiveness of her look sometimes reminded Phyllis of Maisie Miles, though Mariana did not possess the same forthright cockiness. 'The war has taught me one thing above all others; be happy. Just be happy.'

*  *  *

Mick took Phyllis to a dance that night. She should have been on duty, but Mick had had a word with the Operations Room commander.

'Get your glad rags on. We're dancing until midnight.'

Phyllis was taken by surprise. She'd laughed, already deciding that she would wear the mint green dress bought from St Joseph's, a cast-off of dubious heritage donated by someone of social standing – no doubt married to a command centre officer or civil servant. 'Really? Well I don't know about that. I really had it in mind to dance until morning.'

His hesitant smile had pulled at her heartstrings and she knew something was up.

'I'm off in the morning. Pretty routine, but don't worry. I'll be back by the end of your shift.'

'How do you know when my shift ends?' she asked, trying to hide her panic at his words. What was he up to?

His smile gave him a wicked boyishness, lifting one side of his face so it looked as if one eye was on its way to winking. 'I check everything.'

If there were jitterbug numbers that night, Phyllis didn't notice them. The slight roughness of his cheek against hers was as reassuring as his arms round her. When she closed her eyes, she could believe that they were the only people on the dance floor. Behind her closed eyelids, she wished this moment could last forever, but moments never did. Like the minutes and hours, they passed too quickly.

'Do you fancy going to bed with me?'

She opened her eyes and smiled. 'I always fancy going to bed with you.'

\* \* \*

After making love in the small house Mick shared with three other Australians, he smoothed her hair whilst telling her how his vineyard would be. 'Beats sheep. Not so smelly and vines don't need so much acreage. I'll build us a house. Something with a porch and a veranda out front. I think the Eastern Cape will be the right place. There's a coastal breeze, greenery and the soil is good. Just imagine, Phyllis. Just imagine.'

And she did imagine. 'Such a wonderful future.'

'But...?'

That was it with Mick. He could hear the words unsaid as well as those she said.

'I can't marry you until I get a divorce from Robert.'

There was a pause.

'No matter what, you're coming to Australia with me, married or not.'

She buried her face in his chest. There was a time she might have been outraged at what he was suggesting – or perhaps she wouldn't have. Perhaps she would have just been worried at what people would say, her reputation in tatters, but the fact was Mick Fairbrother gave her the confidence to face whatever came their way together.

**12**

---

MAISIE

* * *

The entire stripping room was singing along with 'Chattanooga Choo-Choo', a song which had no relevance to war and held none of the wistful sentiments of virtually anything sung by Vera Lynn. The consensus was that she had a good voice, but there was a time and place for everything. At this moment, working away regardless of the canteen having run out of sugar, and liver yet again on the menu for lunch, they needed cheering up.

Maisie certainly needed cheering up. 'Chattanooga Choo-Choo' reminded her of Bridget and Jonah singing as he belted it out on the piano at the Services Club.

At tea break, the canteen clattered on and the girls round her chattered on as normal. For the first time ever, she felt a profound feeling of isolation. Here she was sitting at a table facing three empty chairs where Phyllis, Bridget and Carole used to sit. One gone nursing, one serving abroad and one promoted to visitor guide. Tea sweetened with something other than real sugar didn't help. Added to that, she could count the currants in the teacake with two fingers.

'No sugar. Would you believe it?' Aggie sat her big backside on one of the chairs. Sitting with Aggie helped negate the feeling of being alone. 'So how's things with your Gran's estate – did she leave you anything?'

Maisie frowned. 'The house – according to the solicitor.'

Aggie eyed her with surprise over the rim of her teacup.

There was also the land, which she reckoned she could well do without. Nobody had much and she'd never had much. They were all chums together in being skint. One thing she valued above all else was having friends. She mentioned none of this to Aggie but changed the subject.

'How's the pub?'

'Standing our ground. Got visited by some American officers who told us we were to have separate nights for black and white soldiers. Curly told them to sod off. Being close to the city docks, we've served all sorts from all over the world, so nobody's gonna tell us to stop now. Either we keep everyone all mixed up, or they can go and dictate to somebody else.'

Imagining Curly and Aggie standing their ground made Maisie laugh. 'It's your pub, Aggie.'

Aggie nodded. 'Our pub and our rules.'

Heads turned as Carole entered the canteen. Office and other non-factory-floor staff had a separate canteen, the idea being that smart office suits didn't pick up the dust and dirt from factory overalls.

Seemingly not worried about that, Carole took a seat and leaned furtively towards Maisie, looking as glamorous as ever though a tiny frown buckled her forehead. Something was bothering her.

'I wanted a word. In private.' She glanced meaningfully at Aggie.

'Don't let me stop you,' she said as she heaved herself to her feet.

'No. Stay.' Maisie signalled Aggie to sit back down. 'Sorry, love. I'm in need of as much company as I can get. Otherwise, I might be another one joinin' up – though they might not 'ave me.' She laughed in a half-hearted manner. Joining up was bound to be an antidote to loneliness, not that she'd admit to anyone that she was lonely. 'Go on, Carole,' she said, as Aggie sat back down. 'You've got a face like a cow's pancake. What's the matter?'

Carole kept her voice low as she told them about the attack. 'Ben was nice. So was his mate, Jan, but it was only Ben who was attacked. He thought at first it might be because he was Jewish – he's had plenty of that sort of stuff in the past, and what with Hitler and what's going on in Germany – he thought that's what it might have been about, except...' She took a deep breath. 'The bloke who attacked him mentioned Eddie Bridgeman and that if Ben saw me again, he'd answer to him.'

Maisie exchanged a look with Aggie. They both knew of Eddie's lust for young girls. Maisie had rescued Carole from him on one occasion with the help of a tough group of Canadians who'd bundled him into a car boot. They'd come from a logging background and were about as big as the tree trunks they had felled for a living. Although seeing Eddie getting his comeuppance made her smile, she wasn't foolish enough to believe it to be the last she'd ever see of him.

'And some bloke's been following me. I was wondering if it was him who'd attacked Ben.' She fiddled with her painted nails as she spoke, her frown undiminished. 'I'm scared that if I go out with any chap, that bloke is going to be following me. That's the way it seems.'

Maisie frowned. 'I don't know 'ow I can help, Carole. 'Ave you bin out with Eric of late?'

Carole shook her head. 'No. He's nice, but I like blokes in

uniform. And as you know, Eric's not very well and dead disappointed that he failed his medical to join the RAF.'

'I don't know what I can do about it. What do you think I can do?'

'Give me some advice. You've got a reputation for handling the likes of Eddie Bridgeman.'

It was true that she'd escaped his clutches. He hadn't bothered her since, but she was older now. At one time, Aggie's daughter, Angie, had lived with him, but he'd dropped her once past her twentieth birthday. The odd thing was that Carole looked older than her years not younger. So why Eddie's interest in her?

Maisie gave her advice. 'At the end of the day, you need a boyfriend that can give as good as he gets. Somebody with the connections and the fists to put up a fight for you, but don't ask me who. Some bloke like Bridget's who comes from another country and class, but he ain't around at present.'

Carole's expression dropped. 'But I want someone who's around. I like to go dancing and have fun.'

'The right one will turn up,' said Maisie with a sage nod of her head. 'Does yer mother know about Eddie and this bloke that's following you?'

Carole shook her head. 'Her mind's on other things. She's met some old geezer who's asked her to move up north. No more lying on her back to make a living.'

'Has Eddie asked you out at all?'

Carole shook her head. 'No.'

Maisie frowned. It just didn't make sense. Why else would Eddie warn off any pair of trousers that fancied their chances? She rested her chin on her hand as she considered the possibilities. 'I don't know what to say until I've had a good think about it. Let me know if yer still bein' followed. Maybe we could do something about that.'

Carole's eyes lit up. 'You mean beat him up until he tells us what it's all about?'

'Something like that,' said Maisie, amused rather than shocked at Carole's enthusiasm for a bit of fisticuffs.

Carole left with a smile on her face.

Maisie turned to Aggie. 'So what do you think?'

Aggie's eyes were averted, looking downwards, eyelids lowered. Her response was slow. 'I'm not sure.' Her eyes met Maisie's. 'Eddie Bridgeman could be saving her for somebody else. He's a pimp, Maisie. When he's finished with girls, he passes them on. They're ruined by then, so no decent man wants them – or that's what most girls think. They hit rock bottom they do...'

'Oh, Aggie, I'm so sorry. 'Ave you 'eard from Angie?'

Angie was one of the girls who Eddie had seduced at an early age. She'd left home to live with him. But Eddie had tired of her. 'She joined the Royal Transport Corps. Learning how to service a lorry last I 'eard. Got one letter from up north and that was it.'

Maisie noticed how small her hand looked lying on top of Aggie's. Ever since she'd joined the factory, Aggie had been the mainstay, the one in charge, the one they went to with their personal troubles. It had always seemed to her that Aggie could punch through problems, not beyond the bounds of possibility given the size of her hands. 'At least she's well out of 'is clutches. Even Eddie Bridgeman can't work 'is wicked ways with the British Army.'

* * *

John Gaunt was an artist and photographer Maisie had met at a bus stop when they'd got into talking about the weather, how packed the bus would be and the poor quality of newspaper. He was a conscientious objector who worked at the hospital as an orderly. He also lived along Coronation Road, not far from the garage owned by George Barton.

'Do you know him?' she'd asked him.

He'd nodded. 'Not well, but enough to know his income isn't entirely derived from the garage business. I heard tell he can't read or write but that he makes enough from scrap metal. Not huge, but enough to be comfortable. I hear he and a partner made a fortune after the war – you know – back in 1918 when the army was getting rid of lorries. Blokes being demobbed bought them and set themselves up in haulage businesses – quicker than the old narrowboats and more convenient than trains. Made a killing so I 'ear, but there was a problem with his partner.'

'Why was that?' Maisie has asked, interested but trying to appear unconcerned.

'Something to do with George being the front man and the other chap preferring to be in the background.' He'd frowned. 'I don't know why. Nothing criminal, I don't think, except that he was foreign. You know what people are like. They prefer the devil they know.' He'd shrugged. 'That's it, though I did hear that George tended to throw it about a bit and the other bloke weren't seen out and about much.'

It was just a one-night stand at first, but this was the third night of going out with him. Maisie never asked him a second time about George Barton. It was enough to know it had something to do with business.

*All work and no play makes Maisie a dull girl.*

Most of the time, the words merely ran through her head. Sometimes she sang it to whatever tune she'd heard ad infinitum on the factory wireless that day.

Tonight she was going for a walk with him and his camera. 'I like that time of day,' he'd said to her. 'Photos have got more atmosphere once twilight falls.'

She'd liked his enthusiasm for something she didn't really understand.

The plan was to have something to eat before she got ready. The geyser supplying the hot water was on the blink, so it would be a case of putting the kettle on the gas for hot water.

There were two items of mail on the coconut mat just inside the door, delivered after she'd left for work. One was a card.

She smiled. 'Sid Bairstow. You're a right Romeo on the quiet.'

'Them Japs must be right buggers,' she'd said to her mates in work. 'They only allow 'im one tatty little card. I bet 'e'd say a lot more if it was bigger – or a letter.'

Her statement had led to a bit of leg pulling, like, 'You're 'oping 'e'll ask you to marry 'im.'

'Bet you want 'im to tell you what you're gonna get up to once 'e's back.'

'Food,' she'd replied. 'He talks mainly about food.' She knew it meant he wasn't eating properly. There'd been rumours about German prisoner of war camps, but the conditions in Japanese camps were said to be much worse.

This card was grubby and his words were written in pencil. Sometimes the words were clear and sometimes less so. She guessed he was using whatever he could lay hands on, possibly no more than a stub shared with others.

*Dearest Maisie, I hope you are keeping well. The Red Cross brought me the letters you've written me over the past six months all at once. Permission to deliver them isn't easy to come by. I don't understand what the Japanese think you might say. Mind you, quite a bit of yours were censored, by our side not the Japs. It's been so long since I saw you last. Can you include a photograph in your next letter? It ain't that I can't remember what you look like, it's just been a while. I want to stare at you while*

*I'm laid here. Looking at you will give me hope. Affection as*
*always, Sid Bairstow.*

His words brought a lump to her throat. She placed the card
behind the clock on the mantelpiece. Just one little card in response
to all those letters she'd sent him. It was far from a fair exchange.

Despite all she said about him only being a friend, she touched
the kiss she held on her lips and placed it on the card. 'Given time, I
might get to love you, Sid Bairstow,' she whispered.

She turned her attention to the envelope, didn't check the hand-
writing but slid her finger into the gap and tore it open.

Unusually, the paper was of decent quality. Most writing paper
nowadays was flimsy, thanks to the lack of imported timber from
Norway and Canada for turning into paper pulp. Before the war,
Avonmouth, Bristol's newest and biggest facility, had been a major
port for the import of timber. Norway had been conquered by Nazi
Germany and Canada was a very long way away, so imports were
much depleted.

Maisie opened the letter.

Brand, Cutler and Co, Solicitors.
Orchard Street,
Bristol.

She vaguely recalled that Orchard Street was up behind the city
centre and just off Park Street. The letter pulled her up, the heading
in particular.

In the matter of the estate of Mrs Grace Theodora Wells.
    We act for Mr George Barton of Barton Garage, Coronation
Road, regarding the will of Mrs Grace Wells.
    As you may know, my client supported Mr Joseph Wells

when he became ill in his later years and, in lieu of such support, a promise was made that following his death and that of his wife, should she outlive him, everything Mr Wells had owned, and subsequently owned by Mrs Wells, would pass to my client.

Mr Barton was somewhat surprised to find that you were named chief beneficiary of the will and that indeed a new will was written. My client does not relish challenging the will in court or your claim to be her granddaughter. He suggests that some persuasion was used to get her to make a new will. However, he would much prefer to avoid any nastiness and come to an agreement that would suit both parties.

In conclusion, my client is prepared to allow you the contents of Mrs Wells' bank account whilst the house in Totterdown and the land in Avonmouth is signed over to him.

Please respond within one month that you accept his terms before we take the matter further.

Maisie no longer felt like eating, washing or going out on the town. She sat in the same velvet-covered armchair where her grandmother used to sit feeling as though the stuffing had been knocked out of her, and she was angry, very angry.

She reread the letter, picking out points that made her grit her teeth and feel like screaming. She had no idea what kind of help George Barton had given her late grandfather. Who could she ask?

Swallowing her anger, she thought things through. George Barton was insinuating that she was not the granddaughter of Grace Wells. Proving that she was would scupper whatever he threw at her. She would take great delight in doing so, but she had to be quick. There was only one person who could confirm her natural father's true identity and he was at death's door in Horfield Prison.

# 13

# PHYLLIS

'Cocoa time!'

Phyllis could only nod her thanks. Cocoa was far less important than talking to the last pilot to land following the latest raid. She kept going until she could finally confirm with the golden words, 'Kite 743 down. All easy.'

Once her heart had stopped hammering, she took off her headset and slugged back a big mouthful of cocoa. It was considered a food and sweetened with honey of which there was an abundance on the island, a valued commodity that went some way to adding a bit of variety to the meagre rations. There was less alcohol, but a nip was added for the night shift, enough to perk up their spirits for the gruelling vigil that would last until 08.00.

It was not yet 08.00 and although all the kites – code word for an aeroplane – were down – some a little worse for wear – everyone knew it was only a temporary respite. For Phyllis, it was a more gruelling wait. Mick's voice had come through loud and clear at 06.00, dawn in this part of the world for most of the year. That was the time he had taken off.

Reconnaissance was Mick's job. OK, he didn't have to scramble into a fighter and give battle, but he did have to encroach into enemy territory. Sometimes he was required to search for enemy vessels entering within a radius of one hundred miles of sea. Most of the time, his job was to fly north to Sicily, just over sixty miles distant, to locate and photograph the airfields of the interior or ports and harbours. To Phyllis's horror, he had a delight in lingering over certain targets such as Syracuse where the bastions of the Sicilian Grand Harbour glowed like gold in the light of the rising sun.

'One day I'm gonna visit that place,' he'd said to her. 'I'm looking down at the history of Europe when I fly over Syracuse. Yep. We'll go there for our honeymoon.'

She'd smacked his hand playfully and told him in no uncertain terms that she might have a say in where they went for their honeymoon, if they ever had a honeymoon and if she ever got a divorce; or settled for the alternative and lived in sin. One thing she'd promised herself was that she would never return to England, to Robert and life with her appalling mother-in-law.

She took out the last letter she'd received from Maisie.

*I don't know whether I should say this, but I saw Robert in Bedminster. He looked at me as though he didn't know me and when I asked how he was he said he couldn't wait to get back to the front. Said his mother was driving him batty. What a turn up! And her doting on him. He even said he had a girlfriend in France. I don't know whether that's true or not.*

Phyllis set the letter to one side, shaken that the domineering man she'd known had changed so much. And a girlfriend in France? She accepted that anything in this war was possible and in a way she hoped there was a sweetheart in his life. Everyone deserved a little happiness.

The station commander blocked her field of vision. He had stepped in front of her, hands clasped behind his back as he checked the clock against his wristwatch.

'The Huns in the sun are late today.'

'Yes, sir.'

The clock set high on the wall was like a great big eye keeping time for them all. How many hours until the next raid? There was usually little more than an hour between them and it didn't matter whether it was a weekday or a Sunday. They were late. Perhaps they wouldn't come.

'Perhaps it's all over,' somebody dared to say. 'Or perhaps not today. It is Sunday.'

The station commander turned on whoever had said it with a withering look. 'Lass, if you believe never on a Sunday, you'll believe anything.'

The clock clicked on – 08.00 hours came and went. A new shift came on, but Phyllis lingered. There was no chatter and few messages going backwards and forwards. Teleprinters weren't clattering; pens were poised over notebooks, earphones were eased off heads, though not taken off completely, just enough so anything urgent could be heard. If that happened, they would be slipped back on.

'You waiting to hear from your Mick,' asked one of her colleagues.

She nodded.

'Why don't you go and get some rest? We can send a message if we hear...'

'No.' She shook her head vigorously. 'I'll stay.'

'Quiet!' ordered the middle-aged man for whom the Operations Room was his kingdom, the place where he reigned supreme.

Chatter ceased. Nobody moved.

The bang of the door opening startled them. An orderly came

in pushing a trolley on which balanced enamel jugs of cocoa and cold water.

'No tea. Only leftover cocoa from last night.' He addressed the Ops commander directly. 'Would you like some, sir?'

First there was a glare, then a wordless grunt as he took the mug. He glanced at Phyllis seemed about to order her off shift, but changed his mind.

No raiders as yet. Phyllis stared at the clock over the top of her mug. Time was moving on. Mick should have reported in by now.

Cedric, the orderly who often had a joke and a laugh with Mick, caught meaning in her look. 'There's a bit of a headwind out there. I think we've got a Gregale coming in.'

The violent wind he referred to regularly brought screaming gales and towering waves and could be the reason Mick was late back.

On seeing the alarm in her eyes, he added a bite of reassurance. 'It'll be that headwind slowing him down.' He made a clicking sound out of the corner of his mouth. 'Mick's got the luck of the devil. No bloody big wind is going to stop the likes of Mick Fairbrother getting home.'

His cheery disposition didn't usually fail to perk Phyllis up and she laughed and agreed that he was probably right. Outside appearances were deceptive. The alarm that had appeared in her eyes remained. Mick was now over an hour late and she had a sick, uneasy feeling in her stomach.

She closed her eyes as she drank more of the sweet alcoholic brew and said a little prayer.

*Please come back, Mick. I love you. I'll go with you to Australia no matter whether we're married or not.*

As tiredness took hold, she finally gave in, picked up her things and headed for the exit. She felt Mariana, who had stayed behind without being asked, looking at her, eyes full of concern.

She followed her and once outside she offered to take her to church.

'All options are open. A little prayer and the lighting of a candle won't take anything from what you believe.'

Phyllis sighed. 'Anything to get him home. Just some little sign...'

The church Mariana took her to was crowded. Churches in Malta always were. Devout locals who went to church on a regular basis were joined by members of His Majesty's Forces. Some were far from being regular churchgoers back home, but when the devil's biting at your heels, as Mick was fond of saying, a little bit of heavenly help doesn't come amiss.

There was something very sacred about a church lit by candles burning in wrought-iron sconces and overhead chandeliers. The flickering candle flames made the eyes of painted saints seem to move and softened the folds of their stony garments. It was easy to imagine there was real flesh beneath those folds.

Head bowed beside her Maltese workmate, Phyllis squeezed her eyes tightly shut. The Latin words, repeated ad infinitum in past wars over many centuries, gave her only a minimum of calm. Thoughts of Mick crept in. Behind her closed eyes, she visualised their future together, grapevines quivering in a warm breeze, a house with a veranda running along its front, bronze skin, both her own, Mick's and the children they looked forward to having.

Mariana touched her arm and whispered that mass was over and it was time to leave.

Outside, the hot sun baked the ground, the buildings and people who couldn't find room to walk in the shade.

Military and civilians, British and Maltese, clustered in the shadows, shuffling forward, bumping into each other and shouting ahead to family members or colleagues.

The quiet shuffling changed, goaded on by something said by

men shouting from the dockyard to relatives in this steady march. News flew from mouths cupped by hands to aid its loudness. In response, the shuffling quickened, heads turning as some great news was passed from those at the front through to those coming along behind. Those who did not speak the language shared enquiring glances. There were murmurs of, 'What the bloody hell's going on?'

Mariana turned to Phyllis, her eyes bright with excitement. 'A tanker is coming in. She's badly damaged, but she has oil. Isn't that wonderful?'

There was no need to exchange words. Hand in hand, Mariana leading the way, they raced up to the bastions where they would have a good view of the damaged tanker coming into the Grand Harbour.

A great tide of people swept uphill, all with the same aim in mind: to see this battered ship limping into harbour. It was hardly the first time this had happened, but there was hope that it would be the last.

Eyes looked skywards from the bastions to a swarm of fighter aircraft, instantly recognised as Hurricanes and Spitfires, diving at enemy bombers, driving them away before they could do any more damage.

Phyllis gazed up at them, looking for him and finally finding her voice. 'I don't see Mick amongst them.' She was hurting inside, yet she felt like cheering. Listing heavily, the subject of many air attacks, the tanker was tied to another ship – she thought a destroyer, but she never had been good at identifying ships.

It seemed hours went by before the crowd dispersed. At no time had they cheered. They were reverent, their thoughts absorbed with how many men had died in order to bring relief.

Mariana touched her arm. 'It's time to go.'

There was sadness in her friend's eyes as well as in her voice.

Phyllis knew she sensed her pain, though nobody could share it with her. 'Come on. Let's get something to eat. My mother does wonders with the rations.'

Slowly, mind numb and having no inclination to eat, Phyllis went with Mariana, aware of a new hopefulness around her. She felt none of this. All those wonderful plans for the future seemed as tumbled and broken as the piles of rubble that had once been buildings.

* * *

Phyllis couldn't remember eating, but perhaps she did. Mariana's mother offered her a chair for the night when the drone of bombers yet again sounded overhead.

Was she only imagining that she had a day off tomorrow? She wasn't sure. It was Mariana who confirmed it.

'Tonight you sleep in our cellar.'

Down in the cool darkness of the cellar, the whole family, from grandparents to great-grandchildren, plus a few stragglers from the street, huddled down.

The chair was all that was available, not that it mattered. In the small moments when Phyllis did sleep, she wasn't in a confined space at all but turning round and around, trying to look beyond the wide horizons that Mick had told her about.

'We'll grow wine and children,' he'd said laughingly, and she'd laughed with him. No matter the intensity of the air raids, the loud explosions, the butterfly bombs, the incendiaries, the noise of Stuka dive bombers and the death and devastation, she'd hung onto that hope, the greatest hope she'd ever encountered in her whole life. The greatest love.

With just a cup of coffee inside her, she left the hospitality of her Maltese friends and stepped out into a morning thick with dust, the smell of aviation fuel, of cordite and all the other explosives used the night before.

On her way back to her billet, she took a detour away from the city. To her great surprise, a bus stopped and without asking where it was going, she got on. Such was her manner that she forgot to pay her fare. Her mind was in a daze. Her eyes were unfocused.

Unseen by her, the bus driver and an elderly woman in one of the front seats exchanged knowing looks before both made the sign of the cross on their chests. She was not the first they'd seen whose mind and heart were likely breaking in unison.

It was a kind of instinct that she was finally outside the city, the ruins of buildings and the stalwart bastions some way behind her. Wherever it was, she could see the sea, wide and unending, a rich tapestry of blues and greens until blending into a hazy horizon.

On alighting from the bus the dry air hit her, the sun blazing. Behind her, the driver and a number of passengers conversed in Maltese, though quietly. More crossing of their chests before the bus moved on without closing the door. It was too hot for that.

Phyllis was unaware of the bus leaving. The sea and sky were one. Being Malta there were few seabirds. A small fishing boat bobbed around, twine trailing behind it, the fisherman's hands jerking in the hope of attracting a big fish to the attached lure.

Had he seen Mick? She shouted and waved. The fisherman, his cap shading his sight, did not wave back.

She walked slowly forward, her feet slipping on the dusty ground. At one point, she stubbed her toe against a stone. It was not a good path. Holding out her arms to either side helped her balance better. Rather than take steps, she slid her feet along the descending path. A few stones loosened by her feet rolled down the steep descent into the rocks and pools below. The scent of salt was strong.

Blueness and more blueness; the sky was unblemished by cloud. Sometimes when a Gregale was forecast, the clouds piled up ahead of it. Clouds, colour and even the roll of the sea meant nothing to her. All she was looking for was one small dot to appear in the sky and get steadily bigger the closer it got to land. If not a dot in the sky, then a larger one on the sea. If Mick wasn't able to fly home, then perhaps he might have been picked up by a fishing boat. Someone had suggested that to her, though she couldn't remember who.

She craved the sea. There were pools between the rocks.

She thought about taking off her jacket. Her fingers discovered cotton; no jacket. Where had she left it? Try as she might, she couldn't remember.

The horizon shimmered with heat, but her legs were cool. She had waded into water. The watery path between the rocks was ill defined and the top of her head was baking. A rest was needed.

Her legs giving way, she sunk onto a rock, the water billowing round her skirt. The scene ahead of her began to spin in circles, like an aeroplane spinning downwards out of control. Was that a message telling her what had happened to Mick?

'No. Please, no.'

She flopped forward, rock to one side of her, water the other. Then her arms fell forward too and in slow motion she toppled to one side, the rock she fell on giving her a glancing blow.

\* \* \*

A little time passed, or it might have been a lot of time. Her hair was wet, streaming like seaweed on the surface of the sea.

'Lady.'

Phyllis didn't recognise the voice and nobody she knew ever addressed her as lady.

A pleasant draught fanned her face. How lovely, she thought. A fan is very pleasant.

She heard voices speaking in a language she didn't understand but recognised. There was a sense of urgency to their tone. More than one set of arms was taking hold of her.

'You have sunstroke. We will help you.'

They sounded kind, but she wanted to tell them that she preferred to go into the sea. Could they help her do that?

'Mick,' she said, and the sea seemed to answer, an inrush of surf kissing the hardness of the rocks.

'You have heatstroke,' someone said in a calm, caring manner. 'You've been out here too long.'

She tried to tell them that she had to wait for Mick and that the sea would be cool despite the summer heat and how wonderful it would be to drown in it.

# 14

## BRIDGET

'Milligan! There's a phone call for you.'

Bridget stopped rubbing her aching feet and looked up. 'Really?'

Caitlin, the Welsh girl who'd replaced Christina, finally reunited with her fiancé, slumped down onto her bed. ''Tis you he asked for and there's only one Milligan round yer that I know of.'

He! Bridget ran from the room and down the stairs to the phone she was told must be used for relatives and emergencies only. Even then, they were supposed to keep the number to themselves and not to hand it out to every Tom, Dick or Harry – which meant no boyfriends.

Bubbling with joy, she exclaimed, 'Lyndon! How did you get this number?'

'I pulled rank with some old battleaxe on the wards.'

Bridget gurgled with laughter. 'Lyndon, you are naughty!'

'Look, there's a letter winging its way to you telling you of all that's been happening, but I got here before it did. My knowledge of your country, my darling, has landed me a real plum of a job. Basically, I'm based in London.'

'That's fantastic!'

'Sure is. I wondered if you might be able to put in for a transfer. I've looked into it. Most of the hospitals in London are crying out for trained staff. And you have done your basic training, haven't you?'

'Only as a trainee, more or less an auxiliary.'

Despite the fact that her face was still wreathed in smiles, his suggestion had not fallen on fallow ground. She needed to explain to him that she wasn't quite there yet, though she had applied for the four-year course that would enable her to become a fully-fledged nurse.

'I thought we could get married there. Neither of us requires parental permission. What do you say?'

The smile froze on her face. 'You've sprang this on me a bit too quickly. I need to think about it, make arrangements and all that.'

For a moment, there was silence. She could imagine his disappointment, hence the silence as he thought through her response.

'I guess I can understand that. Excuse me thinking we could talk about this over the phone. Dead crass of me. We need to meet up and talk about it face to face. After all, we've been apart for over six months...'

'Over seven and a half actually.'

'Too long. Far too long. Do you forgive me?'

'How could I possibly refuse.'

'So there's no new guy on your arm.'

'I would have waited for you forever.'

'That's what I was hoping. Do you know The Duck and Pheasant?'

He was that close by? Her heart raced.

'If it's the one overlooking the pond at the end of the road, yes, I do.'

'I'm presuming you've finished your shift. Meet me there in an hour.'

'Lyndon!' Her surprise was total.

'And I've booked a room. Don't bother with a nightdress – unless you feel you have to.'

The pips sounded. He was gone.

She replaced the receiver slowly, her mind in turmoil. Fate had thrown the dice in her favour. She had two days' leave, although tonight she had promised to wash and set Tilly's hair. By hook or by crook Tilly had managed to get hold of a lemon, great for washing hair. She'd also got enough sugar to make a setting lotion, the real stuff missing from the shops for absolute ages. When questioned, she'd said someone in the kitchens had given it to her. Pressed further, she'd admitted the head gardener at the nearby grand house had plucked the lemon especially from the orangery. They'd all laughed and said she was pulling their leg.

Bridget rushed into the room with a ready apology. 'Sorry, Tilly, but I won't be able to set your hair tonight.'

Tilly's face screwed up as though she'd sucked on the lemon intended for her hair. 'Oh! That's a shame. Caitlin. How about you?'

Caitlin turned another page on the magazine she was reading and didn't bother to look up. 'No can do. Got a date with a bloke from the big house.'

'Really? With one of the officers?'

She sounded and looked surprised.

'No,' said Caitlin, attention still fixed on the magazine. 'With the cook's son. He's on leave from bomb disposal. Asked me to go to the pub with him.'

'Which pub's that?' Bridget asked in an offhand manner.

'The Bunch of Grapes. He plays darts there. Got a match tonight. Asked if I wanted to be on the team.'

'Playing darts? Are you really going to play darts?' Tilly was beginning to sound exasperated.

'I don't mind if I do.' Caitlin looked up at Tilly from beneath her straight-cut fringe. 'Used to play darts back in Magor for the women's team.'

Caitlin, who took great pleasure in pulling Tilly's leg, threw Bridget a wink.

Bridget selected items from her locker and transferred them to a brown paper carrier bag that was just about big enough for an overnight stay.

Getting nowhere with Caitlin, Tilly turned her attention to what Bridget was up to.

'So where are you going tonight that's more important than you doing my hair?'

'I'm staying with a friend.' She determined not to blush.

A slow smile crossed Tilly's face. 'You don't fool me. It's that American chap. You're staying with him somewhere for a night of hot passion. Am I right?'

Bridget felt the first flush of embarrassment cross her face. 'It's none of your business.'

Caitlin chimed in. 'Course it isn't. I took the phone call from her aunt. That's who she's going to stay with.'

Bridget could have kissed her.

Tilly decided she was going to ask around if anyone else could do her hair, otherwise she intended doing it herself. 'I'm sure I can if pushed,' she said as she went off to find somebody willing.

'Thanks for that,' Bridget said to Caitlin once it was just the two of them.

'No need. Her voice grates, her attitude grates and I envy – almost hate the fact –that she can get hold of things easier than the rest of us.' She smiled. 'But at least she has not got your American. Go on. Get out there and enjoy yourself.'

\* \* \*

The Duck and Pheasant had been so named before the time when what had been a village had grown into a town. A ring of grass and trees surrounded a pond where ducks and a pair of swans plied their way through reeds and bulrushes. The old inn, its thatched roof frowning over small windows and rubble stone walls, looked like an old man who'd hunched his shoulders, settled on a favourite bench and stared unblinking at the shimmering water.

Bridget's heart hammered in her chest on seeing the sports car outside, the only vehicle parked there. Lyndon was sitting in the front seat, hand tapping impatiently on the steering wheel. She stopped and watched as he peeled back his sleeve and looked at his watch. She knew she wasn't late and it lifted her heart to think he was desperate to see her

She smiled as she said, 'Hello, Lyndon.'

He barely glanced up before flinging open the car door, leaping out and wrapping her in his arms.

'Bridget.' He swallowed and opened his mouth to speak, but settled for kissing her. In her dreams, she'd imagined this kiss, but nothing could match up to the real thing.

They stood without saying a word, holding hands, drinking each other in.

'I want you so badly,' he said to her. 'I want to kiss every inch of you.'

She pulled a laughingly warning look. 'Not out here. We might be banned from the Duck and Pheasant even before we've gone through the door. And I wouldn't want that.'

His smile was wide enough to crack his face in two. 'Neither would I. I'll get my bag.'

There was a twinkle in the landlady's eyes when they checked in. 'We only got two guest rooms,' she confided to them, her red cheeks like polished apples. 'One at the back and one at the front. I've put you in the front room. It's got a nice view of the pond. The one at the back looks out over our backyard where we store the empty barrels. You don't want to be looking at a load of smelly barrels and bottles now do you.' It was a statement not a question, so needed no answer. 'Dinner at eight all right for you?'

Lyndon took the key. 'That's fine for me.' He addressed Bridget. 'How about you, darling?'

It was just past six o'clock.

'Fine.'

'I thought so,' said the landlady. 'Follow me.'

Their hands fleetingly touched as they climbed the narrow staircase until reaching an oddly shaped door set in an equally lopsided frame.

'It's the oldest part of the building,' said the landlady. 'Don't know if there's ghosts. There might be, but I ain't ever seen one. Lavatory's along the landing. Turn right.'

The room had oak beams and a low ceiling. The bed looked as though it had stood waiting at least a hundred years for them to arrive.

'Thank you.'

'There's hot water in the pitcher there.' She indicated a china ewer decorated with overblown pink roses and sat in a matching bowl.

Neither said a word until the door was shut. Then they looked at each other, their breathing increasing with a desire they'd kept in check for over half a year. Their looks said more than words. This was the moment they'd been waiting for.

'Right.' Lyndon took off his jacket.

Bridget slipped off her shoes.

After that, there was nothing else in the world that mattered more than feeling their naked bodies entwined beneath cool sheets.

'It's been so long.'

'But I still remember every bit of you,' he said to her, his hands exploring every curve.

She moaned in response, touching him as intimately as he was touching her. Not much else was said. Everything was fixed on sensations, the soft caress, the kisses that started with matched lips, then coursed downwards, neck, breast, belly and loins. Eyes closed, it was as if she'd entered another world. There was no war, no room even, just them rediscovering what pleased each of them and there was certainly plenty of that.

'I love you,' he whispered into her hair. 'I was so scared you'd found somebody else.'

'As if I would.'

'Seems to me that everyone is grabbing happiness in the moment. I wouldn't have blamed you.'

Bridget sighed against his shoulder, her lips moving in semi kisses over his warm skin. 'Do you know what? I wouldn't care if a bomb dropped on us right now.' She pressed her body against his, felt the hardness of his muscles and even the beating of his heart. 'We've had this moment. Nothing can take that away from us.'

Their desire was such that they made love again before Lyndon looked at his watch.

'I'm hungry.'

Laughingly, Bridget pulled the sheet over her head and dared him to repeat his exertions for a third time.

He uncovered her face, kissed her again and again, trailing his lips down over her neck, her shoulders and her breasts.

'Do you know what? I'm hungry too.'

He smiled at her. 'I think we're going to be hungry for the rest of our lives.'

The water in the pitcher still held some warmth and the soap, although oddly shaped, smelt as good as pre-war. He washed her and she washed him until he took the flannel from her with the comment that if she carried on doing that, neither of them would be getting any supper.

She brushed her hair and put on a blue spotted dress.

Lyndon stood looking at her, head cocked to one side, hands in his pockets. 'I've got something for you.'

Laying the brush to one side, she asked him what it was.

He held out his right hand, fist tightly closed. 'This.'

In the palm of his hand, he held a ring, the stone dark green and edged with diamonds.

'It used to belong to my father's grandmother. My mother never wore it. She had her own inherited diamonds.'

Bridget gasped. 'Diamonds?'

'The stone in the middle is an emerald. Green for Ireland, where our families originally came from.'

Bridget's heart raced as he put the ring onto the third finger of her left hand.

'There,' he said. 'We're now officially engaged.'

'Yes,' she said, her eyes shining as she looked lovingly up into his face. In that moment, after an early evening of passion, she couldn't possibly refuse. Yes, she had reservations, but she was sure they would come to some kind of compromise – though not just yet. She so wanted tonight to be perfect.

One more deep, lingering kiss and with Lyndon wearing his uniform, they went down to the bar.

Mrs Webber, the landlady, took them through to where a small table had been set up in an alcove slightly apart from their regular customers. 'Thought you might like some privacy,' she said, her eyes seeming to twinkle more than before, almost as though she'd known of the grand gesture that had taken place.

On the occasion when he'd last asked her to marry him, she'd been divided between family and him, especially when he mentioned going to live in America. Now she was divided for a different reason. On Mr Gillespie's recommendation, she'd been urged to apply to become a fully qualified nurse. It had all started with her administering penicillin. She'd found herself relishing the challenge, following in the mould of Florence Nightingale who she'd read about. Also following in the footsteps of Edith Cavell who nobody could help but admire, but how to tell Lyndon? How to ask him to wait until she'd achieved her ambition? It might be that the war would be over by then.

Mrs Webber brought mutton stew to the table. 'More spuds than mutton, but tasty anyway,' she stated with pride.

Lyndon ordered a pint of beer for himself and half a cider for Bridget.

Every so often, she looked at the ring. How could she not accept his proposal?

'So when are you going to apply for that transfer?'

His look bore into her and it was hard to meet his eyes.

She smiled a disarming smile and fobbed him off with a half-truth. 'I'm a bit busy at present, Lyndon, but leave it with me. I'll have a word with Matron and ask her what the chances are?'

He frowned. 'Jesus, Bridget, I'm asking you to marry me. I thought it would be just you I had to ask.'

She grinned capriciously and had the grace to demur. 'My father might have something to say about that.'

'Isn't that a bit old-fashioned?' He didn't look happy.

'Well. It is, but he'd probably appreciate it. And so would I.' She gave his hand a quick clasp and smiled.

The returned smile was reluctant but resigned. 'OK. I get your point. But just sort it with Matron, huh?' His smile widened. 'And we can see the sights of London together.'

\* \* \*

It was late evening in the following day when she got back to her billet just in time to partake of boiled water being poured onto tealeaves left in the pot from the morning.

Caitlin looked up as she came in. 'Well, that was well-timed. I thought I'd be drinking tea alone. Tilly's out with some handsome senior surgeon. Just a fun thing, she told me, nothing serious. If I understand Miss Mathilda correctly, that means that he's married.'

Bridget conceded that she was probably right. Having fun was first priority for Mathilda Fortescue. Short-term romances were the order of the day.

'Have we got sugar?'

'No, but my gran sent me a box of Welsh cakes. I don't know where she gets the sugar and I don't ask... Are you all right?' she asked on seeing Bridget's troubled frown.

Bridget set her bag down on the bed, took off her coat, kicked off her shoes and sighed. 'He wants me to apply for a transfer to London.'

'The bright lights of London! Exciting.'

Bridget pointed out to her that there was still a blackout all over the country and London was no exception. No bright lights.

Caitlin passed her a mug of tea and a Welsh cake.

Bridget took a bite. 'Sweet,' she said as she licked every crumb from her lips.

She could feel Caitlin's eyes on her.

'Are you going to do as he asks?'

Bridget took a sip of tea. It was weak but wet and warm and the thin cake from Caitlin's gran helped it go down.

'He wants us to get married,' she said, meeting Caitlin's gaze head on.

Caitlin drew her chin in, a look of surprise shooting out across the rim of her tea cup. 'What more could a girl want? London and Lyndon; a fun city and a handsome husband. I'd be in there like a shot, so I would.'

'The truth is, Caitlin, I'd never been away from home before. Never been away from my family and never even considered becoming a nurse. I truly thought that was for other girls from posher backgrounds than me. I thought it was the tobacco factory and Bristol forever. Then along came the war. I feel so appreciated here, not that I didn't enjoy my old job, I did, but what I'm doing now has opened my eyes to the big wide world. I'm so grateful for Mr Gillespie's encouragement and appreciative that I'm involved in injecting this new wonder drug. I really feel as though I'm part of making history. I couldn't get that from making cigarettes, or...' She hung her head. 'Or from being married.'

There was a moment's silence, before Caitlin asked, 'What next?'

Bridget shrugged. 'I need time.'

'So you're not going to apply for a transfer just yet?'

She shook her head. 'I need to consider what I really want and try to explain to Lyndon how I feel.'

'Up to you, my queen. You could still be a nurse in London.'

Bridget had to agree that she was right. Lyndon wasn't likely to object to that. 'I don't want to move away from here, not with all this new treatment going on. I was hit for six by the look of joy on Corporal Crown's face when his leg just kept getting better and better. He's going to take me dancing sometime soon.' Her face beamed at the thought of it. The joy she'd felt once he was fully recovered.

'Perhaps you're after a new romance?'

'No,' Bridget replied, vehemently shaking her head. 'Not at all. I will go dancing with him, but that will be it. Anyway, I think he's married.'

'In that case, don't let Tilly know. Oh no. My mistake.' She clicked her fingers. 'Of course you can tell her. He'll be quite safe. She's officer issue only.'

The joke made them laugh. It was a well-known fact that Tilly only dated officers of the very highest rank.

Caitlin got out a small bottle of whisky and tipped a little in a second mug of tea. 'That should give it a bit of strength,' she added. 'Cheers.'

Bridget raised her mug. The tea that had been only lukewarm now burned her throat. 'Thank you Scotland.'

Caitlin responded by pouring each of them another splash of whisky.

'We're going to have a hangover going on like this,' Bridget remarked.

'It'll help you sleep. By the morning, everything will be as clear as day. You'll know what to do. Marry Lyndon, marry the corporal, or even Mr Gillespie –only joking,' she said with a laugh, then added, 'Anything is possible. Anything at all. The war's changed our lives.'

* * *

In the morning, Bridget was still undecided. Lyndon phoned just when Mr Gillespie was doing his rounds, Bridget and other trainees trailing along behind him.

'Tell him I'll phone him back,' Bridget whispered to the auxiliary who had brought the message.

Deep set eyes glared at her from beneath bushy iron grey eyebrows. Mr Gillespie, senior surgeon, missed nothing.

'Is there somewhere you'd rather be?' he asked sharply.

She shook her head. 'No, sir. Not at all.'

'Good,' he said. 'I'm glad to hear it. I've no time for flighty nurses. Dedication. That's all I ask of a nurse.'

And that's what I'm giving, she thought to herself. That's the thing that divides me between love and loyalty, nursing and Lyndon. The trouble was that she wanted both.

# 15

## MAISIE

The inside of Horfield Prison was every bit as grim as she'd expected it to be. The sound of her footsteps flew back at her from the bare brick walls. Every sound echoed, every door clanged open or even more noisily clanged shut. The lighting was dim. The whole place stunk of men sharing confined cells with limited facilities and tasteless, plain food cooked in large batches with restricted ingredients. The smell of potatoes and cabbage made the air taste like soup.

A ring of keys jangled merrily against the hip bone of the prison officer, a lean man with a sunken face and eyes so deeply buried they hardly seemed to be there. It was the jolliest noise Maisie had heard since entering this place.

He stopped outside a cast-iron door, turned a key and there he was – Frank Miles.

If the prison officer looked gaunt, her stepfather looked more so. His skin clung to his bare skull and had the pallid shine of a sickness that would never go away. Her stepbrother Alf had expressed surprise that he was still alive. She could understand why.

She'd been told Frank was in the terminal ward. 'Relatives only,' they'd said. As if anyone else would want to visit the old bugger!

There were three beds in the ward. None of the men lying in them looked likely to try to escape, but still the door was kept locked.

As extra security, the prison officer stood in the corner, far enough away not to hear their conversation – as long as they spoke softly. Near enough to intervene should Frank Miles or any of the other sick souls suddenly regain their health, leap for the door and distant horizons. It wasn't likely. They all bore the same aura of men beyond help and not far off leaving this world.

'Hello, Frank.'

Even though there was a chair at the side of the bed, she chose to stand at the foot, about as far away from him as she could get.

His eyelids opened in flickering jerks. Even once opened, he had trouble focusing on her, narrowing then widening them.

'I need me glasses.'

'Where are they?' Her heart thudded in her chest. She'd prefer him not to see her rather than have to go closer.

'Fred! I need me glasses, so I can see who's come to see me.'

The prison officer stepped out of his corner. 'Right. 'Ere they are.' He stretched the cheap-looking hooks so they better fitted over Frank's ears. 'It's your daughter come to see you, Frank.'

'Stepdaughter,' Maisie snapped. The thought of having ever thought of him as her father made her feel sick.

She reminded herself that she needed to keep him sweet. She had a task that only he could help her with.

'It's Maisie,' she added. Although her tone wasn't quite as sharp, it held no warmth. There was no room in her heart for a man who had beat her mother black and blue whenever he'd felt like it and killed her father. She hated him.

'Maisie?' He sounded pleased.

Was he really glad to see her? If so, there had to be a reason. They'd never been close and never would be.

'Where's Alf?'

'Sailing to South America, I think.'

Alarm suddenly replaced the amenable expression. 'You ain't come 'ere to tell me somethin's 'appened to 'im 'ave ya?'

She was about to shake her head and confirm that Alf was hale and hearty, but had second thoughts. Why the devil had she assumed he would help her prove that she really was Grace Wells' daughter? The old sod was more likely to aggravate the likelihood of her inheritance in any way he could. He must have hated her natural father. She also reminded herself that it was down to the influence of Grace Wells that he was in Horfield Prison. It was Grace Wells that had instigated his arrest following the deaths resulting from him selling rotten meat. What did he have to thank her for? Nothing, but everything to hate her for. The house and everything else Grace Wells had left her crumbled to dust. None of it would ever be hers unless Frank Miles confirmed her parentage. Never in the world would he ever concede the point if he thought she would gain from it. Alf, on the other hand, was a different matter.

'Alf is fine, but it's him I wanted to talk to you about.'

'Eh?'

He looked genuinely interested. Alf, she decided, was the key, but she had to tread carefully.

'Are you going to be here when he gets back?'

His mouth acquired a surly slackness. He swiped at dribble with the sleeve of his prison-issue pyjamas, the stripes faded by hundreds of washes after use by hundreds of other sick prisoners. 'I ain't getting out of yer, thanks to that old cow Grace Wells.'

He spat the words at her. She was right not to mention her true reason for being here. It was the springboard she needed. In her mind, she apologised to Alf for what she was about to do.

'Alf deserves to get through this and come back to something better. Once 'e leaves the sea for good that is. Might want to settle down and raise a family.' She doubted that would be the case. Alf didn't care for women, but Frank, being Frank regarded his son as out of the same mould as himself. Women were lesser creatures, there for the pleasure of men. Never in a hundred years would he ever believe his son's true predilection and she for one would never reveal it.

'Bloody well deserves to.' His voice was as dry as his skin and thin, crackling like sandpaper. 'Still, I put a bit by for 'im. The 'ouse in York Street ain't mine, but there is a bit in the bank. He's welcome to it once I'm gone.'

'Half of it.'

'Eh?' He was thrown off balance.

'Well,' she said, determined to take advantage whilst she could, 'Alf and me are brother and sister, ain't we? Half for him and half for me.'

Though her heart was racing, she smirked with the pleasure of having forced him into a corner, though not the kind of corner where he would surrender, but one where, hopefully, he would come out fighting.

'You ain't mine,' he growled. A coughing fit followed and he was having trouble catching his breath. He pointed at the water, a gesture for her to hand it to him. She didn't move.

Seeing, though perhaps not understanding her reluctance, the prison officer threw her a dirty look. 'Yer you are, Frank. Take it steady.'

Frank gripped the glass with both hands and half emptied it. Once his coughing was under control and the glass back on the table, he turned his murky eyes on her. A finger shook as it pointed right at her.

'You ain't 'aving none of it. Alf is my son. You ain't mine. You're the brat of Jeremiah Wells. That's who you are!'

She arched her eyebrows in disbelief. 'It don't matter whether I am or I ain't. I can still claim and there's nothing you can do about it. The law would recognise me as your daughter unless you claim otherwise, unless you can prove who you say I am. Until then, I'll take what's mine!'

She turned her back on him.

'I'm finished,' she said to the prison officer.

The keys jangled at his waist as he prepared to let her out.

Frank's grizzled voice came after her. 'I'll prove it. You just see if I don't. I'll prove you're the daughter of a mongrel, the grand-daughter of a West Indian. My boy's blonde. You're a bit of darkie. I'll make a will and I'll write it all down. I'll tell everyone who your father was and what he was. You just see if I don't!'

She paused as one more question came to her.

'What about George Barton? He might call you a liar.'

'George Barton!' He nearly choked as he spat the name. 'That scallywag. Partners in crime them too. Wells owning the properties and Barton collecting the rent. And God 'elp 'em if they didn't pay up.'

Though the door was open, ready for her to depart, she smiled at him over her shoulder. 'I doubt you'll bother to write up a will as you say maligning my name, but if you do get round to it, send me a copy.'

'I will,' he shouted after her, too loud for his damaged lungs and throat to cope. 'I...'

The coughing escalated, which made her panic. The last thing she wanted was for him to leave this world before he'd written that letter. And he knew George Barton – as nasty as he was by the sound of it, yet possibly too old now to be as violent as it seemed he'd once been. Her grandparents had been hard people living in hard times. She couldn't blame them for what they'd been. In that moment she promised herself she would do good with her inheritance. What that good might be she didn't know yet, but right would be done.

All she wanted now, for the first time ever, was that her stepfather lived to carry out his threat, the one thing she wanted from him above all else. Everything depended on it, so just for once in recent years she wanted him to live. After that, it was good riddance Frank Miles.

# 16

## CAROLE

Carole smoothed her hands over her hips and jerked her chin at the washroom mirror. She looked good. Her reflection in the mirror told her so. Her only gripe was that her lipstick was much paler than her usual ruby red. Jean Harlow had favoured ruby red, and seeing as Carole had somewhat modelled herself on the glamorous Hollywood star of the last decade or so, ruby red was her preference.

Inclining her head to one side, she pouted at the mirror and said out loud what she was thinking. 'My lipstick is too pale. I only had a stub left and I couldn't find lipstick anywhere.'

Pat was reassuring.

'It's pretty. Anyway, Vaseline makes your lips softer. Shiny too. Very kissable!'

Carole laughed. 'All I need is to test it out.'

'Nobody in the running at present?'

Carole shook her head. 'Not the sort of chap I'm looking for. I want somebody clean and tidy, who wears a suit to work, not overalls.'

'Surely you can't resist a man in a uniform. I know I can't,' said

Jenny, who was currently dating more than one military man. Sometimes they were British, sometimes not. Carole admired her fortitude, the way she juggled one against the other.

'Officer-class only,' proclaimed Carole after going over her lips one more time.

Due to the lack of make-up for sale, melting a little Vaseline with what remained of the lipstick had become quite common.

Jenny's expression became more serious. 'A word of warning, darling; watch out for Reg Harris. He doesn't go over visitors' lists half as much with me as he does with you.'

Reg Harris was an office manager in the publicity department. Jenny was right about him paying her more attention than he did her and Carole hadn't exactly dissuaded him from standing so close. He smelt nice, much better than any of them closer to her own age that tried their hand. She was flattered, but that was about it. She certainly did not want to get involved with a married man.

'He's married and I wouldn't dream of a date with him. I'd get a bad reputation.'

'Just watch him, Carole.' Jenny leaned forward and dropped her voice. 'Maureen Cox fell for him good and proper. Had to leave.'

'I thought she joined up?'

Jenny shook her head, and although Carole knew she had a penchant for spreading salacious gossip, she listened as a home for unmarried mothers was mentioned. Maureen, it seemed, had come a right cropper. 'Our Mr Harris got away with it of course, but that's no big surprise. Most men do.'

Carole took on the information and filed it away. She loved this job and long may it continue. Who would have thought she'd jump from the factory floor to being a VIP escort for W. D. & H. O. Wills, one of the best employers in the country?

Plastering on a smile, she headed to reception, where today's visitors would be waiting in the company of someone from public relations. They turned out to be a mixed bunch, some from local women's organisations with a sprinkling of clergy. They were far from being her favourite visitors, but nevertheless she would treat them as well as they deserved. Her favourite visitors were the Yanks, who always tipped well, secretively slipping her a few pairs of stockings, sweet-smelling soap or candies. All such items were on ration so flew like an arrow to a girl's heart. Dates were also offered, of course. She'd been a bit wary of going out on a date since the incident with Ben getting beaten up. Reg Harris, the public relations manager, knew how to make a good impression on perfect strangers.

The prim-looking female visitors were no exception. The fact was Reg could weigh people up and thus knew the right thing to say. Plain-faced women in tweed, dull hats perched on their heads, stout shoes on their feet, appeared besotted – or at least most of them did.

'Ah. Here's Miss Thompson, your guide for the day. It's this lovely lady who will take you round the factory, beginning with the bays where the tobacco is delivered from the bonded warehouses. She'll explain all that to you – if you wish your lovely ears to be bent with such mundane detail of course. So here you are. Miss Thompson. If you would like to take over.'

His eyes locked with hers when he smiled. She thanked him and smiled back and refused to be unnerved by the extra message she saw there.

She addressed the majority of the group first. 'Ladies. And the gentlemen amongst you. On behalf of W. D. & H. O. Wills, welcome to Number One, East Street Factory. Wills have a number of factories throughout the country...'

Initially the thought of memorising the facts about the company had seemed daunting, but once she got into it, she found learning the script a skill she had not known she had.

The tour went well to begin with. Nobody tripped over anything and if they did hear a few expletives from some of the drivers and labourers, it wasn't mentioned. From experience, the noise of machine drowned most conversation out.

There was less noise in the stripping room of course. Some of the girls were humming or singing along to the muted sound of the wireless. Others talked amongst themselves, through mouths clamped shut, as ordered to do once the visitors came through the double doors.

'This is where the tobacco leaves are stripped from the stems ready to be fed into the machines which shred them into tobacco fine enough for the making of cigarettes...'

It seemed nothing at first, just one of the more austere women stepping away from the merry band, presumably to take a closer look at what one of the girls was doing.

The girl busying herself overlooking other girls stripping leaves, turned out to be Maisie.

'I know you,' snapped the bony-faced woman. A black-gloved finger pointed directly into Maisie's face. 'You're one of Phyllis's friends, one of them who persuaded her to abandon my son, Robert.'

Maisie's jaw dropped as she looked up into the woman's hard-eyed glare.

Carole had never had anything like this happen to her before. She knew leading a party round the factory called for caution, calm and remaining in control of a given situation.

'Please,' she said, approaching the woman. 'Now we don't want any unpleasantness, do we?' The hand she laid on the woman's arm was shaken off.

Hilda Harvey, for that was who it was, would not be moved. All her repressed anger was directed at Maisie. Not that Maisie was going to take it sitting down. She sprang to her feet, the top of her head just about reaching Hilda Harvey's bony nose.

'It weren't me who made up Phyllis's mind to join up. It was you and quite frankly I don't blame 'er. I'd prefer a hundred bombs falling on me to staying another minute under your roof.'

Carole did her best to intervene. 'Please. Ladies.' Once again, she laid a hand on Hilda Harvey.

Accompanied by an icy glare, she was told to remove it.

'I have not finished yet. My son spent time in the sanatorium because of his tart of a wife. He was too good for the likes of her. Too good for any common tobacco girl!'

Carole stood dumbstruck.

Maisie was more outspoken. 'Told me 'e 'ad a French bit back in France. Didn't seem that fussed about ar Phyllis.'

Having come into the room, it was Reg Harris who stepped forward to give Hilda her marching orders. 'Wills' are happy to have visitors but do not tolerate bad behaviour, and you, lady, are behaving very badly.'

'Hussy,' Hilda shouted, pointing at Maisie. 'You're all hussies,' she shrieked, her eyes darting around at the stripping-room workforce.

A few choice comments might have been hurled, but thanks to a warning look from Aggie Hill, everyone held back. They'd been told to be polite when there were visitors and most of them adhered to that. Factory girls they might be, but they were rightly proud of the firm they worked for.

Still protesting, hat now at a slightly askew angle, Hilda Harvey was escorted from the room, instructions following from Reg Harris that she be removed from the building.

Carole mouthed a quick sorry to Maisie, who merely shrugged her shoulders in response.

\* \* \*

The stripping room erupted once the visitors had left.

Aggie strode the length of the room to lean over and mutter into Maisie's ear.

'Is it true that 'er Robert's has been in the sanatorium at Farrington Gurney? Lost 'is marbles after Dunkirk and all that?'

Maisie clenched her jaw. She'd never liked Robert or his mother, but still... 'I'm sorry if it is. I wouldn't wish Farrington Gurney on anyone.'

'You're getting soft in yer old age,' Aggie said to her laughingly.

'Not really,' returned Maisie. Her thoughts were only half immersed in work. The other half of her thoughts were with her stepfather, the house in Totterdown and the easiest way to keep what her grandmother had left her. She'd left her address with Horfield Prison and her visit had proved fruitful. That very morning, she'd received a letter confirming her father's identity; Jeremiah Wells of Totterdown. *'And may he rot in hell,'* Frank had added.

She posted the information on to her solicitor. A response came four days later saying that the opposite side – that is George Barton's solicitor – had backed down and accepted that she was indeed Grace Wells granddaughter. Something else out of the way and, like Eddie Bridgeman, a man she would prefer never to see again.

# 17

## CAROLE

Carole was grateful for Reg Harris intervening when Hilda Harvey had confronted Maisie. She'd never had anything like it happen before.

'Quite frankly, it made me feel rather queasy,' she said to Reg.

His smile was full of charm. 'I was pleased to be of service. No problem with this lot then. Gentlemen every one!'

They both smiled as they looked over a group of BBC people who had come down from the studio in Whiteladies Road. She thought she recognised the voices of some of them.

'Isn't that Tommy Handley?'

A gentleman with a broad face was holding forth with the others on his table. She wasn't too sure what Tommy Handley looked like, but did know that the radio show ITMA – *It's That Man Again* – was broadcast from the BBC studio in Whiteladies Road.

'Couldn't possibly say,' returned Reg. 'I haven't got too much time for radio nowadays, what with the wife being ill.' He frowned at first, then immediately shook it off. 'But I manage. Bit lonely at times though, what with the kids being evacuated. I know everyone thinks the bombing is over and had their kids back, but I'm not entirely convinced. Sneaky devils them Germans.'

'How is your wife?'

Everyone in the factory had heard that she was ill.

His shoulders heaved in a deep sigh. 'Good some days, not so good others. It's just a case of hoping and praying.'

'I do hope she pulls through.'

'Yes. So do I.'

\* \* \*

Feeling sorry for his circumstances and grateful for him ejecting Hilda Harvey, Carole mentioned to Aggie about sending his wife a card, even a bunch of flowers perhaps.

Aggie looked at her askance, then shook her head. 'I'm not sure about that.'

Carole was not so dumb that she didn't know what was at the forefront of Aggie's mind. 'You don't know for sure whether that girl Maureen was pregnant or got called up – not really do you?'

Aggie shrugged. 'There's no smoke without fire.'

Luckily, Maisie came in on her side, the three of them discussing the issue in the privacy of the ladies' cloakroom.

'Carole's right, Aggie. We don't know for sure. Even then, if the poor woman's at death's door, it wouldn't hurt to send a card and a bunch of flowers round. It ain't fer 'im. It's for 'er.'

Although still reluctant, Aggie came round. 'I'll get a collection going. Should be enough to buy a card and a bunch of flowers.'

The matter was decided and the fact that Mrs Harris was ill resulted in enough to buy a card and flowers as planned.

There wasn't much in the way of flowers in the shop. For a start, gardens, parks and allotments had been given over to the growing of vegetables. Summer was fading, which also meant a depleted supply. Luckily, a few women brought in the remaining blooms from their gardens.

On the day they planned to give the flowers and cards to Reg Harris, they found he'd left work early to attend a friend's funeral.

Aggie expressed regret that she'd been resistant at first to Carole's idea. 'We could have bought them sooner,' she remarked.

Carole made a suggestion. 'How about I take them round to where he lives and present them to his wife personally? I think he lives in Queen Charlotte Street off Queen Square.'

'Number 35,' said Aggie. 'Just round the back from me. I could come with you if you like?'

It was agreed that Carole and Aggie would go round there, 'As long as it's not too busy in the pub.' Aggie had added, shaking her head. 'Don't seem to 'ave the energy I used to 'ave. Must be old age.'

'I'll see you later then,' said Carole after reassuring Aggie that she wasn't that old at all.

They arranged to go that evening and although Carole was still a little wary of Reg Harris, she told herself that nothing could go wrong as long as Aggie was with her.

\* \* \*

The Llandoger was in uproar when Carole got there dressed in a mauve cotton dress and lightweight cardigan. May, it seemed, was turning into June and the night was warm.

'Busy,' she shouted across the bar.

Aggie, pulling pints as fast as the beer would come out of the barrel, shouted back that a whole convoy having crossed the Atlantic had all come into port at the same time. The pub had many rooms and snugs coming off the main bar and this evening they were all bursting at the seams with thirsty sailors.

Still pulling a pint, Aggie apologised. 'Sorry, love. I'm run off me feet. Give me an hour or two and I could make it.'

Carole shook her head. 'I'm a big enough girl to go round there by meself.'

'Lovely flowers,' said the barmaid, nodding at the bouquet Carole was carrying.

'Yeah. Better get on and deliver them.'

'Whoever they are will appreciate it.'

'See you tomorrow, love,' Aggie shouted after her.

Queen Charlotte Street was close to both King Street and Queen Square. Being September, it was getting dark, but paying close attention, Carole finally came to the house she was looking for. It looked quite imposing, smart red-brick, the window surrounds picked out in honey-coloured stone.

There were steps leading up to the front door and the knocker was shaped like the head of a grinning lion and made of brass. She knocked gingerly, heard the sound reverberating deep inside. She imagined the hallway having lofty ceilings. Her heart thudded. She'd never stepped over the threshold of such a posh house.

She looked up at the imposing façade, took a deep breath and gave herself a good talking to. *What the hell. You're as good as they are. Go on. Get in there.*

When he answered the door Reg Harris was still dressed in the suit he wore for work. As he'd been to a funeral that day he was also wearing a black tie. He held a glass in one hand full of dark liquid. His smile when he saw who it was nearly split his face in half.

'Carole! What are you doing here?'

'I brought these,' she said, proffering the bouquet. 'And a card. For your wife, seeing as she's so poorly. Would you mind if I give them to her?'

For a split second, he seemed undecided. Eventually he said, 'Well, you could if she was here, but unfortunately she had a bad turn and has been taken to hospital. Still, I'm sure she'd like them. It was a very kind thought.'

'It isn't just from me, it's from everyone. We had a whip-round.'

She nodded vehemently and he did the same.

'Very kind.' He glanced behind him. 'Look, seeing as you've taken the trouble, how about coming inside. The least I could do is give you a drink for your trouble. It's sherry. Harvey's Bristol Cream in fact. Only the best in this house.'

He laughed as though he hadn't really been to a funeral, his wife in hospital and his children goodness knows where, but she counselled that it was his way of coping. Some of the women at the factory maintained that men weren't much good without a good woman behind them.

Tentatively, her heart hammering against her ribs, Carole stepped into the parquet tiled passageway. From there he took her into the living room where she placed what she'd brought on a highly polished side table.

'Do take a seat.'

No harm in that, she thought, thanked him and sat rigidly at one end of a green velvet sofa that looked quite old and valuable. Table lamps with green silk shades threw puddles of light downwards. The curtains were drawn against the darkening evening. Nobody could look out or in.

Turning his back on her he began pouring drinks.

'I'd rather not...'

'Nonsense.'

She looked down into the glass of sherry. Nasty sweet stuff. Some time past she would have told him so, but since her promotion she'd learned to curb her tongue. It wasn't just about improving her diction, she'd learned to think before she opened her mouth.

She took a sip. It tasted as rich and sweet as she remembered it on the few occasions she'd sipped it before.

'Nice isn't it,' he said, almost daring her to say otherwise.

'Yes. Lovely.' She looked down into it, her fingers firm around what looked to be valuable glass.

Seeing her hesitation, Reg urged her to down her drink. 'Well go on then. There's more in the bottle.'

She took as big a slurp as she dared. The sudden headiness made her think it wasn't quite so bad. Another mouthful wouldn't hurt and once that was done, she could make her excuses to leave.

'Have another.'

It was in her glass before she could say no.

'Go on. It'll do you good.'

'Don't you have to go to the hospital?' she said before taking another sweet mouthful.

'No. They advised not to until tomorrow night. Said it was best if she rested.'

'Oh.'

She clutched her glass with both hands. The room was swimming. The sofa she sat on was comfortable and the sherry was beginning to taste better.

Reg smiled, looked at the clock, then looked back at her. 'Are you all right?'

She was barely aware of him refilling her glass each time she took a sip.

'I don't want any more. It makes me feel a bit faint.'

The room was beginning to spin. She rubbed her forehead.

'Perhaps you'd like to lie down.' His voice was as smooth as treacle, so difficult to resist.

Yes, she would. She wasn't sure whether she'd actually said so, but did become aware of him lying her down on the sofa, taking off her shoes, wafting her face with a folded-up newspaper. It felt very pleasant. She didn't feel so hot and even her thighs felt cooler.

She rested both hands on her forehead, unaware of having put the glass down or him taking it from her.

It became hard to work out what was real and what imagined. Her camiknickers were new and she was proud of them. Somebody her mother knew had made them from parachute silk. There was no elastic but there were buttons on the side for fastening. The legs were wide and lace-edged, the crotch easily pulled aside. That's what was happening now! She could feel the tugging, the feeling of a hand and fingers that weren't her own intruding beneath the flimsy barrier.

'No,' she managed to say, and tried to sit up. 'No. Please...'

Her voice sounded ineffectual and weak. His was strong and determined.

'Yes. That's it. Say please again. Say it.'

'Please, please, don't...'

She felt the heat of his thighs against his, then pain.

'No. No!'

She began beating at him with her hands, but he kept thrusting, kept hurting her, totally engrossed by what he was doing, what he was taking from her, so much so that he failed to notice the opening of the living-room door, the dull thud of a suitcase, the fury on the face of the woman who stood there.

'Reginald!'

Reg barely had time to roll off before his wife was beating him about the head with her handbag.

'I just knew it! I knew it!'

The image was blurry, but enough for Carole to see Reg Harris's exposed loins and his hands grappling to bring his trousers up.

'I thought you were at your sister's, my love...'

'Don't give me that "my love" stuff. I know you of old, Reg Harris. When the cat's away...'

'Please...' Tears were rolling down Carole's face. 'He told me you were in hospital...'

'And you thought you'd take advantage. You slut. Carrying on with a married man. Just like the other one. You're all the same you tobacco girls.'

When Carole shook her head, she thought it likely to fall off. She was desperate to explain, but could barely make the effort to tidy up her clothes and get to her feet.

Mrs Harris, her crimped hair tight on her head, grabbed hold of her arm and frogmarched her out into the hallway. She threw her through the front door so violently that Carole landed on her knees at the bottom of the steps. All the while, she tried to explain about the flowers and the card she'd left, signed with good wishes from everyone in the factory.

Her knees bloodied, stockings laddered, she hauled herself to her feet with the help of the few metal railings not gone for scrap along the front of the house.

'Bloody hell! Is that you, Carole?' The beam of a flashlight raked her from head to toe.

Aggie Hill replaced the railings in holding her upright. Carole began to tell her what had happened.

'Leave it until I get a brandy inside you.'

'No.' Carole's response was abrupt. 'Just tea. A cup of tea. He gave me sherry. I told him it goes to my head. Or at least I think I did...'

Her head fell forward and big tears began to roll down her face.

Aggie sighed heavily. 'Let's get a drink inside you, then you can tell me all about it.'

From the shadows, Gerald Crozier watched, face creased with alarm. He'd seen Carole go into the house and presumed it just a social visit. Not so, he thought to himself, seeing and hearing enough to paint a pretty unsavoury picture. The boss won't like this, he thought. He won't like it at all. He'll say you weren't doing yer job, so best not to say anything. Nothing at all.

\* \* \*

Although Aggie had advised her to have some time off work, Carole was there the next day. After Aggie told Maisie what had happened, the two of them made their way to the staff canteen. They weren't really allowed in there, but Carole sometimes popped into their canteen but hadn't done so today.

They found her sitting alone, stirring a cup of tea, watching the spoon go round and around.

'Carole?'

There was a haunted look in her eyes and, unusually for her, dark lines that made her skin look far paler than usual.

They sat down and, despite a few sour looks from a number of office staff, whispered to Carole, asking her if she was all right.

Maisie placed her hand on Carole's far softer one. 'Anything we can do, Carole. We're here to help.'

'That bloke should be horsewhipped,' hissed Aggie. 'I've a good mind to go up to the big office and—'

'No!' Carole's response was swift and sharp. She lifted eyes that held no tears into Aggie's face. 'I don't want to lose my job. I don't want anyone to know about it.' She glanced challengingly from one concerned expression to the other. 'You haven't told anyone, have you?'

Both Maisie and Aggie shook their heads.

'No, chick,' said Aggie. 'I ain't breathed a word of it.'

'Good. I'll get over it.'

'Have you told yer mum?' asked Maisie.

'No. And I ain't going to. She's made herself a new life and ain't keen on letter writing. Anyway, she'll just tell me it was me own fault for going round there.'

'But you weren't to know,' Maisie began, then stopped herself. Carole's mother knew how low men could sink better than any of them. 'All right,' she said, nodding. 'Me and Aggie won't say a word.'

'Promise?'

Liquid eyes looked from one to the other.

They both promised.

At first, they were silent as they made their way back to their own canteen. It became obvious that their thoughts were in tune when Aggie said, 'Let's 'ope he ain't got 'er in the family way.'

Maisie nodded. 'Let's 'ope.'

**18**

## BRIDGET

It was a lovely feeling to see Corporal Arthur Crown up on his feet and dancing which went some way to making up for the fact that Lyndon had gone back to his job.

'You're doing well, Arthur.'

He leaned into her as they glided round the floor of the dance hall to a foxtrot.

'Just don't ask me to dance the jitterbug, eh? A few months' time and I'll 'ave a bash at it, Bridget.'

He'd taken to calling her by her first name and they'd been out on a few times in company with other nurses and patients, all part of the cure, according to the fatherly Mr Gillespie.

It was always a dance. The good doctor, accompanied by his smiling wife and sometimes by his grown-up children, took an interest in seeing the increased mobility of those whom he'd treated with the new wonder drug.

The improvement was there to be seen. The corporal was not the frightened man he had been on arrival with a severely injured leg. Thanks to penicillin, he would not be one of the unfortunates to be fitted with a prosthetic leg. He'd gone from strength to strength.

Going dancing with him was a pleasant break from hospital duties.

'Will you write to me?'

She knew he was off shortly. 'I don't see why not. Have you got your posting yet? Are you back to the desert?'

He tapped the side of his nose. 'Careless talk costs lives.'

She laughed at his reference to the familiar poster. 'I need to know so I can write to you. Or you can write to me first.'

He settled for writing to her first.

They danced a bit more before he said, 'You know, I'm getting fond of you, don't you?'

She shook her head sadly. 'Arthur, you shouldn't. I'm just your nurse.'

'Not to me. To me, you're my personal angel and I'd like to get to know you better.'

Up until now she'd not mentioned Lyndon and the fact that she already had a marriage proposal under her belt. She looked downwards, pretending to be watching the progress of her feet rather than considering how best to let him down – for good.

'I'm happy to write to you, Arthur, but you have to understand that I'm already spoken for.'

He sighed heavily. 'That's a shame.'

'I thought you were too. Married, I mean…'

His expression was woeful. 'I was engaged, but she went off with a Yank. Sent me a "Dear John" letter, only addressed to me, Arthur. Wish it' ad been sent to somebody called John. So there you are. I'm unattached. I was hoping you were too.'

It was hard not to feel guilty. 'I had to tell you, Arthur. It's only fair.'

'Yes,' he said giving a curt nod of his head. 'It's only fair.

\* \* \*

Before settling down for the night, Bridget reread the letter received from home.

*Michael's settled down very well at school, though can't wait to be fourteen and leave. He's going on a bit about joining the RAF, though both me and his father have pointed out to him that the war might be over by the time that he's old enough – pray God that it is.*

*Katy and Ruby have settled in well enough at school too. Molly and Mary are taking their time, but I'm sure they'll be fine. It's early days.*

*Everyone looks forward to your next leave, especially when you come home for Christmas. Here's hoping that you can get a placement at a more local hospital so we can see more of you.*

*Your dad's given up being an ARP as it seems nowadays to be more about drills and drinking tea rather than actually doing anything.*

*There were riots in Bristol of late, but all sorted out by military police. I suppose it's only to be expected with all these soldiers from different nations all thrown into the melting pot and all after the girls!*

*The chicks I bought in the spring are growing well so we should be roasting one or two for Christmas. I've also been saving coupons to put towards fresh things and have managed to put by some tins of salmon and suchlike.*

*Well, that's it for now. Keep well, my darling Bridie, and hope to see you soon.*

Her mother had not enquired about Lyndon in this letter or any others. It was as though she denied his existence.

Bridget wondered if she should mention the family heirloom that had sparkled on her finger when Lyndon gave it to her. Even Tilly had been taken aback by its brilliance and likely value. Once Lyndon had left, she took it off, deciding she wouldn't wear it again until he returned.

Before leaving, Lyndon had told her he wouldn't be able to ring every week, though would try.

'They're sending me all over the place, but keep the faith. You're never out of my thoughts.'

He'd explained he was moving around from one military base to another, lecturing the men from the New World how to treat those of the Old.

'You can write to me at the address I gave you in London and I can catch up when I get back.'

Turning over to face the wall, the sound of her nursing comrades' snuffles and snores plus the plaintive notes of a familiar song drifted into her mind.

'*We'll meet again, don't know where, don't know when...*'

\* \* \*

'Are you all right, Milligan?'

Bridget resumed mopping in and around the beds with renewed vigour, fully aware that her concentration had faltered. There was a lot of sky outside the window, lying like a grey army blanket over the jumble of tired-looking buildings. That's what she'd been staring at when Matron's question had startled her from her daydream. Not that Matron was anything like the dragon Bridget had expected her to be. She was the consummate professional, the mature, experienced woman that younger professionals looked up to. Even the QAs treated her with respect, which was slightly unusual.

There was a distinct separation between hospital nurses, auxiliaries and the elite young women of the QAs, every one of whom achieved officer status the moment they joined. Matrons from each service tolerated each other, showed mutual respect, but there was still a somewhat competitive edge between them.

On the whole, Sister Edith Williams, the hospital matron, was more approachable than Major Farrell of Queen Alexandra's. But Bridget was likely in trouble if she'd been noticed for losing concentration.

Sister Edith stopped and barked a firm command. 'As soon as you've finished, come along to my office.'

Bridget applied herself more thoroughly to her task. Perhaps her application to become a fully qualified nurse hadn't met with approval. She had little to recommend her; no further education certificate because none had been on offer, but she did have good reports from her old school. She'd presented all this, but perhaps, given her background, she might not be accepted.

At eleven o'clock precisely, she knocked on the door to Matron's office and was given permission to enter.

The walls of the office were as dull as any in the hospital, but somehow exuded a warmth some others didn't have. Paint and crayon pictures created by childish hands added much-needed colour and a jumble of tomato plants, leaves dry and tomatoes bright red, formed a tangled display along the window ledge and on top of a filing cabinet.

What looked like real porcelain cups and saucers sat on a tea tray on a table with barley twist legs in front of the window. Matron was pouring tea.

'Sit down, my dear. I've added milk but no sugar. Is that all right?'

Bridget felt an upsurge of nerves. Had she been turned down?

A little tea had slopped into the saucer no doubt when the tea had been poured.

The same with Matron's tea. 'Whoops. Waste not want not.' Saucer was tipped into cup and accompanied with a smile, an invitation that she should do the same.

'Right,' said Matron after taking a sip. 'You were a bit far away this morning. Is there any particular reason for that?'

Bridget shook her head. 'No. Not really.'

On Lyndon's last call, he'd lost patience with her procrastinating about marrying and moving and slammed the phone down. Since then, she'd heard nothing.

She felt matron's eyes on her. 'Milligan, it's sometimes a curse to be young. The world is full of options when you're young, all of them very exciting. Now I don't know your exact circumstances, but I have noticed you've been a little distracted this last week. I have to ask you before we go any further whether you still wish to train as a fully qualified nurse.'

'Yes! Oh, yes, I want it more than anything in the world!'

The words spoke for themselves, drowning out the other choice. Having two options was tearing her apart. All this last week, she'd been unable to concentrate, because she was so divided as to what she should do.

Matron smiled and drew a manila folder across from one side of the desk and onto the blotting pad in front of her. Still smiling, she opened it. 'You've been accepted on the four-year training course. Four years of working on the wards whilst studying towards your finals.'

'I've been accepted!'

'You have. Congratulations.'

Bridget's hands shook even more as she took the confirmation letter and read it, once, twice, then three times, until intoxicated with success, she felt quite dizzy.

'This is wonderful.' She could hardly breathe, but there was more to come.

'Unfortunately, we cannot accommodate you here. Our modest teaching facility is being converted into a ward for amputees in need of learning to walk again.' Matron sighed. 'Prosthetic limbs have come a long way, but it's still an uphill struggle. You've been offered a place in London.'

Bridget's face dropped – not with disappointment but the vagaries of fortune; Lyndon wanted her in London. It was almost as if somebody had waved a magic wand in answer to her heartfelt wishes. There was only one thing left niggling like an unreachable itch.

'How about penicillin? I've become very interested in its use. To see men who might have lost their limbs or died from their wounds recovering so quickly is quite wonderful.'

Matron smiled and clasped her hands in front of her. Unlike the smooth hands of the more upper-crust QA matron, they looked as though she'd done hard work at some time. 'That's why you've been selected. You've mixed and administered this new drug. Your interest and skill were noted. It's London because the demand for that experience is higher there. I'm sure you'll do very well.'

\* \* \*

Bridget went to bed that night feeling more hopeful than she had for a long time.

That night, the words of 'We'll meet again,' drifted once more across the quadrangle and to her were more poignant than they had ever been.

# 19

## MAISIE

The bank holding her grandmother's bank account was in Queen Square, not too far distant from Mr Pomeroy's office. It all seemed so grand; Queen Charlotte Street for the solicitor and now Queen Square for the bank.

Maisie was as unfamiliar with bank managers as she was with solicitors, but she wasn't going to let unfamiliarity put her off. She strode in with confidence, dressed in the female equivalent of a man's suit; a plum-coloured jacket with peplum that snugly fitted her waist and a matching box-pleated skirt. The pleats on the skirt were a little wider than utility allowed simply because it was of pre-war vintage. A simple white shirt, also pre-war and made for a boy, plus a blue and red tie, black suede court shoes and black hat with a plum-coloured feather stuck in the band completed the outfit. Everything was second-hand, including the shoes which were a size too big, but a bit of newspaper folded and stuffed in the back sorted that problem.

Mr Day wore a monocle, had a bald head and his suit smelt of mothballs. Even so, he had an air of authority, allied with old-fashioned courtesy for the 'little woman' who had asked to see him.

'Miss Miles. Do please take a seat.'

The chair he offered was so wide and so high it looked to have been made for at least one and a half people, almost two. When Maisie slid back too far, her feet didn't reach the floor, so she adjusted herself and sat slightly forward.

'Thank you. I've been given these papers by the solicitor who acted for my grandmother, Grace Wells. They explain everything.'

Pushing his monocle more firmly in place, lips pursed in a stance prepared for perusing, he took the papers. After eyeing each in a perfunctory fashion, a look of something approaching surprise came to his face. If he had had any preconceptions that she might be a vulnerable woman, they disappeared. If she was anything like Grace Wells, vulnerable was the last word you'd use to describe her.

He looked at her with the eye that wasn't obscured by glass. 'Very interesting. Your grandmother was a greatly favoured customer. I would consider it a pleasure to assist you in any way I can.'

Maisie kept her back straight and looked him in the eye. She needed his professional advice but wasn't going to have him think her stupid. Before coming here, she'd sat with her eyes closed and made herself speak like her old friend Phyllis and her new friend Carole. Speaking properly was sometimes necessary if people weren't to think you ignorant.

'Firstly, I would appreciate you confirming the amount of cash in my grandmother's bank account that is to be transferred to my name.'

'Certainly.' The monocle was readjusted. He went out to the outer office and brought in a ledger. His countenance had the look of a man looking to ingratiate himself. 'Would you like tea?' he asked.

'No thank you.'

Her outward confidence hid a little nervousness. Drinking a cup of tea would mean a speedy visit to the lavatory.

'Right.' He proceeded to open the ledger, turning over pages until he came to the information he sought. 'Ah. Here it is. As of yesterday, your grandmother's account, including accrued interest, amounted to two hundred and sixty-five pounds.'

Maisie pretended to tally this with the piece of paper she took from her handbag – a letter from Phyllis dated three months before. She hadn't heard from her since. 'That tallies with what I've got written down here. Now, about the house; how much do you think it's worth?'

'Are you considering selling it, if so I know someone who—'

'No. I intend living in it.'

She'd already thought about renting out a room. A little rental income would do very nicely.

He made a kind of puffing sound as he considered. 'No more than a hundred pounds, I should think. It's Totterdown, so not as sought after as anything north of the river, for example Clifton.'

To Maisie, one hundred pounds seemed a fortune. Added to what was in the bank account, it was quite colossal to someone who'd never had more than five pounds in her pocket at any one time.

'That's...' she took a deep breath. 'Very much the figure I had in mind.'

Mr Day was now examining the third item her solicitor had given her. 'This land at Avonmouth...' He sounded almost awestruck. 'I'd have to check sources who might know better than me, the city council for a start, but a piece of land in Avonmouth...'

He sounded stumped and although she'd managed to fudge her knowledge of the bank account and the house, she could only visualise Avonmouth as a muddy mess that nobody was really interested in. She'd even considered giving her share away to George

Barton purely to keep the peace. Mr Day's eyebrows lifted towards his hairline when she made mention of it.

'Miss Miles. I think that would be very foolish of you. The city council has plans post-war to extend the docks at Avonmouth due to the size of ships becoming bigger and not able to navigate the River Avon into the city. The docks need more space and so they have a need to expand to land round the port. A few years ago, your piece of land was just a marshy field. Nobody wanted it. It's gone up in value since then, but if the city council stick to their plans, it's likely to be worth at least two thousand pounds.' He glanced down again. 'Hmm. I stand corrected...'

Maisie was now on the edge of her seat and giving her portion of the land away to George Barton had flown out of the window.

Both the eye with uninterrupted vision and the one behind the monocle met hers. 'According to this, it's two acres. Two by two is four. Four thousand pounds. You could end up being a very rich young lady, Miss Miles. Very rich indeed.'

'Thanks to my grandmother, Grace Wells. And my father. And my grandfather.'

Sensing her thoughts were heading in an unknown direction, he peered at her.

Maisie grappled with her thoughts. She'd always been known as Maisie Miles, daughter of Frank Miles. But she wasn't his daughter. By her stepfather's own admission, she never had been. So why should she be Maisie Miles any longer?

'Do you think,' she began, clenching one hand tightly inside of the other, 'is it possible for me to change my name? To become Maisie Wells?'

'Yes,' he replied without hesitation. 'Mr Pomeroy is the best person to advise you on that particular subject. But I have heard of the procedure. If you've a mind, you can have it changed by deed poll.'

Maisie too did not hesitate. 'Yes. I've a mind.'

\* \* \*

Bank managers and solicitors: well, whoever would have thought she'd ever gain entrance into the offices of either of them?

She walked to the bus stop, her mind buzzing. Money? A house? The prospect of very much more money. The thing she relished above all else was the prospect of no longer being Maisie Miles. She'd loathed her stepfather and he hadn't had much time for her. Even her mother had feared giving her love and attention because Frank would have given her a back-hander for being too soft. Desperate to keep the peace and avoid being brutalised, her mother had conformed to his wishes. Love and affection had been sadly lacking at the house in North Street. She owed Frank Miles nothing. Sad to say her feelings weren't too dissimilar for her mother.

*Maisie Wells, Maisie Wells, Maisie Wells!*

She wanted to shout it out loud. Even more so, she wanted to rub it in with Frank Miles that she'd discarded his name and adopted that of the Wells family. How would he react? she wondered.

So engrossed in hopes and dreams in a world she had never thought to achieve, she walked right past her bus stop. She came to on realising that she was going round Queen Square for a second time – or it might have been a third.

'Excuse me...'

The woman addressing her was well dressed and vaguely familiar. Hair that once had been bright blonde had the ashen look of turning grey. The wide brim of a felt hat shaded one half of her face, a black net veil clung crisply from the brim to her jaw.

Maisie eyed her querulously. 'Hello.' She frowned. 'Do I know you from somewhere?'

'Yes. My husband works at Wills. I attended a retirement do a while back of a long-serving employee. I recall you handing me a cup of tea.'

'Oh yes. Of course.'

Maisie only vaguely recalled the retirement do: so many employees stayed for years, for life in fact. She just about remembered Mrs Harris. She'd been wearing the same hat, half of it covering her face. Somebody had said her face had been scarred in one of the bombing raids, the result of an incendiary bomb falling close by.

'Do you know Carole Thomas?'

'Yes. I used to be her supervisor when she worked in the stripping room. How are you now?'

Although the hat brim and veil partially obscured her features, Maisie detected a quizzical frown. 'I'm fine. The accident was some time ago.'

Now it was Maisie who frowned. 'But your husband said that you were ill. We had a whip-round and bought you flowers and a card and Carole offered to deliver them. As for your husband, his behaviour was despicable.'

Mrs Harris squared her shoulders and pursed her lips. 'You're lying. Reg bought the flowers and I don't know anything about a card.'

'Then he's lying.'

'I want her sacked. She had no business coming round to my house when I was away, throwing herself at my husband.'

If there was one thing Maisie hated, it was someone trying to shift the blame onto someone else. This woman was loath to blame her husband and, from her own dealings with Reg Harris, Maisie knew he had a silver tongue. Carole was no saint, but she'd gone round with the flowers and card out of the goodness of her heart.

Maisie was having none of it. Now it was her who squared her shoulders.

Maisie jabbed her finger into Mrs Harris's ample bosom. 'Your old man is a right stinker. Strikes me the management should know about 'is shenanigans and I've got a mind to tell them.'

She couldn't do so of course. Carole had sworn her to secrecy, but this woman was either stupid or just turned a blind eye to her old man's weaknesses.

'Don't give me that load of old rubbish,' said Mrs Harris, eyes blazing and shaking her head in a manner that betrayed her disgust. 'She came round to ensnare my husband. I know her sort...'

'Because he's done it before. There's been other young girls out to snare him. Pull the other leg, Mrs Harris!'

'How dare you?'

Maisie laughed in her face. 'Come on,' she said, hands perched on hips. 'Be honest. Ensnare your 'usband? Well, from what I know from factory gossip, it don't take much to do that! And deep down you know it for a fact, and mark this, Mrs 'Arris. A whole load of us put in a few bob to buy that bouquet and card. That's a lot of witnesses to the truth, don't you think? As for your old man, scarpered a bit quick and that's for sure. Suddenly joined up? At 'is age?'

Mrs Harris eyed her indignantly. 'He wanted to do his bit.'

Maisie adopted a cocky pose, one hand on her hip, head held to one side and daring in her eyes. 'Was that why? Not because 'e wanted to get away from you? Or repercussions? And what about your kids? Still evacuated? For their own safety or 'is convenience?'

'Our children are at boarding school. At Red Maids, as a matter of fact.'

Maisie barely held in a surprised gasp. Red Maids was a very old public boarding school in Bristol. It was also expensive. 'Really?

Them places cost a lot of money, and your old man don't earn enough to stretch to that kind of thing.'

'My parents pay, if you must know.' Mrs Harris's voice was faltering and her face was turning red with embarrassment.

Sensing she had the woman on the defensive, Maisie raised her voice so that passers-by looked in their direction, their footsteps slowing so they could hear the row better. 'Forced 'imself on young Carole, 'e did, and that's a fact. Now, if you don't mind, Mrs 'Arris, I've got important things to attend to.'

Assured that victory was hers, Maisie stalked off feeling even more elevated than she had been at the bank.

It wasn't long after she'd left Queen Square that the smile dropped from her face. All she hoped was that Carole wasn't knocked up and in need of someone like her grandmother, someone who could put things right if all else failed.

Something about this situation, the collection for an employee's wife, the coming together of her and Aggie sticking up for Carole, was so typical of the close camaraderie between the girls at the factory. No matter what, she was still one third of the three M's and as such couldn't bear to change her name. With due reverence to the tobacco girls, she would remain Maisie Miles. She was one of them and always would be.

# 20

## PHYLLIS

'You'll be all right there. It'll be a bit of a change for you.'

The new station commander was as sensitive in his treatment of his staff as he was in barking out orders. It all depended on circumstances, but overall he acted the father figure for his staff.

Although Phyllis appreciated him arranging for an RAF officer to ferry her out to the RAF airfield at Ta'qali where a small relay station had been set up, she felt numb, spoke only when she couldn't avoid it, pain like a knife slicing away at her heart.

The truth was that she didn't think anywhere would help her with such all-consuming grief. It lay on her shoulders dragging them down with pain and sorrow. Her sleep was haunted by a vision of Mick smiling at her in that cheeky way of his, even though his 'kite' was diving into the sea. It lay heavily in her stomach, leaving no room for food. No wonder her skirt was in danger of falling down. She'd lost inches.

Mabel, an officer-class aircraftwoman, insisted the change of scene would do her good. 'You'll come back to us feeling better.'

Mabel had possessed a disarming smile. Somebody said that

her sister was a nun – not just any ordinary nun, but a mother superior.

Phyllis didn't care much where she was. She would do her job, but that didn't mean to say she had to be happy the rest of the time. Life, she'd decided, would be empty from now on. Mick had not turned up and there was no word about his whereabouts. There was always a waiting period between a plane going down and the possibility of a body being found by a boat or floating into shore.

She preferred not to think of him floating into shore and to some extent accepted that he wasn't coming back. Along with his wonderful plans for their future and growing grapes in the Australian sun, Mick was gone.

The station at Ta'qali, was some distance inland. The captain repeated what her station commander had said that a change of scene would do her good.

The sight that met her eyes made her doubt that. Red flags dotted the dusty ground round the perimeter of the field.

Captain Trevor Vernon noticed her reaction. 'I presume you know what those flags are.'

'Unexploded bombs.'

'I'm afraid so. Priority was given to those that fell on the runway. Can't have planes not being able to land, can we.'

'No,' she sighed, feeling dejected at the sight of them and what they represented. There weren't enough UXB – unexploded bomb personnel – to cope with the wholesale bombing of the island. She knew that in London alone there were at least six divisions of UXB people. Here in Malta there was just one and even that was a bit ad lib – sappers of the Royal Engineers without training in defusing, learning as they went.

The hut at the edge of the airfield was small and cramped. An overhead fan looked a godsend. Even though the season was cooling, it was still hot. Unfortunately, as the day went on, Phyllis found the fan to be a temperamental beast, stopping and starting whenever it felt like it.

Everyone told her they were pleased to see her, and that she'd drawn a cushy number. She herself knew the reason was that she wasn't fully concentrating on her job back at the Lascaris War Rooms. A little peace and quiet and a far-reaching view beyond the window gave her chance to wonder, but not for long.

A swarm of Stukas came in from the north, their engines throbbing before the noses of the aircraft pointed downwards and they screamed their war cry. They were some way to the west and flying in the direction of Luqa, a bigger airport closer to Valletta.

Used now to talking into the mouthpiece and at the same time typing out the report, the time raced and the raiders bombing Valletta turned tail when faced by the new squadrons of Spitfires. It seemed the bombing was not over yet and the exuberance of a month or so ago was premature.

A man in uniform, she didn't know who, saw her pallor and told her to go outside. 'Just don't go anywhere near the red flags.'

She said that she wouldn't, but in a way she didn't care. If a bomb did explode, at least she'd be with Mick.

The sound of a truck seemed far away because she was far away. The red flags suddenly owed likeness to dark red gladioli of the kind that had grown in her mother's front garden back in Marksbury Road. That was back in the days when Robert used to call round for her. When she'd mentioned the gladioli and how much she'd liked their colour, he'd sneered and told her they were vulgar. No doubt his mother had thought the same. Everything he'd believed in was handed down by his mother.

'Stop! Stop right there! Don't move. DO NOT MOVE!'

The directive was full of warning and commanding.

Phyllis stopped.

'Now step backwards. As much as possible, place your feet in the steps you took to get there. Backwards!'

Her first inclination was to turn round and berate him for shouting and making her nervous. Her second was to freeze as panic set in.

'I'm no good at going backwards.'

Her voice trembled. She clenched her fists and jaw. The red flag she'd compared to gladioli fluttered close to her knee. An unexploded bomb was just inches away.

'Wait there.'

She barely heard his footsteps and certainly didn't feel any vibration. It would have been easy to deny his existence until his front was warm against her back.

'Now I'm going to put my hands on you. Just say yes. Don't nod.'

'Yes.' Her voice trembled.

His palms were hot on her shoulders. 'Place your feet on mine.'

Luckily, flat shoes were the norm when on duty. You could run to the shelters faster in flat shoes. She didn't say that. She was too frightened.

She did as he said, placing her feet on his, whilst his hands gripped her shoulders.

Bit by bit and very slowly, he took backward steps. At one point, she thought one foot was sliding off. Well aware that one wrong move and it could be the last thing she would ever do, she pulled her thoughts back from distant horizons and concentrated. Hardly daring to breathe, she let her body go loose, trusting in his strength to take her back through the fluttering flags that bloomed like flowers until finally they reached safety.

Just as she was about to thank him, he got in first.

'Where did you think you were, you stupid bitch! You trying to send us all sky bloody high!'

The man who'd carried her backwards on his feet, was red with fury – or perhaps the heat – or both.

Over his shoulder, she spotted a couple of grinning men in army uniforms.

'I'm sorry...'

'You would have been, though not around to say so!'

He stomped off towards a lorry piled with an assortment of useful-looking things including a tripod, used to retrieve a bomb from deep in the ground.

'Well don't just stand there, get to work!' he shouted at the men.

It seemed they too were in his bad books.

This was all too much. She'd come here hoping to forget, hoping to heal if only to a small extent.

'Don't you yell at me, you monster!' Hot tears coursed down her cheeks. She felt like a bomb herself and likely to explode.

He stopped in his tracks and glared at her over his shoulder. For a moment, he looked likely to say something but didn't. He turned away and shouted instead at the others in the lorry.

'Come on, get yer asses into gear. We ain't got all bloody day!'

Phyllis ran to the lavatory and once there let it all come out, puking into the lavatory bowl until there was nothing left in her stomach. Wiping her mouth, she eyed her reflection in the mirror, only it wasn't her reflection she was seeing. It was Mick she saw there and was suddenly filled with anger.

'Why did you leave me, Mick? Why weren't you more careful?'

It wasn't until she remembered the open window and saw the soldiers – sappers, she realised, Royal Engineers tasked with the job of defusing unexploded bombs. They were looking her way and then at each other. They'd heard everything.

* * *

Later, as the sun began to dip like an orange ball into the cooling sea, Phyllis sat in the shade, gulping back water after yet another raid had flown in and flown out again.

One of the sappers came over and offered her a cigarette.

She shook her head. 'No thank you.'

Without saying another word, he sat down on what bits of a stone wall were still intact. The stones were still warm and often stayed that way until January and February when the rains came and drenched everything with chilly northern wetness.

He didn't look at her but gazed over the dry fields, where scrubby trees clung on between dry stone walls and earth baked the colour of the Sahara Desert.

'You mustn't blame Sheraton for acting like that. We've had a shit day – sorry – a very difficult day.'

'I've had a shit month… or is it two months.'

She felt no empathy, no sympathy. She had her own concerns.

The sapper drew on his cigarette, his eyes still fixed on the landscape. Phyllis kept her eyes trained in that direction too, imagining the heat rising up from ground still baking from the daytime heat.

'We lost a mate of ours today. Sheraton blames himself, though God knows that ain't true. We dug up this Italian five-hundred-pounder. Used magnets to stop it exploding in our faces. For some reason, the Jerries use steel connectors. We use brass on our bombs. Steel reacts to a magnet. Brass doesn't.'

Phyliss took a deep breath. She didn't want to hear any of this. She didn't want his company. All she wanted was to sit quietly alone and feel sorry for herself.

'Sorted this one. Got it onto a handcart. That's the only way we can get a bomb through the narrow streets and out into the country so we can detonate safely. We got to the outside of the city all right, even managed to heave it onto the back of a lorry. Left Nobby Clark with it whilst we disconnected the tripod we'd left earlier from another job. We all had it in mind to go out on the booze. We were tired. Dog tired...' His voice faded and she noticed the fatigue, heavy in his voice, in his eyes, on his face.

His chin almost rested on his chest, his elbows rested on knees, hands and cigarette loose between them.

He shrugged. 'That's the way it goes. One minute you're with your mates and next minute they're gone.'

She had no need to ask what had happened. She could see it in the stance of his shoulders, the way he seemed to slump as though every bone had left his body. Up until this moment, she'd felt that she was the only one suffering, the only one who'd lost someone dear to her. This sapper, his eyes red from lack of sleep, his young face furrowed with the tiredness of an old man, deserved her respect and empathy.

Spontaneously, without a thought that it might make her seem fast, she kissed his cheek.

Cigarette hanging from his fingertips, he stared at her and then responded in kind. They stared at each other. Suddenly everything was clear. He'd lost someone and she'd lost someone. The mouth that connected with hers was hungry for release. Throwing themselves at each other made sense.

When they broke, he looked at her searchingly.

'Live for today,' she said, thinking of Mick and suddenly accepting he was gone. This sapper was here. 'That's all we can do isn't it.'

His mates on the lorry, the words 'Danger, UXB' painted in white on the side, were calling to him. He gave them a wave of acknowledgement before turning back to her. 'Are you off duty now?'

She nodded. 'Yes.'

'We can give you a lift into town if you want.'

She nodded again. 'Yes. I want.'

\* \* \*

Tom Sullivan was easy to talk to. He'd lost mates and, like her, he had also lost the love of his life. Talking helped overcome the constant desire to look back, to somehow change what had happened. Nothing could change it of course. Some people pined for years, but not everyone. In some there was a need to reaffirm that they were still alive, and in doing so address the odd feeling of guilt that they had not bought it as many had.

They'd talked at great length about their love life: he'd told her about Rosa, his Maltese sweetheart who he'd met at a British Council tea dance. She'd been killed in an air raid. She'd told him about Mick and the plans for the future which would now never happen. Work also figured. She recognised he needed to talk away what he did more so than she did. There was as much urgency to his talking as there was to their lovemaking. Both were a form of escape. Making love was a desperate, hurried experience, their way of blocking out the reality of the world around them.

He lit up one cigarette after another as he told her about the many close shaves they'd had.

'The lieutenant's the real expert. Been in bomb disposal from day one. I kind of just tag along.'

'I think you do a bit more than that,' she said to him. 'Go on. Tell me about your job.'

She too wanted to talk and also wanted to hear him detail the work he did. Detail, even of something she didn't have much knowledge of, helped her cope.

He explained to her about rigging up a tripod above an unexploded bomb to drag it out from the crater in which it sat. 'Damned Germans. Some of the timing devices are booby-trapped. We had one way back during that big raid when HMS Illustrious was in harbour. Bombs bloody everywhere. We were doing OK until we had a five-hundred-pounder with a booby trap. The lieutenant made the decision to get it out to the cliffs and chuck it in.'

She knew he was talking about Dingli, where she and Mick had often sat gazing out to sea and talking of their future. The cliffs were sheer there, nothing halfway down for a bomb to bounce or get stuck on.

Tom had a faraway look in his eyes. She knew he was back there and needed to be dragged back into the here and now.

'Did it work? Did it explode?'

He came back from wherever he'd been and grinned. 'It did that all right. The local fishermen had a right old field day. Got one of the best catches ever without needing to go too far out. Fish floating everywhere – even sharks.'

It was the most she'd laughed in weeks. Tom laughed too.

'I'm off on leave shortly. Home. England,' he said. 'On duty until then. Perhaps we can get together when I get back.'

'Yes. I'd like that.' She curled her naked body close up to his. 'In the meantime...'

'Yeah. Carpe diem – seize the day.'

\* \* \*

Her senior officer let her off lightly for not going back on duty when she was supposed to. Phyllis was fine with that and, following her request, was even given permission to see Tom Sullivan off on the ship taking him to Gibraltar, where he would board an aircraft back to England.

She was just winding down from duty when the news came through that an enemy bomb had exploded in the residential area of Gzira.

'Three blokes killed, including an officer. Just about to go home on leave too. This war! This bloody war!'

Being buried in an icy avalanche could not have been as cold as she felt now.

The station officer noted this. 'I'm sorry. Did you know them?'

'I might have done.' Her voice was barely above a whisper. 'Do you know their names?'

Recognising shock when he saw it, he was careful how he answered. 'Let me get you a cup of tea. Whilst you're drinking it, I can find out for you.'

Even before he came back with the tea, she knew Tom Sullivan's name would feature.

'Dead,' she said, before her commanding officer had chance to confirm. 'Tom Sullivan is dead.'

# 21

# LYNDON

*July* thought Lyndon as he stared out across the flat lands of the East Anglian countryside. Not a hill broke the unrelenting flatness. Like my life, he thought. Flat and uninteresting. You've never broken a bone, never fired a weapon in anger – deer hunting with the old man back home didn't count. And that's how he was feeling, as though he didn't count.

OK, he had the right credentials for informing the guys fighting this war about Britain and the British. His father had told him that a desk job was more likely to prepare him for taking over the company than fighting. He fancied his mother had nagged the old man about not wanting Lyndon to do anything so stupid as fighting on the war front.

'I want to do my bit.'

He'd kept on long enough to get him back to England, but the hankering to do more than lecture on local customs and attitudes would not go away. The feeling of being worthless would not go away.

The Flying Fortresses on this particular station in rural Lincolnshire carried out daylight raids over Germany. Industrial and military installations were their main target, but that didn't mean bombs didn't go astray and land on cities. The thing is he wanted to go up there. Sure he was helping the war effort, but in a safe and laid back way. He wanted to see what combat was really like, but passengers weren't allowed – not officially anyway. But unofficially?

'I'd like to see some action,' Lyndon declared to a bunch of young bloods he'd grown particularly fond of.

It was sheer lunacy. He didn't need to do it. He'd been told by the crew that he was crazy for even suggesting it.

'Let's get this straight,' quipped Gabriel, lieutenant and pilot of Molly Malone, the Flying Fortress that habitually flew night missions over Nazi Germany. 'You want to be shot at out of choice?'

Lyndon had said that he did. 'I'm fed up with sitting around on my butt in London with nothing to do. Getting sent here was my big chance to see some action.'

The crew of Molly Malone laughed at what they considered to be his total naivety. 'Hell, man, Uncle Sam trained us to do this.'

'And they trained me to tell you about England, Ireland, Scotland and Wales.'

'Yeah. You've done a pretty good job of that. Can't wait for the next leave. I'm aiming to use what I've learned to chat up the dames.'

'How you going to do that?' asked Panda, whose real name was Pandapholous but ease of communication had truncated this to Panda.

The whole plane was shuddering; the blades on the four engines spinning at what he considered breakneck speed but the crew regarded as idling.

One by one, a line of these mighty iron war machines were heading down the runway, their size and bomb loads requiring them to be well spaced from each other.

It both delighted and reassured Lyndon to hear them talking about how they would win a girl's attention and a few dates once they came back from their mission. None of them mentioned not coming back. Neither did they mention those who hadn't come back from the previous mission. He'd learned they never did. It was bad luck to do that.

'You got a girl,' asked Panda as Molly Malone eased in behind the plane readied for take-off in front of them.

'Sure I do.'

'Back home?'

'No.'

'Is she British?'

'Yes. She is.'

'She ain't gonna be happy with you going into battle.'

The pilot chipped in. 'Neither's our commander if he finds out we've got a stowaway. Keep your head down buddy or we ain't going nowhere!'

The induced flippancy of these young men, some no more than boys, was drowned in noise as the joystick was pushed forward. Runway, airfield and the hastily brick-built buildings became a blur, then gradually distant as the plane's nose turned skyward.

There was a jolt as the landing wheels were hugged up into the fuselage. They were up and flying level, the sea ahead of them and beyond that mainland Europe.

'Great. I could do with a coffee. How about you, sir?'

Lyndon had never quite got used to officer status and it still took him by surprise when somebody called him 'sir'. He kept looking round, assuming his father or another older man was the one being addressed.

Conversations about girls resumed along with an invitation for him to join them for a night out in the local town before going back to London.

'But only if you have us down there to stay with you in London. That's the Big Apple over here, right?'

'London is big – but it's been badly bombed.'

'Bet there's still bars and clubs though. Dance halls and lots of girls there?'

He assured them there were.

'East into the darkness,' said one of the crew – Lyndon didn't know who.

The conversation, which had carried on in the same vein for some time, stopped as land was spotted. To a sailor long at sea, the sight of land came as a great relief. To a Flying Fortress, it signified the opposite. Conversation became minimal as the crew followed the procedure of night flying into a battle zone and more importantly flying out again.

A few more miles and a shower of flak lit up the sky and puffs of smoke exploded round them. The plane rocked with each blast. There was swearing, mumbled Hail Marys and orders from the pilot to put out a fire or stuff something in a hole that had suddenly appeared.

It seemed like an age before the order was given to open the bombing door. A surge of fresh air came upwards. The bomb aimer's eye darted between charts and instrument. Finally, after a few negatives, he gave the affirmative. The bombs were away.

Lyndon fell against the giant aircraft's framework as it banked steeply away from the area where they'd dropped their load. His thoughts were as jumbled as his limbs. How did these guys cope with this? He was scared and if anyone had asked would have freely admitted it. But these guys, most younger than him, kept up the brave façade – just as he was doing. And that's what it was, a façade. Beneath the chirpy optimism was pure, unadulterated fear, their voices rising, screeching orders and responses – scared to death.

He also felt something else: exhilaration. He'd heard guys say that being close to death was the most exciting time of their lives. Like sex, said some of them. He hadn't really known what they'd meant – not until now. Fear and exhilaration were bedfellows and he'd never forget it.

Suddenly, the Fortress was banking away from the explosions.

'Home,' shouted Panda. 'We're heading home.'

Feelings of it being all over were blasted by a close one. The floor beneath Lyndon's feet heaved upwards, shrapnel flying everywhere. A hole appeared.

'Damn. The landing gear's taken a hiding.' Panda, Lyndon's nearest crew neighbour, sounded worried.

'Is it still there?' Lyndon asked.

'I think so. Let's just hope it works when we need it to.'

The white flares from ack-ack batteries continued to explode all round them and sent the plane rocking.

'No bandits,' exclaimed Panda. 'That's lucky.'

'Yeah. Sure.' Lyndon had been party to enough air force lingo to know that bandits were enemy fighters. They had not been attacked by enemy fighters. A small mercy, but enough of one to make him feel eternally grateful to a god he'd not totally believed in. In these circumstances, he could understand the hushed prayers going on round him and said one himself.

The flashes of explosions in the night sky became less frequent and finally fell away, along with the coastline they had crossed. There was nothing now except the dark expanse of the North Sea gliding like glass below them.

It seemed to Lyndon that the whole crew had exhaled a single breath of relief. Someone began playing a mouth organ. Hesitant but determined, the conversation went back to their favourite subject: girls.

'You still on for taking us on a sightseeing tour of London?' they asked him.

He was shaking from head to toe. It was hard to assess whether they were doing the same.

A call from the cockpit came back asking if everyone was OK.

'Nobody bought it. Isn't that something?'

Lyndon caught sight of Panda's beaming face. There was both hope and relief there: relief that they'd all survived, hope that they would continue to do so.

As the control tower of the airfield came into sight, Lyndon found himself overwhelmed with a great sense of having put his life at risk – and possibly theirs – out of sheer cussedness. He'd no business being here. It wasn't his place. It was theirs. Bridget had prevaricated about his offer of marriage, his insistence that she had to come to London. This had been his retaliation, yet the only person it was likely to harm was himself. He wasn't trained for this. He was a passenger amongst warriors. He'd learned his lesson at least for now The experience had stirred something deep inside. A challenge had been thrown down and he felt obliged to be more of a warrior than what he was at present.

\* \* \*

Skipping breakfast, Lyndon rang the hospital to speak to Bridget and explain why he hadn't been in touch – not that there was any viable excuse. As the phone rang, he rehearsed a speech of outright contrition. Pressure of work was one excuse, though after flying out with the guys on the Flying Fortress he'd feel a fraud saying that. Nothing could come near the pressure those guys were under.

'I'm sorry, she's not here.'

Panic set in. Had she already found somebody else? Things moved fast in wartime.

'Can I leave her a message and a phone number?'

'I'm afraid not. She's been accepted on a training course in London.'

'London!' He couldn't believe what he'd been told. She'd gone to London anyway. She was waiting for him there.

'Can you give me an address?'

He sensed hesitation, guessed he was speaking to the matron. Perhaps if he proved he wasn't just some casual acquaintance...

'Is that Sister Williams? The matron?'

'Yes. It is.' Her steely tone had turned less wary.

'I'm Lyndon O'Neill, Bridget's fiancé. I think we met in passing.'

He was clutching at straws. He crossed his fingers for luck. Perhaps he had met her, but the moment eluded him. Fingers crossed she wouldn't ask him to confirm where and when they had met.

'Ah yes.'

He breathed a sigh of relief.

'Though you won't find her in London just yet. She's taken some leave with her parents before taking up her London appointment. I presume you have their address?'

'Yes,' he replied, relieved that he now knew where to go. 'I do.'

## 22

### MAISIE

The end of July brought two sets of news. The first left her unmoved. Her brother Alf wrote to say that his father – her stepfather – had passed away.

*I can't get back for the funeral and, knowing your feelings, wouldn't expect you to go. I just thought I'd let you know.*

Aggie Hill who had lost a bit of weight of late, came and sat with Maisie as she sifted through Sid's cards between nibbling an oatmeal biscuit and sipping her tea. Maisie took in Aggie's features. Her cheekbones were more pronounced than normal, and there was a kind of waxiness to her skin. 'You OK, Aggie?'

'Course I am,' Aggie snapped. 'Never mind about me. Tell me about Sid.'

Maisie knew better than to persist. Aggie's mind was as strong as ever.

'He don't say as much as he used to. Still draws, though they're so small I can hardly make them out.' She frowned and held one of the cards close to her eyes.

'Let me take a look.' Aggie put on a pair of spectacles bound with a sticking plaster on one side where the frame had been damaged. Getting a replacement was almost impossible. A sticking plaster had to do. Aggie took off her glasses and rubbed at her forehead. 'I can't make 'em out either. You need a magnifying glass. That should do it.'

'You're right. I've got one back 'ome. I'll see to it tonight. Do you want a biscuit?'

Aggie, her eyelids drooping, shook her head. 'No, I ain't got no appetite of late.'

'Are you feeling all right?'

'Tired. That's all.'

Maisie didn't believe her. 'Why don't you go up and see the nurse? She might suggest a tonic.'

Aggie glanced up at the clock, put on her glasses and looked at it again. 'Yeah. I might as well. There's time. See you in a few minutes.'

When Aggie didn't come back and it was getting close to time to get back to work, Maisie paid a visit to the lavatory. Just as she was about to push open the door, she saw Carole waving from the end of the corridor.

'Maisie. Can I have a word?'

'Sure you can, but it'll 'ave to be through the door of the loo. I'm desperate.'

Unperturbed, Carole followed her in. After a brief look about to ensure nobody was around, she leaned against the cubicle door and very quietly said, 'Maisie. I think I'm up the spout.'

A pull of the chain and Maisie flung the door open. 'What? Are you sure?'

Crestfallen, Carole nodded. 'Ain't seen me best friend for two months now.'

'Oh, darling, I'm so sorry,' said Maisie, her hand rubbing up and down Carole's arm.

Carole shook her head. 'I don't know what to do. I just don't know what to do!'

Maisie felt for her. She'd been a right little cow when she'd first started at the factory, but she'd changed since then. A lot of that change in attitude was down to Maisie. And now this!

'What about yer mum? 'Ave you told 'er?'

'Not bloody likely. Anyway she's still up north, she's moved in with the old geezer she met a while back.'

'Look,' said Maisie, glancing at the clock, 'we ain't got much time to talk about it 'ere. How about we go out for a drink at the service club tonight? We can talk there without interruption.'

They arranged to meet at eight, which gave Maisie time to check Sid's cards. The poor lad deserved some attention, bless his little heart!

As Carole and Maisie went their separate ways, Maisie remembered that she'd sent Aggie up to see the factory nurse.

On checking the far end of the room, it surprised her that Aggie had not returned to her seat. She didn't feel too worried. The nurses in the health centre were sticklers for getting people to rest and Aggie certainly looked as though she needed that.

Gertie Blake, of similar age to Aggie, came rushing in. The look on her face was enough to turn Maisie's blood cold. 'Aggie's been taken away in an ambulance. One of the nurses told me she'd been taken very poorly. Didn't say what it was though.'

Her head ached with worry. All afternoon she kept looking up at the clock, half expecting that Aggie would come bouncing in saying that it was all a false alarm. But she didn't come back, bouncing or otherwise.

Only minutes after the whistle went that evening, Maisie was crowded into a phone box with a couple of the other girls from the stripping room plus Carole. The hospital refused to impart any information.

That night instead of going to the Services Club, Carole and Maisie took the bus, then hurried to The Llandoger Trow. The atmosphere of the old Jacobean inn was sombre, a world away from the rowdiness that usually pulsated within its ancient, plastered walls. Some nights it was enough to knock the plaster off the walls!

One of the few regular customers caught Maisie's eye. He wore a flat cap and was grim-faced when he jerked his head towards the bar and the door behind it that led to the private accommodation. 'Curly's out back. Don't want to come into the bar. Not under the circumstances.'

Maisie closed her eyes. Earlier she'd convinced herself that Aggie had been overworking and would be out of hospital soon. Now she felt sick.

'Is she…' Carole's voice faded away.

Maisie shook her head. 'She can't be.' Aggie was larger than life, too big for death to claim her so easily – yet the atmosphere…

The old man in the flat cap caught sight of her pale face and pulled out a chair. 'Sit yerself down, love. I'll get you a drink. Funds don't stretch to a brandy, but I can get you 'alf a cider. Yer mate too if she wants one.'

Shaking her head and too shocked to answer, Maisie sank into the chair.

Carole's hand briefly glanced on Maisie's shoulder. 'You stay here. I'll get the drinks and find out what's happened.'

Maisie nodded. Her breathing was coming thick and fast and her head had begun to ache.

'Knew Aggie well, did you?'

She nodded. 'We worked together.'

The old man, face seared with broken veins, sighed. ''Tis the natural way of things. We all comes' into the world and we all goes out. I don't get upset about it any more. At my age, there ain't no point.'

It was as though she'd turned to ice. Her whole body had become rigid with shock. She felt the old man eyeing her with a mix of pity and resignation. She fancied he said something, but it was as though his voice was far away. All she could think of was Aggie not being around any more.

Carole came back from talking to the barmaid, who, like everyone else in the pub, was subdued.

Even before she opened her mouth, Maisie could tell from the look on her face that Aggie was dead. The sickness inside turned to emptiness as though she hadn't eaten for days and, what's more, had no wish to.

'Something to do with her stomach. Seems she'd been having stomach problems for a while, that and... you know... down below. Women's problems.'

'I wish I'd known.'

'How could you? If she wasn't saying anything, you couldn't be expected to know.'

'I've got to tell Bridget and Phyllis.'

Carole seemed suddenly distracted by the wheezing of old wood rubbing on cast-iron hinges.

Maisie turned round to see Lyndon poised at the pub door. His gaze swept over the rickety old tables, the men in flat caps, their gnarled fingers gripping the handles of even older pewter tankards.

Bridget swept past him, stalled for a moment before a sombre look was swiftly replaced with one of joy.

'Maisie!'

Hugs were accompanied by moist eyes.

'I didn't know you were due back,' said Maisie, weeping for the moment, for Aggie having left her world and Bridget yet again stepping into it.

'Not for long. I'm off to London. I'm becoming a proper nurse. I'm staying at home for the moment, though I have to say it's a bit squashed. Lyndon has made other arrangements.' She hunched her shoulders with happiness, glanced sideways at Lyndon before there were smiles and more hugs including one for Carole. She turned back to Maisie. 'I heard through the grapevine about Aggie,' she said before Maisie had chance to ask how she knew. 'Mrs Devlin from three doors down told Mum. Lyndon was waiting for me at home. We went to the hospital and were told she was gone. From there, it wasn't far to come down here and check on Mr Hill.'

'Seems it was something to do with her stomach,' said Maisie. Her expression twisted with guilt. She really should have noticed and not been so wrapped up in her own affairs.

Not appearing to notice her consternation, Bridget carried on. 'I saw Rita. She told me Aggie had been to see her a few months back when the doctor told her that it was cancer and there was little they could do about it.'

'And she 'adn't told anyone? Oh, Bridget, I only wish I'd known. I might have been able to do something instead I was all wrapped up in other things...'

'No you wouldn't. There was nothing you could have done.'

'Helped her a bit more at work?'

'She wouldn't have thanked you for drawing attention, making her look weak. Aggie would have hated that.'

Lyndon went off to get everyone a stiff drink. He came back with the brandies the old man hadn't been able to afford. Maisie didn't mention the old man, but his kindness and his quip about coming in and going from this world had stayed with her. Aggie was gone and here was Carole knocked up through no fault of her own. It angered her, or so she had thought, yet what the old man had said rang so true.

The intention tonight had been to discuss Carole's condition and what to do about it. Instead they talked about Aggie and what they might have done differently.

In the meantime, Lyndon and Bridget exchanged loving looks, Lyndon's hand caressing Bridget's arm.

'We're getting married,' said Lyndon. His smile faded a little when he added, 'Once Bridget gets up the courage to tell her parents and I get up the courage to tell mine.'

Bridget frowned and covered his hand with hers. 'And a few other things. But we'll sort everything out. I'm sure we will.'

Perhaps more might have been said if the pub door hadn't creaked open again, damp and dark sweeping in from outside.

In swept Angie, Aggie's daughter, who Maisie hardly knew and Carole not at all, and who Lyndon and Bridget hadn't seen since he'd been involved in a mass observation project when she'd barged in, upset her parents, and barged out again.

Angie ignored the condolences from everyone, barrelled her way to the bar and headed for the door to the pub's private quarters.

'Who's she?' asked Carole.

'Aggie's daughter,' Bridget replied.

'Poor Curly.' Maisie wondered how Angie would handle the meeting with her estranged father. Aggie had gone some way to accepting her daughter regardless of Angie's involvement with Eddie Bridgeman. Curly Hill had not. Eddie had not only extorted money from him for some years, but he'd seduced his daughter, barely fifteen at the time. There was a lot of bad blood to get over. Under the circumstances, she hoped this might be the time when the wounds would finally heal.

Could she do anything to help? Well she could but try. After dabbing the wetness from her eyes and buoyed with determination and a firm jutting of her chin, Maisie got up from her chair. 'I won't be a minute.' She addressed Dora the barmaid. 'I want to see Curly.'

'That don't mean you can. It's family only back there.' Wearing a defiant look, Dora rubbed vigorously at a wet tankard.

Maisie reminded her of the time awhile back when she lived here. 'Me and Aggie go way back both at the factory and 'ere. Don't you remember me livin' 'ere?'

Dora cocked her head to one side as she thought it through. 'Yeah. Go on then.'

In the back room, Curly was sitting in an overstuffed armchair with a cat on his lap. Along with the cat, he was staring into the glowing coals of the old black range. Angie was hovering in the middle of the room, looking unsure of whether to approach or get the hell out. She was pretty much as she was when Maisie had last seen her tripping up the steps into the pub on the arm of Eddie Bridgeman, though perhaps less blowsy. Her hair had reverted to its natural colour and her make-up was less obvious than it used to be.

'Dad. You can at least talk to me. She was my mum. I'm upset too.'

Fragile teardrops clung to Angie's eyelashes.

Her father continued to stare into the fire as though he hadn't heard her, but Maisie wasn't fooled. She saw his jaw flex each time she spoke.

Father and daughter. What wouldn't she give to have known her own father and for her mother not to have suffered abuse at the hands of her stepfather. She had a great urge to knock their heads together. Reining in her frustration, she said instead, 'Mr Hill? It's Maisie. I worked with Aggie. You were kind enough to let me stay here for a time. Do you remember me?'

The sound of her voice jolted him from his unrelenting stare. He looked round. The firelight picked up the wetness that had pooled in the wrinkled crevices beneath his eyes. 'Maisie? Yeah.' He nodded warmly, though the loose skin of his neck flexed and trembled, a sure sign of the grief-stricken restriction of tears. 'My missus was very fond of you.'

The warmly expressed comment was specifically aimed at her, his daughter totally ignored.

Maisie felt Angie look and gave her a swift nod of recognition. She kept her voice steady.

'I was very fond of her. We all were. I'm so sorry for your loss, Mr Hill.'

'Thank you, Maisie. It was kind of you to come. Much appreciated.'

Now she had his attention, she jumped in with both feet. Blow the consequences.

'You too, Angie. I wish I'd had a mum like her. And a dad like yours. I never knew my real dad. Wish I 'ad. It wouldn't 'ave been perfect though, would it? We would 'ave fallen out as families do, but in the end, they'll be there. Anyway, that's the way it seems to me from the outside looking in.'

There descended a sudden stillness in the room, the hint of a lull before a roll of thunder; a storm that might pass, but might also give full vent to all the pent-up anger.

Angie stood rigid, staring unblinking at her father, willing him to look her way.

Rigid of stance, Curly Hill looked perplexed, unsure whether to continue staring away from his daughter or turn to look at her.

Sighting a chink in Curly's armour, Maisie made a last effort to knock through.

'There was an old man in the bar out there. He said he'd got used to the fact that we come into this world without wanting to and leave it without wanting to. That's life. Best to make amends whenever we can and take everything, good and bad how it comes. Who knows when we're going to leave this life. Once we're gone, there's no going back, no forgiveness and no regrets. That's what he said.'

When she saw Curly's eyelids flicker, she knew she'd broken through. Not that the old man had said all of what she'd claimed, but elaborating – lying a bit – didn't matter as long as it brought father and daughter back together.

One more thrust and it would all be over.

'Aggie would have wanted you two to forgive and forget. Curly? Angie?'

A slight hesitance broke in on Curly's part.

Angie appeared more flexible, desperate to make up for what she'd been and what she'd done. She took a step forward, urgency written all over her face.

'I don't 'ave anything to do with Eddie Bridgeman any longer, dad.' She sounded like a little girl craving forgiveness. 'And I've got a job on the buses. I'm a clippie. Sharing a flat with another girl who works there. It ain't much, but I'm on my way to making my own life. Thinking of getting married, too, to a bus driver.' She gave a nervous laugh. 'I'm going to be a respectable woman, Dad. One Mum would 'ave been proud of. One I 'ope you'll be proud of.'

The storm broke in a flood of tears on both sides. Even Maisie had to brush at her eyes.

Daughter threw her arms round her father's neck, Curly patting her back as they both cried onto each other's shoulders.

A job well done, thought Maisie on leaving them there.

* * *

Maisie watched Carole disappear out back into the pub lavatory before telling Bridget in confidence about her unexpected inheritance.

'I don't mind admitting I was knocked off me perch. I did write to you that she'd died. You did get it, didn't you?'

'Yes, I did receive it. What a surprise.'

'It was. Now that Aggie's gone You two are the only people who know, so I'd appreciate you not mentioning it in front of Carole.' Her dark lashes fluttered over her equally dark and beautifully expressive eyes. Keeping it secret had weighed her down. Sharing it with Bridget made all the difference.

'Will you tell anyone now?' asked Bridget.

Maisie glanced into her half glass of cider which was slightly green in colour. A colour like that, plus the bits of what looked like sawdust floating round in it, meant it had come to the pub direct from a farm. Farmers with apple trees were doing a good trade in the West Country, beer and spirits being in short supply. 'I don't want anything to change. I want to be a tobacco girl forever, and if they thinks I'm getting a bit above meself, I won't fit in. I won't be a tobacco girl any more. Do you see what I mean?'

Bridget said that she did. The factory girls were products of the same background; their families didn't have much and it was very probable that they would never have much either.

'You might think about it in a few years though, depending on promotion.'

Lyndon was a bit more sceptical but promised not to say anything.

'We're off now,' Bridget said, once Carole was back from the lavatory and they'd made arrangements to meet up for the funeral. 'It's going from here isn't it?' she asked, her voice dropping.

'Yes.' Maisie jerked her chin in a stiff and affirmative nod. If they hadn't been in public, she might well have burst into tears.

'At St Mary Redcliffe,' Carole added. 'So's the internment. Lovely inside, it is. I'm sure Aggie would appreciate it.'

Bridget thanked Carole for the information. She remembered

Carole as a bit rough round the edges when they'd first met. Her pronouncements this evening made her sound as though she knew the inside of the old Elizabethan church as if she was a regular member of the congregation. Carole, she suspected, had never been inside any church, let alone something as grand as St Mary Redcliffe.

'What's bugging you?' Lyndon asked once they were outside.

'Me,' she responded. 'I was thinking an uncharitable thought.'

'Which is?'

'That Carole's never been inside any church and certainly not St Mary Redcliffe.'

'You're right,' he said. A heavy frown beetled his brows as he took her hand and held it tight between his upper arm and his ribcage. 'Tut, tut.'

'What?'

'That was an uncharitable thought. You'll never go to heaven thinking things like that.'

Bridget returned his mocking smile. 'According to my mother, I won't anyway if I fail to marry within the Roman Catholic faith.'

'Ahuh!' Lyndon nodded sagely. 'My mother might think the opposite.'

'Oh dear.'

'One thing above all else we're going to have to avoid is inviting my mother and yours to our wedding.'

'It worries you?' she said blithely, almost amused at the prospect.

'One war at a time, huh?'

She laughed. 'You're right. I think it's something we have to keep to ourselves.'

'Darling.' He turned her so they were facing each other. His look was intense. 'I don't care about the wedding. A wedding is a short-lived ritual. Our marriage will be for the rest of our lives. I promise you that.' With one strong finger, he raised her chin so that their eyes met. 'I love you, Bridget.'

She smiled. Any doubts retained about their relationship had flown away like birds released from a cage.

'And everything I am is for you, Bridget. My heart is in your hands.'

Silently they walked hand in hand, the cobblestones damp and slippery underfoot. In peacetime, the street lights would be flickering into life, pools of gaslight making the cobbles shine. The blackout had stolen the light, she thought, just as it had the precious years of their youth, for some the last years they would ever have. But her mind was made up as was his. The war would not steal their future.

* * *

Back inside the pub, Maisie bought them another half cider each.

Carole shivered. 'Feels cold in here.'

Maisie felt obliged to agree and wondered whether it was because warm-hearted Aggie was no longer in residence. The old place with its lumpy walls, flagstone floor and heavy beams couldn't possibly be the same without her.

Such a sad occasion, but the past was gone. They all had a future to face, a slightly unpredictable future as far as Carole was concerned. The girl needed advice and encouragement. Her mother was unlikely to be much help, but she'd suggest telling her anyway.

Carole ran her finger round the rim of the glass but failed to get it to ring.

'You don't get it, do ya? My old lady couldn't care less about anybody 'cept 'erself. She's moved in with this bloke and I'm not welcome. Less welcome once she knows I'm up the spout.'

'Are you sure?'

'Sod it, yes.'

Maisie bit her lip. 'Well. It's not been quite as we planned,' said Maisie and sighed. 'What with Aggie going. Got to tell you, Carole I'm gutted.' She shook her head. 'I still can't believe it.'

Carole's head fell forward and Maisie was sure that the blonde fringe was hiding a tear or two.

'Here. Take my hankie.'

Carole took it and gave her nose a good blow.

Sullen from Aggie's death and feeling responsible for Carole, Maisie wished the hands of the old clock standing stiffly in the corner would go backwards. 'If' was a small word, but pretty big under the circumstances; *if* either she or Aggie had accompanied Carole when she'd taken round the card and flowers to the house in Queen Charlotte Street; *if* only they hadn't had a whip-round and bought them in the first place. At the root of everything was the biggest if of all; *if* only Reg Harris hadn't told such a bunch of lies or plied Carole with goodness knows what and taken advantage of her. There were a whole host of expletives waiting for expression, preferably when Reg Harris was around. But he wasn't. Rumour had it that he'd joined up or transferred to Wills Swindon factory. Temporarily, some said. Well, one day he would be back and then he'd have got a piece of Aggie's mind. As it was, now it would only be a piece of hers.

'I'd still like to ask your advice,' said Carole. 'But not here,' she said softly. 'In private.'

'Yes. In private. I'll do all I can to help you. If only Aggie...' She swallowed the sob and the words. There were no words to describe how she was feeling, but they remained in her head... *was here*. They'd be in the back room chewing things over. Out of the question now.

Maisie frowned as a thought came to her. 'How about you come and stay with me this weekend. I'm not doing anything. We could have a bite at lunchtime and then go to my local on the night. Just don't wear too high a heel,' she added with a smile. 'You'll see why when you go walkin' down the street I live in.'

'That would be lovely,' said Carole, forcing a smile. Her eyes remained tearful.

* * *

At home, once the front door was closed, the blackout curtains pulled and her shoes slid from her feet, Maisie sat down. Tea would have been good, but she just couldn't be bothered to put the kettle on. Aggie's passing had happened too bloody quickly!

Then there was Carole... She'd had noticed her dashing out to the toilets in work at regular intervals in the hope that her 'best friend' had arrived.

Disappointment hung like a dark veil on her face. Carole remained pregnant.

Maisie dozed and dreamed that the enamel bowl and length of rubber hose her grandmother had used to abort babies had found their way back into the house. They shouldn't be doing this, she heard herself say.

She banged her head on the chair back when she jerked awake. The house felt cold because she hadn't lit a fire.

Head and shoulders aching, she used the chair arms to straighten herself and saw that her handbag was lying over one foot.

Making tea had seemed like a good idea, but like a pet puppy, her handbag demanded her attention containing as it did, the cards from dear old Sid. It was a big relief that he at least was still alive – thank goodness.

Cradling the handbag on her lap, she drew them out and she

went through them one by one. The words he'd written were just about discernible. The tiny drawings were not.

A magnifying glass was needed. Her grandmother's eyes had been failing badly towards the end of her days and she'd often used a magnifying glass if only to check her bank statements, bank statements that Maisie now knew had reported a very decent balance of her account. Cards clutched in one hand, she got up from the chair and approached the sideboard drawers.

'Now, where are you,' she muttered as she searched through one of the two long drawers that spread the width of the heavy piece of furniture. Beneath the drawers were two equal sized doors.

A silver handle of Victorian vintage glinted like treasure amongst the fish knives and forks, a set of napkin rings unused for years, and a silver thimble, also unused for some years.

'Got you.'

She hesitated, stared at the silver embellishments, the clear cleanliness of the glass. It was sad to accept that the last hand to hold the decorative silver handle had been her grandmother. It looked and probably was expensive. Maisie knew that if she searched through her grandmother's ledgers, she'd likely found it had been pawned in lieu of a loan payment.

Pushing those particular thoughts out of her mind, she settled back in the chair to concentrate on the job in hand.

'Sid,' she said softly, taking a deep breath before commencing on her task. 'Now what are you going to tell me – if anything?'

On close inspection and without the aid of the magnifying glass the drawing on the first card looked like a man's face. Beneath the smooth sharpness of the lens, it still resembled a man's face.

'Just a man's face! Sid, are you having fun with me?'

On fingering the next card, the first one fell to the floor. She picked it up and looked again, this time upside down. There was something about the drawing that made her take a second look.

She gasped, hardly able to believe what she was seeing. There it was, a secret message from Sid, not in words but as a drawing.

The light-coloured area that had been a face right way up showed up against what she'd thought was hair as a whole figure, a sticklike figure. The hollow that had been an eye was a man's head hanging forward, sticklike arms at an awkward angle above and behind him, wrists tied. The dark strip that had been a nostril was now a gash in a man's body.

No gasp this time, for her breath felt trapped in her throat. Sid was telling her what was happening in the prisoner of war camp. Without doubt, the other postcards with their small drawings would tell a similar story. Pushing the prospect of having nightmares aside, she ploughed through each of them, seeing stick men with little flesh, some in cages, some looking about to drop or lying dead, eyes staring from sunken sockets...

Nightmares would come, but to her it was small suffering in comparison to what poor Sid was going through. Barbarism on the other side of the world. Nothing that happened in the city of Bristol or anywhere in Britain could equal such cruelty. Now, after everything that had happened today, it was her that was crying.

## 23

### AGGIE'S FUNERAL

It occurred to Maisie that the crowds hanging around in King Street to witness Aggie Hill's funeral might not have been so numerous back in peacetime.. Aggie's extravagant funeral was filling a need in hearts aching for a distraction from these dire times.

The funeral cortège was a sight to behold. Four horses wearing plumes of black feathers between their ears and purple-edged caparisons over their backs stamped their feet and snorted steamy breath. The hearse was a black japanned affair, the stout oak coffin with brass handles clearly seen through glass etched all round with crystal like ivy leaves. White chrysanthemums donated by keen gardeners shone like stars in the many wreaths mainly composed of greenery since flower gardens had been turned over to growing vegetables.

It seemed to Maisie, sombrely dressed in a black coat with a brown fur collar, as if the whole of King Street, plus Aggie's work-mates from the tobacco factory, had braved the cold air and the slippery cobbles to see their old friend off. It was some comfort to realise that Aggie, the undisputed mother hen of the stripping room, was well loved. Who she wondered would take over?

Two undertakers wearing dark clothes and top hats sat up front of the hearse. Two more, mutes with sad faces and bowed heads, walked immediately behind. Faces she didn't know bobbed around above dark clothes, peered over shoulders, pushed their way through. In the midst of them, she espied a familiar face. Reg Harris was here! Bold as brass standing in the crowd, the brim of his trilby hat tilted over one side of his face, cigarette fixed between his lips.

Bridget clocked her old friend's darkening expression. 'Maisie, you look as if you'd like to shoot somebody. Anyone I know?'

'Reg Harris.' So bitter was the taste on her tongue, that it was hard to keep her voice low. 'Of all the bloody cheek.'

There was an instant intake of breath from Bridget. 'I'm surprised Carole isn't screaming at him.'

'She doesn't want anyone to know, or otherwise she might.'

As it turned out, Carole became livid, all reserve thrown aside. 'You creep! You swine! You've ruined my life. You owe me.'

Maisie and Bridget tried to drag her away.

'He isn't worth it, Carole,' said Bridget.

Maisie, never willing to back off easily, screwed her face up and thrust it close to his. 'The likes of you should be in prison. I'd hang you if I had my way.'

His thin black moustache stretched with his smile, shiny and slippery like a worm. 'Oh really?' There was mockery in his voice and on his face. 'She asked for it. Came round to my home when she knew I would be alone.'

Maisie glared angrily, her stomach reeling with nausea at the sight of him. 'The police should know about you,' she growled.

He laughed. 'You know as well as I do what they'd say; she knew that I would be alone.'

'We only heard your missus was ill, not that she was in hospital. Carole wasn't to know that you were alone.'

'Oh, come on. Right little floozy that one. Asking for it.'

'You...'

Reg ducked and looked surprised when Maisie lashed out.

Between them, Bridget and Lyndon dragged Maisie back into line.

'I wanted to punch 'im.'

'So we noticed. So did everyone else for that matter,' hissed Bridget.

Face red with anger, Maisie let herself be taken back to where everyone from the factory was eyeing her with a mix of pride and consternation. Trust Maisie to speak her mind.

Out of the corner of Bridget's eyes, she saw Eddie Bridgeman who'd obviously overheard. His look was as dark as midnight. He turned aside, grabbed the arm of one of his aides and said something. The other man looked addled, lips rubbery as though not finding the right words.

Reg Harris noticed nothing. To her mind, he must have been born with that arrogant sneer on his face.

Attention fixed on Reg Harris, the hard jaw of Eddie Bridgeman clenched harder before he moved off to join the funeral procession. One last glance and she could half believe that it wasn't him, but nobody could do malice like Eddie Bridgeman. Taking a tight grip of Maisie's arm, Bridget steered Maisie back. 'We're moving off shortly. Let's sort this later, shall we?'

'I thought I saw...'

'Who?'

Maisie obediently turned to face forward. 'Never mind. I must be imagining things.'

The hearse moved off, the two mutes walking behind them with heads bowed, top hats tipped slightly forward.

In turn, shoulders shaking with sobs, walked Aggie's husband, Curly Hill, supported on one side by his daughter Angie, on the other by...

Maisie froze. Surely not?

Carole jabbed her in the ribs with her elbow. 'Eddie Bridgeman! Didn't expect to see him here.'

'Neither did I.'

Carole looked confused. Her face was pale anyway, but she looked as surprised as Maisie that Eddie Bridgeman was in attendance.

'Angie used to live with Eddie,' Bridget reminded them.

'I know.'

'Perhaps Angie asked him to be here and such was Curly's sense of loss that he hadn't had the strength to protest,' suggested Bridget. 'Well,' she said, shrugging, 'it's one possibility.'

'I suppose it is,' murmured Maisie. A long column of people, Maisie and Carole included, followed the hearse along the Welsh Back, the cobbled road leading to Queen Square and onward towards St Mary Redcliffe.

Maisie concluded that Eddie's presence was all about history. They were all residents of the same manor, and although he preyed on them, there was something about family and community. Good or bad, they'd all known each other for years.

The employees from the tobacco factory stayed together, a mixed bunch of girls and a few foremen, Wills having given them leave to attend.

'Production's going to be down today,' muttered Maisie.

In the chill splendour of the five-hundred-year-old church, their breath warmed the air and the singing of 'The Day Thou Giveth Lord Has Ended' warbled from shaky voices.

Back at the Llandoger the wake began quietly enough but quickly developed into a noisy party atmosphere. Aggie had been popular, and a lot of the girls regarded her as the mother they'd never had.

'Cheers to Aggie. And no nonsense from you, St Peter, or she'll be sortin' you out!'

There was much laugher, much drinking and, despite shortages, enough food to make it seem like a party rather than a wake. Spam sandwiches, fish paste sandwiches and, amazingly, a whole ham, plus a platter of fairy cakes and jam tarts were spread out on the bar.

Curly attempted to thank everyone for coming, but his voice broke into sobs before he could get it out. Angie took his place.

'Thank you all for coming. My mother would 'ave liked it. Now 'elp yerself to food.'

Eddie came and stood close to her side, his suit finely cut, his hair slicked back and smelling of something expensive. He raised a glass. 'Drinks are on the 'ouse. And I'm footin' the bill. Eddie Bridgeman, at yer service.'

'I don't get this,' murmured Maisie, shaking her head.

'Don't knock it for now,' said Lyndon.

Sensing Maisie was going to ignore Lyndon, Bridget offered her advice. 'It's not the right time, and anyway, Aggie's gone. It's no longer our concern.'

Maisie had to admit that she was right. With Aggie gone from the factory, they would no longer be calling into the pub where Aggie had ruled supreme, just as she had in the stripping room. The two worlds had separated forever.

Eddie Bridgeman raised his glass in a toast. 'Here's to Auntie Aggie.'

'Auntie?'

'Birds of a feather,' said the old man in the flat cap who had been in the bar on the night Maisie had come to see what had happened. 'Knock spots off each other, but related. You didn't know that?'

Dumbfounded, Maisie shook her head. She looked for Carole, but couldn't see her.

'Anyone seen Carole Thomas?'

Nobody could confirm exactly where she'd gone. Still seeking the arrival of her 'best friend,' thought Maisie, the most welcome monthly period she had ever wished for.

\* \* \*

Unbeknown to Maisie or anyone else, Carole had been waylaid, grabbed and tugged back behind the bar and into the small vestibule just in front of the living room door. 'I want a word,' said Eddie Bridgeman.

Carole stared at him, her eyes as big as saucers. 'Leave me alone.'

Her voice trembled. She was so scared she wanted to pee.

Eddie did his best to sound reassuring. 'Don't be frightened.'

His grip lightened. She swallowed hard. 'What do you want?'

Eddie's face was oblong in shape. His brow was square. His eyes were deep pits in deep hollows. Overall, he did not own a handsome appearance, but he did have the look of a man who inspired fear. In fact, he couldn't recall the time he'd last smiled. All the same, he tried it now when he asked, 'I 'eard you 'avin' a go at that bloke.'

'Reg Harris.'

He nodded. His expression darkened. 'Are you all right, girl?'

Her mouth was as dry as the bottom of a birdcage, but from somewhere, goodness knows where, she found enough courage to speak. 'What's it to you?'

Eddie stared at her. He still had trouble believing that she was his daughter. She looked more like her mother than him, blonde and curvaceous. After a bit of soul searching, not a thing he regularly went in for, he thought back and recalled that his mother had been blonde – a lot like Carole in fact. He'd had time for his mother, but none for his father. The old man, the bloke who'd wore braces with silver clips and cufflinks resembling skulls, had taken off them braces at times and used them on his back. The scars were gone, but inside they were still there. When young, it was Carole's mother who'd given him love – until the world moved in – until blood was out and he became a chip off the old block. That had been when his dad had become proud of him.

'Thanks to me, you're the man you are, as 'ard as me. And I made you that way, boy. Right? I made you.'

The old man had been right and, oddly enough, Eddie had respected him for it, though never loved him. His love had been reserved for his mother, as beautiful as a butterfly – just like in the old music hall song.

'You remind me of someone special,' he said and meant it. Carole did remind him of his mother.

Carole folded her arms and held herself upright. It made her look defiant, she thought, though she didn't feel it. 'Who's that then?' she asked as cocky as you like.

Eddie took a deep breath. 'Never you mind. I want you to know that you can always come to me if there's trouble. If that bloke's done you wrong...'

'What's it to you?'

'I'm interested in you. I want to take care of you. This bloke, Reg 'Arris. Are you fond of 'im?'

Carole looked at him in shock. 'Are you kidding? He's a creep and he... he... took advantage,' she finally blurted.

She couldn't help it. She burst into tears.

Eddie took the clean white handkerchief from his breast pocket and gave it to her. A few minutes ago Gerald had given him the gist of what he suspected. Carole had just confirmed it.

Carole blew her nose and dabbed at the tears.

Eddie said nothing but just stood there staring at her with anger boiling in his eyes. 'No need to explain. I've 'eard enough. Here...' He handed her a bundle of five-pound notes. 'Take care of yerself. Get rid of it if you want to. I wouldn't blame you.'

Carole was shivering in her shoes. He scared her. She felt like a doll that he could play with and throw away when he had no need of her. Not that he'd tried to take advantage, yet.

She flinched when he stroked her cheek with one cold finger. 'You come to old Eddie if you need to.' His voice was soft, oddly gentle. He sighed, chewed on a cigar he took from the inside pocket of his well-cut suit; not a black suit. Dark grey, but the whiteness of his shirt made it look black. There was a flash of silver grey lining. He'd decided it was time for confession. He felt good doing it.

'Me and yer Ma 'ad a thing going when we was young, but I wanted to get on. Didn't want to settle down. All I wanted was to be somebody and 'ave everybody call me "sir" and wait on me 'and and foot when I stood at the bar of me own club. Do you understand what I mean?'

She wasn't sure what she was supposed to answer but said the first thing that came into her head. 'You split up with mum, when she was young.'

He nodded. 'Yeah. We split up, but not before you came into being. Now do you know what I'm saying?'

Lightening flashed. Thunder rolled – or at least it felt that way. It was suddenly as though the room was spinning like a top and a whole host of colours had dispersed the black of funeral clothes.

She stared at him open-mouthed.

He laughed. 'Yeah. I can see by yer face that you're gettin' it. Yer mum's gone off with a bloke, but yer dad's still 'ere.' He gently ruffled her hair as his look turned serious. 'I ain't 'avin' anybody taking advantage of my little girl.'

She recalled the man who'd sprung into a shop doorway. 'You had me followed.'

'I didn't want any bloke thinkin' 'e could 'ave 'is way with you.'

She thought of Ben, his bloodied face. 'Ben was nice. You had no right, not like Reg Harris.'

She looked to where Reg Harris was swigging back another drink, as though he was king of the world and nothing could touch him. Many people were here from the factory to pay their respects, but why him?

She felt Eddie's eyes on her, the smile having dropped from his face.

'This other bloke; did 'e do what I think 'e did?'

Carole felt sick, nodded and closed her eyes, not to block out the spinning but the memory of Reg Harris. Of all people it was Eddie who was forcing her to face it.

She nodded. 'He raped me. I think I'm up the spout.'

Eyes turning as black as the ace of spades, he appraised her silently, then leaned in close and whispered in her ear. 'I promise you he'll pay for it. That toerag will get 'is comeuppance, or my name ain't Eddie Bridgeman.

Once he'd gone, she stood shaking. Her head was reeling, her blood running cold, then hot flushing her face.

Covering her mouth with her hand she ran for the toilets, burst in and regardless of the queue, barged into a cubicle and threw up into the bowl.

# 24

# MAISIE

'Temple Meads! Again! I've never been in this station so much since the start of this bloody war.' Maisie smiled apologetically at Lyndon. 'Excuse me language.'

He threw back his head and laughed. 'I hear worse than that on the bases I give talks to. Still. All that's about to change.' He grinned at Bridget and hugged her close. His dream had come true. They would both be based in London – at least for now. He'd said nothing of feeling ashamed that his job was too cosy, that he was seriously contemplating applying for active service. It scared him, but he felt duty-bound and it had all begun when he'd gone up with the bomber crew of the Flying Fortress and felt terrified, guilty and thrilled all at the same time. He felt the spoilt little rich boy, doing a cosy job whilst other guys were putting their lives on the line.

Maisie attempted a stab at humour. 'Seems I'm always saying goodbye to someone here, never hello.'

'One day you will.'

Maisie nodded. 'Sid was the first I saw off from 'ere.'

'And one day he'll be back.' Bridget smiled and Maisie smiled back.

'You bet!'

They exchanged a look of understanding. Bridget was the only person she'd shown the cards to. They'd been in what had been Grace Wells' front room and had opened a walnut cocktail cabinet, got out a bottle of damson wine and drank the lot. As tears poured down their faces, they'd used expletives that nice girls weren't supposed to use to describe the wretched war.

'Shame on you, Bridget Milligan. I wouldn't 'ave thought you'd known words like that.'

Bridget had laughed. 'I learned them from you.'

'Take care of yourself,' said Bridget as Lyndon gently ushered her towards an open carriage door.

'You too.'

Their clasped hands gradually slid along their arms, their looks holding, their smiles only just.

Lyndon kissed her on the cheek. 'Good luck with everything. Any help with all the financial and legal stuff, don't hesitate to holler!'

She laughed through her tears. 'I will.'

Doors began to slam the length of the train. Bridget, Lyndon pressed behind her, continued to wave and blow kisses.

Maisie wanted to turn her back on them purely because she couldn't bear it that her old friend was leaving again. It was Bridget who had coined the phrase, 'Three Ms'. With hindsight she realised that the phrase had been applied to make her feel accepted. She'd not wanted to work at the factory, had felt she might not belong. Bridget and Phyllis had made her feel that she did.

One last wave before the sound of strained metal intensified and the train disappeared into a pall of white smoke.

She stared at the greasy, grey space it had left, along with the smell of soot and the feeling of emptiness. Pulling a handkerchief from her pocket, she gave her nose a good blow. Never had she felt so alone, so isolated.

'You all right, love?'

The soldier had a kitbag weighing down one shoulder. He was young and sounded local.

She returned, perhaps a little too brusquely, that she was fine.

'Sorry. I didn't mean to intrude.' He turned away, then more quickly turned back. 'You sure you're all right?'

Maisie nodded. 'I've just seen a friend off. I'm a bit upset, OK?' The brusqueness remained, though less than before.

He looked genuinely concerned. There was kindness in his eyes. 'Course you are.' He half turned away again, then turned back. 'Fancy a cup of tea?'

She curbed the challenge that he was trying to chat her up. What with Aggie, Carole and all the other things going on in her life, she craved a diversion.

He led her to the station café. Although there hadn't been any raids for a long while, the windows were still crisscrossed with white tape. Paper chains made from newspaper and just about anything else were strung across the ceiling. Bits of ragged tinsel festooned round cold metal lampshades glittered as best it could.

'My treat,' said her new friend.

She didn't argue. She was too tired to argue. The war had caught up with her, drained all her energy, made her yearn for the days of peace before the war had started.

'Fancy a biscuit? Or a tea cake?'

She declined. 'Just tea.'

He held up a hand in acknowledgement.

He came back with the tea. 'There you go. Not sure you wanted sugar, but I put one cube in. That's all they've got. Cubes. I prefer two myself.'

He'd bought himself a teacake. Maisie found herself counting the currants, which were easily spotted through the thin scraping of margarine.

She took a sip of her tea and thanked him. 'It's hot.'

He grinned. 'But not strong. Doubt it ever will be until this lot is over.'

She smiled at him and couldn't help but notice that his eyes were blue and seemed a bit out of place in his tanned face. 'You just got back?'

He chewed, swallowed and nodded. 'As cold as it is, I'm glad to be here.'

'What battles you bin in?

'I ain't done any fighting.'

The moment she saw the look of embarrassment on his face, she knew what he was going to say next.

'You're a conchie – conscientious objector.'

'Indeed I am.'

'But you're wearing a uniform.'

He pulled the kitbag about so she could see the red cross on a white background on the other side. 'I joined the medical corps. I prefer to save lives than take them.'

In the past, she might have cut and run; there was plenty of condemnation for those who didn't want to fight. It wasn't so much that she disagreed, it was that it made her feel awkward. This war had divided her from her friends and poor old Sid was going through hell in a Japanese prisoner of war camp.

'My name's Alan,' he said, thrusting his hand across the table.

She took the proffered hand. 'I'm Maisie. So where's home?'

He shook his head in an almost apologetic manner and poked a finger into his ear. 'London, but I've been assigned a position in a prisoner of war camp in a place called Pucklechurch.'

'Pucklechurch? It's just a village. You're going to find that a bit different to London. And you'll finally meet the enemy. Does that worry you?'

'No. I won't be fighting them and they won't be fighting me.' He grinned. It was quite an attractive grin and although she told herself to ignore it, she was finding him as attractive as his grin. His voice was nice too.

'I know Bristol pretty well, so my plan is to get transport in and catch up with my old haunts.'

'You lived here?'

'I did indeed. I was teaching typing. That's what I do. I did it for a while in London before they caught up with me and insisted I serve.' His kitbag fell over. As he reached down to retrieve it, she saw the name on the side and felt sick. Alan Stalybridge, the father of Phyllis's baby.

Not seeming to notice her reaction, he took a packet of Woodbines and offered her one.

'No thanks.' She clenched her jaw. Alan Stalybridge. A typing teacher. Phyllis had learned typing at evening class. And this man, Alan Stalybridge had left her pregnant.

Suddenly she no longer wanted company, especially his company.

'So where do you work, Maisie?'

'Stripping tobacco leaves at Wills,' she finally offered. There was a bitter taste on her tongue when she asked him if he'd ever known any tobacco girls.

'No,' he said, stubbing out his cigarette with grim determination. 'I don't think so. Well,' he said, glancing up at the clock, then checking the time on his wristwatch. She guessed she'd needled him. 'I'd better be off. I'd like to get to my billet before it gets too dark. I understand it is damned dark in the country.'

'Yes,' she said, seeing him anew, wishing she could tell him all she knew about him. 'Very dark.'

He left abruptly, heaving his kitbag over his shoulder.

She wanted to shout out after him that the baby he'd fathered had died, that Phyllis had entered a loveless marriage for the sake of the child. The fact that it had also been in some small way to save her reputation was neither here nor there. All she'd really wanted was to learn to type and improve herself. A useful skill, never could anyone have foreseen that the military would have need of it. And so Phyllis was serving in Malta and all Maisie could hope for was that she would one day return. In the meantime, smug looking and a little too sure of himself, Alan Stalybridge was to blame for all of it.

# 25

# PHYLLIS

Back in July thousands of men had set sail for Sicily from Malta and although they were fighting for every inch of ground, in September the allies had landed in Italy.

'We're having a party tonight to celebrate the allied advance on the mainland,' said Charlotte, a charming but slightly wild girl who had grown up in English boarding schools between bouts living with her parents in India.

Phyllis was less than keen. 'I'm not sure I want to. It's too hot.

Charlotte flopped onto the bed beside her and gave her shoulder a shake. 'Of course it's hot. This is Malta. Phyllis, darling, you can't go grieving over your man forever. Life is for living and you being glum is not going to alter anything.'

'Easy for you to say.'

Phyllis didn't want to be reminded of her loss and she had no wish to be goaded into a future she might not want. Might was the operative word. In the meantime, Charlotte's relentless enthusiasm irritated. It wasn't that she was nasty, just naive. She was of a certain class who, although regarding themselves as British, were far removed. Charlotte's father had been something to do with the railways. Her mother, so it seemed, had done little except watch polo, gossip and drink Singapore Slings at the country club. Housework was done by servants and the whole family had led a standard of life they would never have acceded to back in the old country. They were Indi- orientated not British, though it would have floored Charlotte to hear that. She floated around in her own little world, loving the attention of men in uniform, though only those of officer class, and looking down her pert little nose at anyone not British, even the colonials.

Smelling of the lemon juice she'd washed it in, Phyllis's hair fell forward as she looked down at the floor, unwilling to meet Charlotte's perfectly made up and slightly aloof expression. What did she know?

Charlotte wasn't giving up. She nudged Phyllis with her elbow and leaned in close. 'I can guarantee you'll meet someone special tonight. I've dropped the word in a certain ear. A major, no less. He's very interested. I told him you were a redhead with a super figure and grieving for a lost love. And of the right class of course...'

'Stop it!'

Taken by surprise, Charlotte's eyebrows rocketed upwards.

'I've had enough of this, Charlotte Vincent. Now get this straight. I ain't one of your lot, floating around without doing a stroke of work – *real* work. I'm a tobacco girl. I worked in the factory that makes Woodbines. And I grew up with a widowed mother in a council house on an estate in Bristol.' She gave a light laugh. 'And to think I wanted to talk like people like you. Wanted to improve myself. Well, I'm telling you now, that after a few weeks with you, I realise I was totally wrong. My old mates at the factory are worth ten of you. At least they're honest and don't give a damn if someone is posh or poor. So tell your major I'm not interested in stuck-up toffs likely to look down their noses at me. I'm a factory girl, a tobacco girl, and that's that.'

Angered, she slammed the door so hard that stone dust was dislodged and sent fluttering in the air round her.

For a moment, Phyllis stood with her arms crossed and tears stinging her eyes. Charlotte had lived a sheltered life. She'd never been through what Phyllis had been through. Or made the mistakes; Robert and Alan for a start. Why hadn't she been strong enough to resist?

Way back, Maisie had said, 'What you after, Phyl. What the bloody 'ell are you looking for?'

She'd laughed off the comment, but with hindsight she knew that, as usual, dear Maisie Miles had hit the nail on the head. Phyllis loved attention and she loved to be loved. Perhaps that was why she'd given herself so easily and also why neither Alan nor Robert had left her with any great sadness. Mick was the only one she still longed for, the only one she was finding it almost impossible to get over.

The sound of footsteps on the cool marble staircase heralded the arrival of Beattie, a steward with the navy who made it her job to collect post for all females, no matter army, navy or air force.

'Four for you, Harvey. Aren't you the lucky one.'

'Thanks.'

Flipping the letters between her fingers, Phyllis decided there and then that she wasn't going back into her billet and put up with Charlotte continuing to apply pressure she could well do without; better to be alone with her old friends even if it was only via a letter. Only briefly did she glance at the postmarks, taking it for granted who they were from. It would be a pleasure to have them to herself and throw her mind back to a different place and a different time. Friendship was very important when it was all you had left.

She was off duty, it was late morning and the wintry sun was as warm as it was ever going to be. A coat would have been a good idea, but Phyllis shrugged her shoulders and decided it would be warm enough to sit on the rocks across the road.

Each grand façade of Whitehall Mansions overlooked rocks of yellow ochre frilled with green waves and creamy foam. A large flat rock in the corner looked inviting. On hot days this area was packed with service personnel diving off the rocks or sunning themselves.

Small children screeching with laughter were dipped into the deep water and jerked out again. A great game for the young.

Mick might have drowned in that sea, though some way from here.

Pushing such daunting thoughts to the back of her mind, Phyllis wrapped her skirt under her, uncaring of how dusty it was going to be once she got up.

As she'd already guessed, the first letter was from Maisie.

*Hi Phyl. I hear you're not being bombed so much now the battles in North Africa are over and more supply ships are getting through.*

Most but not all, thought Phyllis. There were still shortages, but at least local fishing boats were not being so badly affected now the blockade was lifted. The hospitals were busy. She'd seen the hospital ships bringing in the injured. Hundreds of years ago, Malta had been named the Nurse of the Mediterranean – even after the knights of St John the Hospitallers, the knights who cared for the sick, were confined to history. It had been so once again in what was now being called the First World War, back in 1914–1918. Once again it was playing its part in providing care for those injured in the horror of this, the Second World War.

*It will upset you to know that Aggie has passed. There's a big gap in the stripping room without her. We miss her. And with you and Bridget gone, it just leaves muggins here. It's lonely without you two, though I do have young Carole.*

*I hear the divorce came through. You're hardly the only one. I heard tell that the Marriage Guidance Council shut down before the war but had to reopen double quick. The divorce courts are sitting all night, thanks to this war. The world's changed and so have we, but there, life goes on whatever it is.*

*Bridget will, of course, be writing to you separately. From your letters, your chap Mick seems nice.*

Phyllis jerked her attention from the page and out to sea, straining to see what wasn't there. Sometimes she pretended that a black spot in the sky was his plane returning. Such a thing was impossible, but hope really did spring eternal. Mention of him being nice had created a vision based on his appearance and their conversation the last time she'd seen him – talking about vineyards and their time together after the war.

'Dusty hills and scrub turned green with vines. Grapevines love sunshine, you see, and, well, back in Oz we've got oodles of that.'

Yes, her divorce had come through. They would have been married straight away, but instead here she was, single again, but with no prospect of marrying the man she had really, really loved. She should have written to Maisie and told her, but she couldn't the pain cut too deeply.

The urge to collapse into a heap and shed tears onto the dusty rock was strong, but she held back. It was something Maisie had said about life going on. Other people had spouted the same clichéd saying, but it was different coming from Maisie. Not just was she the one with the old head on young shoulders, she had a way of saying things that made it more believable. These words were only written on paper but oozed all that Maisie had been and was.

A young couple sitting some distance away looked up when she sniffed loudly.

'You all right, love?'

She managed a smile. 'I'm reading a letter from home.'

'Oh yeah. They make you feel homesick, don't they?'

'Yes,' she answered, maintaining a fixed and decidedly weak smile. 'They do.'

Tucking the letter into her coat pocket, she turned her attention to the other three. One of them was from her mother, a diary of her exploits up north when new hubby was there and when he was not. It seemed she'd made a lot of friends but hated it when he was away.

*I find it hard to fill my time. I don't like going to dances without him. There are so many single men around and it doesn't take them long to get fresh.*

No mention of missing him, no statement of fear, the dread of him not coming back.

The next letter was obviously from Bridget and didn't just make her smile, it made her envious. She too mentioned Aggie and how bereft they'd all been. Being methodical in her writing, she related the minutiae of her job very precisely and to some extent without emotion. Then suddenly she was crowing about the benefits of penicillin and how she'd seen a man, who at one time would have had an amputation, be cured with this new medicine.

*They're calling it the magic bullet. The young corporal injected promised that if it worked he would take me dancing. It did work and he did take me dancing. He offered a lot more than that, but I had to tell him that I was engaged.*

*Lyndon is over here lecturing to the American forces on*

*British foibles. He went along as an observer on a bombing raid over Germany and came back a bit shaken. Ever since then he's been musing on joining a combat unit. I hope he doesn't.*

*I'm only training to be a nurse, but feel I can better look the likes of you in the eye when you come home – whenever that is. Can't wait for us to get together and be the three Ms again. Heady days.*

*Love to you and your man. Bridget.*

'Love to you and your man,' Phyllis repeated the words softly then sighed. The letter from her old friends had taken some time coming, the sea route not entirely back to normal just yet. What wouldn't she give to turn back the clock and be one of those care-free factory girls again? After thinking about it, she wasn't so sure. Those precious moments with Mick would never have happened.

Before continuing, she closed her eyes, her lips moving in a silent prayer for Aggie. May her soul rest in peace. Dear old Aggie!

Tucking Bridget's letter away, she turned her attention to the last one and frowned. The envelope looked official. It had a stamp on it that she couldn't clearly read. A red cross. All letters weighed light nowadays, but this one was exceptional. It was, she finally decided, a telegram and her heart lurched. 'What have we here?' She used her fingernail to open it. There was just one piece of paper inside and just a few words.

*A very nice nurse from Idaho is writing this letter for me. She refuses to let me exert myself, though I keep telling her it's my legs that took the bashing, not my arms. A quick outline: I crashed, Sicilian partisans rescued me and kept me safe. I'm a bit battered but still alive here at the American base hospital just outside Catania where I eventually ended up. See you soon. All my love, Mick.*

Never had she scrambled so quickly up those rocks and back over the road. The door she'd slammed earlier crashed against the wall as she burst back into her billet.

'Charlotte. Am I right in thinking there's an RAF unit in Catania. And an airfield? The whole works, like there is here?'

Charlotte was a picture of indignation but before she could answer Phyllis grabbed hold of her not too gently and gave her a shake. 'My fiancé is there. Sicilian partisans took him there. He's alive. I thought he was dead, but he's alive.'

'But I thought that the UXB bloke...'

'No,' said Phyllis, shaking her head, eyes bright with excitement, feeling more excited than she had for quite a while. 'He was just a friend...' A friend. She felt quite cruel saying that, but it was the truth. 'Mick went on a reconnaissance mission over Sicily. His plane went down. I thought he was dead, but he's alive. He's alive!' She screeched the news at the top of her voice.

Charlotte, who seemed privy to intelligence information gleaned from officer friends, eyed her with a puzzled expression before replying to her earlier question that there was an RAF base in Catania.

'Then I can get a transfer!'

Charlotte shrugged. 'I suppose so.'

Her decision was instant. Again the door banged open, but before it had time to bang shut, Phyllis held it open. Ecstatic was the only word to describe how she felt. 'That party you mentioned...'

'Yes.'

'A beach party?'

'Yes, it's...'

'Count me in. I need to celebrate.'

The time living with Maisie gave Carole comfort, but she was still loath to have anyone at the factory know her condition.

'I've already told you that I don't want anyone to know.' She squeezed her eyes shut, her fists clenched in desperation. 'I don't want this baby. How could I? Each time I look at it, I'll see him – Reg bloody Harris!'

Maisie sighed. 'You don't really have a say in it.'

Carole tilted her head back and glared at her, jaw clenched but bottom lip quivering.

'There's ways of getting rid of it. Gin for a start. And laxatives you can get at the chemist. Meg Jacobs told me there are.'

'So I hear.'

'And there's women who'll get rid of it for me. I've got money. I can pay.' She didn't tell Maisie that the money had been given her by Eddie Bridgeman when he'd confessed to being her father. Somehow she couldn't bear to touch it, but for this...she would. 'Can you find one for me, Maisie? Can you? Please?'

Maisie bridled and avoided facing Carole's pleading counte-nance. The very thought of abortionists making money from getting rid of babies made her angry. She could still remember the day when she'd first walked into this house and realised that her grandmother had made money helping girls like Carole. She hadn't liked it then and she didn't now.

She shook her head hard sending tendrils of hair flying round her face.

'No. I don't. You could die, do you know that? You could DIE.'

She strongly emphasised the last word.

Maisie's emotions were tumbling all around. She couldn't bear the thought of an aborted baby in this house where so many such operations had been performed. Even the thought of the baby being adopted filled her with sadness. What if it was me, she asked herself? The answer came quickly. She would keep it, love it and give it all the care she could.

Carole slumped glumly in her chair. 'I want to go back to work. I love my job, but how can I go back with this belly?'

Maisie was nothing if not resourceful. 'You need a corset.' Maisie grinned. 'I've got just the thing.' She shot upstairs.

She'd taken most of her grandmother's clothes to an exchange so that others might benefit. Many adult clothes were good for cutting down for slimmer women or children. Some things, however, were a little too personal – or too old-fashioned.

After a quick rummage, Maisie came down with a very old-fashioned corset, complete with laces that could be tightened to suit.

Her feet thudded back downstairs.

'How about this?'

At first, Carole gasped, then joined in the laughter as she breathed in and Maisie pulled the laces tight. The result was surprisingly effective.

'Amazing,' said Carole, patting her stomach.

Maisie stood with arms crossed, looking at her.

'What?' said Carole on seeing the look on her face.

'I was thinking that Reg Harris 'as got off too bloody lightly.'

Carole grimaced. 'So do I. That bloke ruined my life.'

'Deserves for 'is to be ruined,' said Maisie. 'Still, you never know. Might get 'is just desserts yet.'

\* \* \*

It was Saturday and Carole had volunteered to accompany a regular ambulance driver who would teach her the basics of driving. 'We've staged a bit of a rehearsal to see how you get on. It's on a bomb site and we're going to pretend that there are bodies still buried there. You never know, we might find a real one.' Supposing her squeamish, he laughed at his little joke.

Bomb sites were drab affairs and although weeds were doing their utmost to break through and break down the tumbled rubble, it would be some time before they were flat enough to rebuild.

When they arrived at the scene, bell jangling, there were men on the site and a bulldozer was pushing earth around. A foreman appeared to be giving instructions, pointing here, waving his arm there.

Mr Oxton, her driving instructor, told her that there wasn't really much point in them being here as all the bodies had been recovered some time ago when air raids were still happening.

'So we just sit here? Can't I go in and help?'

'No. Let the lads get on with their work.'

She sighed. This wasn't quite what she'd envisaged. Driving seemed more about sitting down than actually doing something. 'Noisy beast,' declared Mr Oxton, referring to the bulldozer.

Just as he said it, the noise lessened, the bulldozer coming to a standstill.

A man standing in front of the digger bent his knees, looking closely at something on the ground in front of him. The foreman left his safe perch on top of a slab of brickwork and joined him. Together, they peered downwards. Pushing his hat onto the back of his head, the foreman looked right at them sitting there in the ambulance and waved them over.

'Hiyup,' said Mr Oxton. 'Looks as though they've found something. Bring the first-aid box – just in case, though…'

He didn't need to finish his sentence. Carole guessed they'd found a body. She only hoped it wasn't a child. It would be bad enough if an adult, but a dead child would be just too awful.

'I will not be sick, I will not be sick,' she muttered as she trod carefully across the uneven ground, first-aid bag weighing her down on one side.

Beside her, Mr Oxton shook his head. 'I don't think you're going to be needing that bag.'

A hand showed stiff and filthy above the expanse of dirt and debris.

Mr Oxton looked at Carole. 'Better see if there's a pulse,' he said to her.

'Do I have to? It's a corpse.'

'Procedure,' came the reply.

Stomach churning, she knelt down, her hand trembling, fingers numb as she placed them where she would detect a pulse – not that she expected to.

'Dead,' she said. Stiff from days of no pulse, the hand remained upright, one finger pointing accusingly upwards.

'Right,' said the foreman. 'Let's have some shovels here – but go gently. The less damaged, the more likely we can identify the poor sod.'

Carole thanked God she hadn't eaten anything that morning or it would have been up by now. She turned to leave, but it seemed Mr Oxton had other ideas.

'Let's see this through. Thing is,' he said, frowning, 'it's been a

long while since the bombs hit here and that hand looks too fresh
to have been here for a couple of years, don't you think?'

'I suppose so.'

"Ello, 'ello,' he exclaimed, looking to where a uniformed bobby
was making his way cautiously across the site. 'Looks as though
they've nabbed a passing copper.'

'What we got then, Fred?' The police constable addressed the
foreman whilst resting his hands on bended knees and peering at
the steadily emerging body.

'Don't rightly know, Ted, but it do seem a bit queer. I thought all
the bodies had been dug up from here ages ago. To my mind...'

'This one looks too fresh.' Ted got out his notebook. He looked
up and saw Mr Oxton with Carole beside him. 'Hello, Archie. You
confirmed the death, 'ave you?'

Mr Oxton made a sideways jerk of his head, indicating Carole.
'Miss Thomas took the pulse.'

The bobby saw the lovely though rather pale face and straightened. He beamed at her. 'Miss Thomas, I'd like you to witness the
uncovering if you would. It would help me with my notes – if you
don't mind that is.'

'You've no choice,' Mr Oxton murmured out of the corner of his
mouth. 'Watch him, mind. Ted is a wolf in a copper's uniform.'

'I'm on my guard,' returned Carole.

The police constable turned and smiled at her as she made her
way back to him and those carefully scraping earth from the body.

For no apparent reason, his gaze dropped to her feet. The smile
dropped from his face. 'Well,' he said, poking a finger at the rigid
rim of his helmet, enough to set it at a more jaunty angle. He
pointed. 'Look at that ground. Full of rubble, yet here,' he pointed
down at the growing mounds of earth to either side of the body, 'it's
earth. Nowhere near as stony.' The charm dropped from his face to
be replaced by a contemplative frown. 'Dig a bit more, but I'm

thinking I might need a second opinion. Is there a police box around 'ere?'

'Over by the market I think, Ted.'

\* \* \*

Ted Baxter injured at Dunkirk, on recovering had opted to join the police rather than going back into the army. Naturally observant and with an eye on promotion, he took every opportunity to forward his career. Today he reckoned his observance would reap big rewards. He knew he was right about this body. It was too fresh to be a long-lost victim of a bombing raid. He glanced yet again at the stony patch, then back to where the men with shovels waited for him to finish looking so they could get on with exposing the corpse.

'Hold things till I ring the station.'

PC Ted Baxter set off in the direction of St Nicholas Market. The market had existed since the Middle Ages, a place of flag stoned alleyways, arched ceilings and deep cellars used for storing wine, port and sherry.

Mr Oxton asked Carole if she'd like to go back to the ambulance whilst they awaited PC Baxter's return.

'I've got a thermos flask there. We could have a sip whilst we wait.'

The men with shovels also halted and drank stewed tea from a saucepan bubbling away on a makeshift brazier.

Carole put the first-aid bag in the footwell of the ambulance and gratefully accepted a sip of tea.

'You all right, love,' Mr Oxton said to her after she'd supped all she could. 'Only, you look a bit pale.'

'I'm fine. It's just all a bit unexpected.'

'You can say that again.'

The return of PC Baxter signalled the resumption of labour.

'I've got to see this through, especially now the police are involved,' said Mr Oxton. 'How about you?'

Her face burned. It could have been the tea, but it was a bit stuffy in the ambulance, the windows closed and steaming up all the time they'd been sitting in there. 'I could do with the fresh air.'

They got down from the ambulance and walked to where a trio of men were examining what they'd found.

Baxter gave the nod. 'Carry on, lads.'

'Shovels only,' ordered the foreman. 'And very gently, scrape rather than dig.'

The scraping didn't take long to reveal the corpse. A man wearing a brown suit and a shirt that used to be white. The tie was not in its usual position between the shirt collar but tied tightly round the neck.

'Clear his face with your hands,' ordered the foreman. 'Let's see the bloke's face.'

Calloused hands more used to heaving shovels gently cleared the dirt away from the man's face.

With grim expressions, those that had dug him free looked down at him.

'Well. There he is,' said Baxter. 'Anyone recognise him?'

There were mutters of no and shaking heads.

Carole saw the face, gasped in astonishment, then promptly fainted.

# 27

# BRIDGET

The head surgeon had arranged a party for his patients and staff on the occasion of the birth of his first grandchild. A band had been sourced from a very obliging contingent of army personnel, and the excitement was palpable.

Lyndon had phone just a couple of days before to say he had leave and if she could swing it...so she did.

'Well, you're a lucky dog going home,' said Edna, one of Bridget's colleagues. She said it laughingly, then added, 'You're going to miss all the fun.'

Bridget smiled secretively. 'I'm taking my fun with me. My beau is home on leave. It's been weeks since I saw him. We're off down to Bristol to stay with my parents.'

It wasn't strictly true. The Milligans' council house had only three bedrooms and too many children. Used now to having her own bed and her own space, Bridget couldn't contemplate sleeping with her sisters and, anyway, she wanted to sleep with Lyndon.

Travelling down by car, they had arranged to eat lunch with her parents before going on to stay with Maisie. Bridget had taken the opportunity to write beforehand and see if she had room. The answer had come back swift and sharp.

*Of course I've got room. Three bedrooms and one with your name on it. Just one thing, Carole is staying too. She's got nowhere else to go and anyway, I get a bit lonely living here by myself. She's going through a bad time at present. Hope that's all right.*

All right? Bridget was over the moon. Saying that she was staying overnight with Lyndon at Maisie's might not go down well with her parents, but she was over twenty-one and the choice was hers.

*   *   *

it was raining when Lyndon picked her up early in the morning. The windscreen wipers swept the water away on the outside. On the inside, it was necessary to keep a window open to help prevent condensation. Even then, she had to use a cloth to keep it clear.

'Have you got the whisky?'

'Yep. And the tinned cake, dried egg, doughnuts and cigars. All thanks to Uncle Sam.'

'I've got the cooked ham.'

She took another swipe of the screen. Her donation to the family feast was nothing compared to what Lyndon had brought. The US forces were well supplied with food – no wonder they bred such big men.

Lyndon kept his eyes glued on the road, saying little except to complain about the weather and driving on the wrong side of the road.

'Our side,' Bridget corrected him. 'Anyway, I thought you would have got used to it by now.'

He grunted that he couldn't figure it out.

She was ready with the details. 'Because your right arm is your sword arm and you need it free to fight and so does your opponent.'

'My sword arm?'

'That's the reason behind it – or so I'm given to understand.'

'Handy to know – if I happened to be riding a horse and carrying a sword. In the meantime, can I remind you that this is an American Forces car and the steering wheel is on the left and the sword fighting side is on your side!'

The conversation remained light. At the back of both their minds, only mentioned intermittently, was the question of Bridget's parents' response to their marriage, done in a rush of enthusiasm with a three-day licence. The whole escapade had been exciting and passionate, a few forces friends invited to partake in the celebration afterwards, the physical passion of their love expressed as a married couple in a three-quarter-size bed in a room above a local pub. There'd been no time to invite Maisie up from Bristol, though she had sent a telegram.

The excitement had gone. The love was still there, but still, there were bound to be recriminations. Lyndon had sent a telegram to his parents. Bridget had opted to tell her parents face to face.

'We're both over twenty-one,' Lyndon reminded her. 'We don't need our parents' approval.'

'I don't want them being upset.'

He knew this was what she was thinking, could see it by the way her hands were knotted together in her lap. She'd be devastated if they disapproved.

\* \* \*

'Oi Mister. You a Yank?'

The kids of Marksbury Road swarmed to the spot where they'd pulled in, the white star on the side of the vehicle drawing them like curious bees. It was that white star – American vehicle – that had given them access to enough fuel to drive here rather than catch the train.

'Yep. And I've got Hershey bars and gum.'

'Better get inside before they have you turning out your pockets.'

'Here come the cavalry.'

Bridget's siblings were being held in check at the front door, their faces expectant.

'We're having Albert and Victoria for lunch,' said Mary, one of Bridget's younger sisters.

Lyndon raised his eyebrows. 'Really|?'

Bridget grinned as she enlightened him. 'Mum's been raising chickens.'

There were hugs and kisses, clamouring for attention, cries of amazement as chocolate, sweets and gum were handed out – though not without a warning from Mary Milligan that none should be consumed until after Christmas dinner.

'So you've arranged to stay with your friend, Maisie?'

There was a searching look on her mother's face.

'Yes. She's got three bedrooms and looking forward to seeing us.' She didn't mention that Carole Thomas would also be there. Three bedrooms and four people. Her and Lyndon sleeping together. 'It's her own house,' she said to her father.

'A lucky girl,' he replied as he puffed on the cigar Lyndon had lit for him. 'Fancy that. Still single and with her own house. Is she courting?'

'Not really,' said Bridget. 'She does write to someone she met years ago. He's in a Japanese prisoner of war camp.'

Her father shook his head sadly. 'Poor devil.' He turned to Lyndon. 'And how about you? What are you up to?'

'Doing as I'm told, sir. I hope you're OK with me as a son-in-law.'

'It's not down to me. You're both over twenty-one and old enough to make up your own minds. Isn't that right, Mary?'

Mary Milligan smiled weakly. Laying her apron aside, she'd gone out to the front door to welcome them in her best Sunday dress. Now she put it back on again, tying the strings in swiftly and impatiently. 'We all make our own choices.'

To Bridget's ears, it seemed an odd, slightly unfinished thing to say. Whether Lyndon noticed or not, he called for glasses and the bottle of whisky to be opened.

'Well, I'd like you all to toast to our happiness.'

Glasses were raised, whisky for the adults and lemonade for the kids.

The prospect of a secret being shared lent excitement to the exchanged look between Bridget and Lyndon, the man she loved.

Lyndon proposed the glasses should be refilled. 'I've got an important announcement to make about that happiness.'

'I won't refuse,' said her father, giving that intense look as though already guessing what was about to be said.

Her mother looked more apprehensive, as though fearing what it might be about.

Lyndon made the announcement. 'I'm somewhat relieved that you approve of us getting married, because the truth is, we already have.'

'Two days ago,' added Bridget. 'By special licence.'

Her parents gaped. The kids hooted with delight.

'Cheers,' cried Sean, her sixteen-year-old brother, his glass of lemonade looking suspiciously doctored with a dash of whisky.

'Hooray,' shouted Molly.

Mary, on the other hand, frowned deeply. 'Does this mean I won't be your bridesmaid?'

Bridget held the little girl by the shoulders, amazed at how quickly she'd grown. 'When this war is over, we'll have a church blessing. You can be a bridesmaid then.'

Her father shook Lyndon's hands. 'Welcome to the family, son. Congratulations to you both.'

Her mother kissed her cheek. 'Good luck, Bridie.' She waved her hand in front of her face. 'My goodness,' she whispered. 'These hot flushes.'

Deep down, Bridget knew it wasn't the onset of the menopause upsetting her mother. She'd always had reservations about her and Lyndon. The O'Neills were wealthy, the Milligans far from it. To her mind, it was only right that a man should maintain his family and Lyndon would do that. Her heartbreak was that he would take Bridget away from her loving family to the other side of the Atlantic.

Bridget's father took Lyndon to one side. 'And what do your parents have to say about this?'

Lyndon grinned. 'I've sent a telegram. Could be some time before I hear.'

Patrick Milligan patted the firm, young shoulder. ''Tis your life, my boy. 'Tis your life.'

'And Bridget's.'

'Yes. And Bridget's.'

Happy chatter bubbled all round her, her mother bustling round the table, keeping everyone's plates topped up, refusing Bridget's offer of help.

'Well I'm helping anyway.'

If anything, her assistance seemed to spur her mother on to greater effort, hovering over the kids, making sure her father had his fill of roast potatoes – especially the extra crispy ones.

'When are you going to have babies?' Katy asked her.

Her mother's response was sharp. 'Don't ask stupid questions, Katy, and get on with your dinner.'

'All in good time,' Bridget whispered to her. Her eyes stayed on her mother, who'd barely stopped long enough to sit down and eat her own dinner.

It had never been easy to have privacy in an overcrowded house, but Bridget waited her chance. She'd seen the look of surprise but something else on her mother's face. Later, once the kids had headed to the park to find conkers, Bridget followed her mother into the kitchen.

'Mum.'

Bridget caught her mother's busy arm. Their eyes met.

'Tell me you're happy for me, mum.'

Her mother stopped scraping the remains of the chicken into a stockpot, looked down into it as if by some odd quirk the words she wanted – needed – to say might be lurking there. 'I'm shocked. This isn't what I expected at all.'

Pain stabbed at Bridget's heart. 'Mum, I didn't mean to hurt you, but...' She had sworn to Lyndon that she would say nothing for the moment until his posting came through. She swallowed and it all gushed out. 'Lyndon is joining a bomber squad. He feels guilty about being behind the scenes and preaching at young guys carrying out such deadly missions. He felt he had to step forward and be counted.' Her hair fell round her face, cloaking the consternation she was feeling. 'Carpe diem. That's what we both said. Seize the day.'

'I know what it means. I'm Catholic, remember?' Her mother's voice was strident. A tear trickled from one eye. 'I didn't think he would marry you. Men can promise you the world and not deliver.' She sniffed and wiped her hand across her face. Her eyes were downcast. Finally she raised them. 'I knew somebody like that once back in that other war. He let me down.' Her eyes glistened. 'So, you see, I am happy for you my love. Happier than you could ever imagine.'

## 28

### MAISIE

Even after so many months, the stripping room at the tobacco factory seemed less vibrant without Aggie's huge presence. The prospect of another winter of war didn't help things.

Maisie had been allotted two school leavers to knock into shape. She couldn't help looking at their awestruck faces, their wide-eyed surprise at the noise of machinery, the flood of women making their way into the canteen, the laughter, the gossip. To some extent and despite her youth, she'd also taken over Aggie's role of mother hen.

Yet there still seemed to be a yawning gap at the table where she'd once worked and reigned supreme. Her chair was still left vacant as though she might return from the canteen or lavatory at any minute and would expect it to be there.

Besides reminiscences about Aggie, the death of Reg Harris was raked over again and again, everyone seemingly having their own theory as to what had happened.

'They reckon it was suspicious circumstances and it's ongoing,' said Gertie Spiller who had kept every newspaper article written on the event.

'I wonder who did it?'

'P'raps 'e got caught with his doodah where it shouldn't 'ave bin.'

It was widely acknowledged that Reg Harris had always been too free and easy with his hands and his private parts.

Maisie listened, smiled and said, yes or no or maybe; Carole was close-lipped about Reg's attack on her. Maisie noticed her holding her stomach in each time Reg was mentioned.

Carole still had a pretty face and as always her make-up was immaculate, but still the dark lines beneath her eyes still showed. She was the one who had been there when his body had been discovered, but she refused to talk about it.

'Too upsetting.'

Secretly she confided in Maisie that she hoped he'd gone to hell.

'We all reckon some bloke did 'im for messin' about with 'is wife, daughter or sister. What do you reckon, Carole?'

'He fancied you, Carole.'

'Yeah,' laughed Gertie. 'It could 'ave bin you? Did 'e try it on, did 'e and you did 'im in?'

Carole looked at Maisie, then drank half her tea. Maisie slid her cup across the table. 'I ain't thirsty. Have mine.'

Carole didn't refuse.

'Are you out tonight?'

Carole shook her head.

'Home alone?'

She nodded.

The seed of an idea that had germinated in Maisie's head now began to grow.

'That's not good for you.'

Carole shrugged. 'I don't 'ave much choice.'

'Yes you do. You can move in with me.'

A reluctant smile appeared on Carole's lips. Maisie felt a sudden and very warm sense of relief. It was the first time she'd seen Carole smile for ages. She patted the sleek white hand with its beautifully manicured nails.

'I'm here for you. If there's anything you want. Money. Anything, I'm here.'

The grey circles beneath Carole's eyes suddenly seemed less grey as her face turned sunny. 'Thank you for being such a good friend, Maisie.'

'That ain't a problem. As for Reg Harris whoever did 'im in deserves a bloody medal as far as I'm concerned.'

# 29

## PHYLLIS

Permission to travel to Catania had been refused which Phyllis had fully expected. The war was still going on and military considerations took priority.

'At least you know he's alive,' counselled Barbara, who reminded Phyllis of Bridget with her careful judgement and wise counsel.

Phyllis heaved a big sigh. 'I can't wait. I wrote a letter to Bridget and another one to Maisie when I thought he was lost to me forever.'

'Now you'll have to write to them again and tell them you're bursting with happiness.'

'You're right. I thought I knew what love was but didn't know at all until I met Mick.' She laughed. 'I told Bridget and Maisie that spinsterhood might suit me very well, that I would grow geraniums and get a cat.'

'And what did your friends say to that?'

'Bridget wrote back with words of sympathy and that my heart would mend.'

'Well there you are then. Coming to the party tonight?'

Phyllis sighed. 'Why not?'

She didn't tell Barbara what Maisie had said, but she'd definitely been more blunt.

*Come on, Phyl. You're too good-looking to be alone for long. Blokes flock to you like moths around a flame.*

'Come on. Let's celebrate at this party tonight. You can borrow my silk dress if you like.' Barbara flicked at the skirt of a sea green dress embroidered with poppies round the hem and sleeves.

'You don't mind?'

Phyllis loved the dress, the sea green suiting her Titian hair and creamy skin.

'I wouldn't offer if I did mind. Let's face it, Phyllis, it suits you better than it suits me.'

*Yes*, thought Phyllis, holding the dress up in front of her whilst eyeing her reflection in the mirror, *it does suit me*.

Lights went on all over the island. The war wasn't over, but the Germans were too busy fighting battles in Northern Italy and France to worry too much about a small archipelago in the Mediterranean Sea.

Bars had thrown their doors wide open; if the locals weren't in church, they were picnicking and partying at the water's edge, along with the army, the navy and the Royal Air Force.

It seemed to Phyllis that they only had to walk a few feet and a man in uniform would take her in his arms, twirl her round and, if he was quick and lucky, grab a kiss.

Drinks were offered and accepted. The air was humid but nobody took any notice. Everyone was overjoyed and predicting that the end of the war was at last in sight.

'Be over by Christmas,' somebody shouted, tot of whisky raised in a toast.

Somebody pointed out that something similar had been said back in 1939.

'And in 1914,' someone else added.

The mood was infectious and Phyllis couldn't help but join in the party. Only when a flash of sheet lightning lit up the sky did her eyes turn seawards. There was a slit of light where the sun had set, its dying light reflected on the bank of marbled clouds.

For a moment, it held her attention. Staring at the sky had become a habit these last years, waiting for Mick's plane to reappear each time he flew on a mission and now she knew he was alive, waiting for him to come home.

When the rain came, some ran for shelter, with the exception of those who were too drunk to care. And lovers. Phyllis saw a few couples melt into the shadows, their intention to celebrate with more than beer and spirits. She wished she was one of them.

The rain got heavier, puddles forming on the hard ground, streams of water flowing along cracks and gullies, filling holes in the road until what remained of rock and concrete became stepping stones to cross from one side to the other.

'Let me take you for a drink, darling.'

The hand of a drunken sailor reached out to her. She batted it away.

'No thank you. I don't want a drink.'

'Well how about you let me rub you down with a rough towel?'

She pushed him away again as he tried to grab her for a second time. 'No.'

He was getting to be a nuisance. She looked around her, seeking help, but it was hard to see anything, the rain having plastered her hair to her head.

'Stuck-up cow. Ain't I good enough fer you?'

'Please.' She pushed him away again.

'Well I'll teach you, you little tart...'

Suddenly he was falling backwards away from her, his legs staggering under him until he was sprawling in three inches of water.

She thanked whoever it was over her shoulder and, without turning round, began to pick her way through the steadily rising rainwater.

'Take my hand. Take my arm. Take my life.'

Her legs almost gave way. Her breath felt sucked from her body.

'Mick!'

Her hair was soaking, her dress was soaking and her feet were wet through.

She shook her head in disbelief, was afraid even to turn round. There had been so many occasions when she'd thought she'd seen him, thought she'd heard his voice purely because she wanted to. She had never wanted to accept that Mick was dead, never wanted to go on living without him.

Water trickling into her eyes, she turned slowly, afraid that the vision of Mick Fairbrother would be washed away in the rain.

'You're drenched.' In the fragile light from inside a bar, she saw the upturned corners of his mouth, his smile just as she remembered.

'Mick?'

'It's me.'

'No.' She shook her head. 'This is a trick. If I touch you, you'll vanish.'

'Touch me and see.'

Her whole arm shook as she reached out, her fingers lightly landing on his shoulder. 'Mick.'

'Phyllis. I'm back.'

# 30

## MAISIE

It was a bittersweet experience finding the sweet little nightgowns once given to Phyllis for her baby. Maisie smiled down at them as she fingered the soft, lawn material and rows of smocking stitch. 'Here,' she said, on giving them to Carole. 'These are brand new. They've never been worn.'

'Are they yours?' Carole eyed her speculatively, presuming that Maisie had once been expecting a baby.

Maisie shook her head. 'No. They belonged to a friend.' Again she ran her hand down the soft flannelette. Phyllis had lost her baby. She was going to make sure that Carole didn't lose hers.

The enamel bowl used by her grandmother to end pregnancies was gone, left at the end of the street for somebody to take. She'd gone back to check and found it gone.

The rubber hose was a different matter. Nobody was likely to take that, or if they did might question its use. Fearing they might guess the truth, Maisie had buried it in the garden. Her mind had turned to Phyllis wondering what she would say if she learned that the father of her child, Alan Stalybridge, was back. Not that she'd mention it. Water under the bridge, she'd thought. Let sleeping dogs lie. The old and well-used sayings made her smile.

It was Saturday evening and Maisie had cooked haddock for supper. Once the dishes were done, they sat there knitting matinee jackets and bootees for the baby.

For a while, they listened to the music playing on the radio.

War news mostly referred to Italy and US victories in the Far East. Everyone agreed that at least now it was going in the right direction, but there still seemed a long way to go.

'I wonder how long now until the war's over. Your little 'un needs a world at peace, not bloody war!'

Maisie stabbed her knitting needle through the loop and clattered on. It had never occurred to her how lonely she was until Carole had moved in with her. Once the baby arrived, there would be three of them and the prospect thrilled her; more so than Carole – or so it seemed.

Carole remained oddly silent. The needles moved hesitantly, progress on the bootee seemed at a standstill.

'What is it, Carole?'

'Nothing.'

'Don't tell me it's nothing. You're never going to get one bootee done, let alone two, at the rate you're going.'

Expression sombre, Carole's hands and knitting fell into her lap.

'I hate knitting. I told you I did,' exclaimed Carole through clenched lips.

Maisie carried on knitting, blithely thinking ahead to that wonderful time when the baby would arrive. 'Think of how sweet it will look. And all your own handiwork.'

'Mostly your handiwork, Maisie.'

Maisie heard the accusation in Carole's tone of voice.

'Yes, but we have to be ready...'

'No,' Carole exclaimed, lunging forward in her chair, eyes blazing, her fists fiercely gripping the chair arms. 'I will never be ready for this baby. Never! It's you that's trying to make everything right, Maisie, but it won't happen – not for me anyway. I was raped, Maisie and it disgusts me.' Maisie's jaw dropped and so did her knitting. Carole's beautiful eyes met hers. She'd always been jealous of those eyes, their blueness, that along with her clear skin and light blonde hair. She'd once described her as having a 'butter wouldn't melt in her mouth' look but had later changed her mind. Could she have been right in the first place that something less than nice lurked beneath the shining surface?

'Carole. Everything is going to be all right.'

'It won't be. It can't be. I don't have a job or even a widow's pension. The bit I'm going to get for the baby isn't going to go far. I need to make a living.'

Maisie sighed. She'd done everything in her power to chivvy her along, to make her feel more positive about its arrival. She'd even managed to obtain baby wool, though the woman in the shop had charged her the earth. Carole's knitting didn't grow at anything like the pace of Maisie's. Deep down Maisie knew she was hoping the clothes wouldn't be needed, that the baby wouldn't go to full term.

'Look. I've got enough money to pay you to be my housekeeper once you ain't earning. That way you'll 'ave a bit of cash and be at home with the baby anyway. I'll even look after it when you want to go out of an evening.'

Carole shook her head. 'I don't feel that's right.'

'Why?'

'It's my problem, my choice. If I can't get rid of it, I'll give it up for adoption.'

Although a true statement, Maisie hated it; she hadn't meant to get so involved, to feel some ownership of this child. At the beginning, all she'd meant to do was to support Carole through this difficult time, but things had changed. Maisie had a deep-seated yearning to be part of the baby's life and Carole talking about giving it up for adoption filled her with alarm. Fuelled by that alarm, her mood turned spiteful.

'Well that's gratefulness for you.'

'Please don't get like that, Maisie.'

'I've done everything for you and you repay me like this. Well, thank you very much!'

Carole's expression was pained. 'Please. I know you've done heaps for me.'

'Beyond the call of duty,' grumbled Maisie.

'Thanks for the ring too.'

She flicked a finger at the engagement ring Maisie had thought to buy in order that everyone believed her story.

'Well, we couldn't have you linked with the death of Reg Harris. That would be real trouble.'

There was a sudden intake of breath on Carole's part. The knitting and needles fell from her hands as she slumped back in the chair. One hand ended up resting on her belly.

Instantly alarmed, Maisie let her own knitting fall and leaned forward. 'Carole. I'm sorry. I didn't mean to say that. Are you all right?'

Breathing more heavily than normal, Carole caught her breath then nodded. 'Just a twinge.'

'My fault. I shouldn't 'ave mentioned...' Not wanting to say his accursed name again, Maisie took a deep breath. 'Him,' she said with an air of finality. 'Fancy a cuppa?'

Carole nodded and managed a weak smile.

Once the kettle was on the gas and the cups and saucers were sorted, Maisie rested her hands on the scullery sink and stared out of the window. Sid sprang immediately to mind. Somebody in work had asked her why she rarely dated.

'Because Sid will expect me to be yer when 'e gets back.'

Sid was always the excuse she gave. It was debateable whether he actually received all the letters she wrote to him in which she detailed everyday life. All the same, she wondered if she was living in hope of Sid's return. Initially she'd been quite blasé about him, saying he was just a friend, but now... She *willed* him to survive and if she had to say she would wait for him, even marry him, she would do that.

The whistling of the kettle interrupted her thoughts. She made the tea and took it in.

Carole had laid the knitting to one side and was sitting quite still, a faraway look in her eyes.

'Here you are.'

Aware she had been caught day dreaming, Carole jerked her head round too quickly to hide the tears spilling onto her lashes.

Setting the tea to one side, Maisie knelt down beside her, felt her forehead, stroked her cheek. 'What is it, love? What's the matter? You can tell me.'

The tears that had stained her lashes dropped onto her cheeks.

'It was my fault, Maisie. Reg, I mean.'

Maisie frowned. 'What the 'ell are you talking about?'

'It was my fault. I killed him.'

At first, Maisie persuaded herself that some aspect of pregnancy had unhinged Carole's train of thought. On reflection, she discarded that particular possibility. 'Right. First things first. Drink your tea before you say anything else.'

Firmly but gently she handed Carole the cup and saucer into which she'd put two sugar lumps and nothing in her own. No matter that she had money, rationing still dictated how she managed the supplies of food.

Carole had a very ladylike way of sipping tea, her small finger held aloft from the handle. She took one sip after another.

Assuming she was about to hear more, Maisie left her own brew to cool and waited. There was no denying Carole's manner, the look of a sudden decision being made.

She raised her tear-filled eyes to Maisie. 'It wasn't my fault that I got pregnant. Honest it weren't!'

'Of course it weren't, love. Of course it bloody weren't.'

'But it was my fault that he was killed.'

She took a big gulp of air. Her eyes were big and round. 'You know what Eddie Bridgeman was like with me. As if he owned me.'

A shiver ran down Maisie's spine. He'd been like that with her once but she'd always kept one step ahead. Just out of reach. Her mouth was dry. She feared what she was about to hear. 'I know,' she managed to say.

'He collared me at Aggie's funeral. Said he'd overheard somebody talking about me, asked if it was true. Told me he'd take care of Reg Harris and not to worry.' Her eyes again met those of Maisie. 'He called up here. I didn't like to tell you.'

Carole bit her lip as she awaited Maisie's response.

The last person Maisie wanted on her doorstep was Eddie Bridgeman.

'I didn't want to worry you. He asked if I was all right. He gave me some money and said that if I needed anything else just ask. Even a flat to live in. He said if I wanted to give up the baby for adoption, he'd fix that too.'

Maisie passed her a man-size cotton handkerchief. 'Blow your nose.'

If she read Eddie the same as she had of old, it seemed he wanted to set Carole up as his mistress. The baby didn't count. Get it adopted and it seemed that too was what Carole wanted.

Her dark curls flew round her face as she shook her head. 'How could he be so bloody cruel!'

'No. No. You don't understand.'

Carole gave her nose another blow and mopped at her eyes. 'I'm going to tell you something in secret. You must promise never to tell anyone. Nobody. Do you promise?'

With unbridled apprehension, Maisie promised.

'Eddie Bridgeman is my father. He told me so at Aggie's funeral.'

Maisie's jaw dropped. 'He told you that?'

Carole nodded, turned away and sniffed into the handkerchief. 'And he gave me money. What a predicament, eh? I'm carrying a kid fathered by a monster, and my own father ain't much better.' Her tear-filled eyes turned on Maisie. 'Can you blame me for not wanting this baby? Can you blame me for wanting it adopted?'

\* \* \*

Maisie sat up until nearly twelve that night looking into the fire. She didn't want Carole to have her baby adopted. It was Carole's baby, yet she felt an inner need to protect it, almost as though it was hers. She didn't want a child brought up with strangers. She'd had a bad enough childhood growing up with a stepfather. What if this baby's adoption turned out the same?

A plan was slowly forming in Maisie's mind, a plan she could barely believe she was making. If Carole allowed it, she would take the child, then Carole could always have access – if she so desired. She even thought about moving far away so it wouldn't be easy for Eddie Bridgeman to track her or his grandchild down.

Eddie Bridgeman's grandchild! What a predicament it was.

But what if the baby was hers and not Carole's? What if they pretended it was hers and that Carole had gone away? It seemed a preposterous idea; sheer fantasy. But at least she had plans.

Tonight she would sleep on these plans. Tomorrow she might very well put them into motion.

# 31

## PHYLLIS

Mick Fairbrother was much thinner than Phyllis remembered him. For days, weeks, after his return, she couldn't stop staring at him.

Her Maltese friend, Mariana, asked if she would like to come to church and give thanks. Without a second thought, Phyllis said yes. 'I never believed in miracles, but I do now.'

'I'd like to stand in another place that's witnessed a miracle,' she'd said to Mariana. 'Not a church in Valetta. I'd like to take a ride out to the one in Mosta.'

'I understand.'

In the quiet coolness of the domed church in Mosta, she lit a candle and, with her head veiled, gave thanks.

Back in April of 1942, an enemy bomb had crashed through the beautifully painted dome of this church. Although it wasn't confirmed for sure, there were over three hundred people inside hearing mass. They should have all been killed if the bomb had exploded – but it did not. The hole in the dome had been hastily patched and army bomb disposal had made it safe. Tom had been one of that team who had risked their lives to make it safe and she recalled him talking about it.

Once outside in the bright sunlight, she felt a great sense of peace and contentment. Hope had returned and the days of miracles were not over.

'You lit three candles,' said Mariana. 'Just as I did.'

'A prayer of thanks for Mick, one for old friends and the third for all those young men fighting their way into Europe.'

'Amen,' said Mariana. 'Mine was for all those I love and everyone, everywhere.' She laughed lightly. 'I'm unsure the church will have enough candles to go round. But never mind. God will understand. Are you meeting Mick tonight?' she asked as they climbed onto the bus. As with all buses on the island, it was brightly painted and had been manufactured by the Bedford Motor Company, some way back in the twenties and even before.

'Oh yes,' said Phyllis. 'Do you know, I'm getting to hate him being out of my sight, just in case it's all a dream.'

There was a pause in conversation on the crowded bus where the seats were narrow and many passengers were forced to stand. On a hot day like today, it was hardly the most comfortable ride.

Once back in Valletta, the conversation went back to Mick and also to Edward, the young Maltese gunner Mariana was engaged to. It wasn't the first fiancé for Mariana. Andrew had been an armourer at Ta'Qali but had been killed in a bombing raid.

'I intend coming back here when this is finally over,' said Phyllis thoughtfully. 'I mean, look how peaceful it is now. A bit battered, but it's survived.'

Mariana agreed with her. 'The islands have survived many battles; first the Ottoman Empire and then Napoleon. We adapted and came through. We will do the same again.'

'The country or its people?'

'Both.'

They walked on, Mariana aiming for home with her family and Phyllis back to her billet at Whitehall Mansions.

'Do you sometimes think of Tom?' Mariana's question caught Phyllis off guard.

She answered truthfully. 'Yes. I haven't told Mick about him.'

'Will you?'

The question had sprung to mind a few times. Each time she'd shied away from confronting it. Was it best to say nothing or own up?

'I don't know how. I mean, I do, but I'm afraid that if I tell him that might be the end of us. I don't want us to end, not after we've found each other again.'

They stopped at the end of the stone paved alley where Mariana lived. A woman threw a bucket of water over the hot slabs and a cat ran for cover. Lines of laundry baked from washing lines was strung from second-floor windows.

'Have faith, Phyllis. God sent him back to you for a reason. That reason can't possibly be for you to lose him again. It wouldn't be worth God's effort.'

There was merriment in Mariana's eyes as she said it. Mariana had a puckish sense of humour, but she was also very religious. Phyllis respected her for that and had much appreciated her accompanying her to the church in Mosta. She had no doubt that the miracle that had happened there would be retold to future generations. She hoped the same for her and Mick's story.

Once they'd smiled and waved goodbye, Phyllis' thoughts returned to their conversation. Should she not say anything about her moment of passion with Tom? How would Mick take it if she did?

There was something about seeing the patched-up dome of that church that made her want to confess and however Mick took it was meant to be. All she needed was the courage to tell him.

It was whilst Lyndon was away that Bridget was enrolled on a two-week course in East Grinstead.

The hospital consisted of a series of low brick-built huts. Before arriving, she'd been informed that some groundbreaking work was going on there.

'I've had experience of administering penicillin when it first came out,' she declared, not without a sense of pride at her achievement.

Matron eyed her with a tight smile. 'I know. You've shown great aptitude as a nurse and also interest in the incredible strides forward in modern medicine. However, this is not about medicine but surgery. Have you heard about the guinea pig project?'

In that moment, it seemed Bridget's heart floated up into her mouth, such was her sudden increase in pulse rate. 'Isn't it a burns unit?'

'Yes. In the main, the patients are RAF pilots and air crew who have suffered severe burns. There is also an attached unit where some experimentation is going on in treating those who've suffered injuries to their eyes.'

The matron had the looks of Margaret Lockwood, quite a surprise really.

'Nurse Johnson will show you to your quarters, then it's a case of knuckle down and get to work. I do hope you don't mind hard work.'

'Not at all.'

'Good. Learn from it. We will report back to your tutor.'

Nurse Johnson introduced herself as Violet.

'I'm Bridget.'

'Do you have a sweetheart?'

She nodded. Admitting to having a sweetheart was one thing, being married was another. For now at least, she was Nurse Milligan.

'Is he in the forces?'

'Yes. American Air Force. Bomber crew.

'Oh.'

There was something about the way she said it and the expression on her face that made Bridget think she was a little surprised she was there.

It wasn't until her first foray onto the ward that she understood the reason why. Not one patient was without bandages round the head, though some had bandaged hands as well.

'It's called skin grafting. New skin is added once the burned skin has healed.'

Her head was reeling from the very first and it was difficult to keep a neutral expression and it wasn't just about the bad burns. Those who had undergone surgery no longer had the faces they were born with. Some had had to have their eyelids reconstructed, some their cheeks, jaws or noses.

At night, Bridget cried. Violet heard her.

'It's normal,' she said. 'You need to cry where the patients can't see you. They don't need our pity, just our compassion.'

'I understand.'

Her words were only partly true. Hidden by the darkness, Bridget lay in bed and prayed for Lyndon, prayed he'd never be injured so badly as to end up here and felt oddly guilty denying he was her lawful wedded spouse.

\* \* \*

At the end of the two weeks, Bridget was back on her normal nursing training course, assisting on the wards, attending lectures and demonstrations on medical procedures.

It was ten in the morning. The lecture was about applying the correct dressing for various types of wounds on different parts of the body. The lecturer's voice was an unending drone, totally bereft of undulation, thus making the subject sound even less interesting than it was.

The leaves of the sycamore trees outside the windows drew Bridget's gaze. Not that she actually saw them. Finding it hard to shake visions of brutalised faces, she'd slept fitfully. What kind of bandage suited a face burned beyond recognition? More to the point, how did they cope seeing a face that was no longer their own? And what about encountering the reactions of their sweethearts, mothers, wives and children; even total strangers staring at features so changed by injury and then surgery?

Air crews who'd crashed in flames; why oh why had Lyndon chosen to become one of them and how would she cope if he...

The voice of the lecturer sharpened and became louder.

'You would all be wise to pay attention.' Less of a drone and directed at her.

Bridget felt the dig of an elbow from Nurse Anne Jones sitting next to her.

'Back to work,' said Anne once they'd finished. 'I could have sat there all day.'

'I can't wait to get back to work. I thought I was going to fall asleep back there.'

It wasn't true. She wondered if she'd ever sleep again after those two weeks in East Grinstead; at least, not until Lyndon came home safe and sound.

\* \* \*

Excitement helped disperse the worst of her fears when a telegram came from Lyndon to say he was coming home on leave. There was just one problem. She was on duty for the days stipulated. Better to work this weekend and leave the days she required free. She turned to a fellow nurse.

'Anne. You wanted the weekend off. Care to swap with me? Lyndon's coming home for three days during the week.'

Anne readily agreed. It was her mother's birthday that weekend and she was desperate to see her.

'There won't be much of a party, but fish paste sandwiches and seed cake go down a treat with a bottle of brown ale.'

'Thanks a bunch, Anne.' Bridget gave her an almighty hug.

'Watch it,' said Anne as she patted her breasts. 'You're squashing my finest assets.'

They sailed through their work for the rest of the day, happy they were both going where they wanted to be and who they wanted to be with.

Bubbling with excitement, Bridget left her shared room at the nursing home – nurses were not allowed to live anywhere except in the home. The excuse that she was visiting an aunt made her giggle. Three days of bliss.

Finally arriving in Kensington she ran up the stairs to the flat she shared with Lyndon when she was off duty for an extended time, bristling at its emptiness without him being there.

The hours dragged and the minutes passed too slowly. Bridget had prepared everything, cooked a welcome-home dinner, spread out a white linen tablecloth and laid it with fine crockery and cutlery.

Once she'd done everything, including bathing, washing her hair and applying make-up, it was time to change out of uniform and into her favourite dress. When there was nothing more she could find to fiddle with, she stood looking out of the window, aching for Lyndon to come home, to feel his arms round her, to lie in bed and hear his gentle breathing.

Across the leafy square, a big black car was pulling in. It was very shiny, and although she was no expert, she guessed it was very expensive. The driver opened a rear door and a woman got out who looked just as expensive as the car.

A sudden pang of jealousy struck her, not out of envy for the woman's clothes but something more deep-seated. The woman was likely of the same class as Lyndon, had been well educated, been brought up used to servants, used to being at the pinnacle of a class system that kept aloof of the lower orders. She'd heard the term stick to your own kind. Know your place. As far as Bridget was concerned, her place was with Lyndon.

So here she was, living in Kensington until the war ended and they would head off to America.

White stucco on the grand facades of elegant houses gleamed like frosted icing on a giant wedding cake. Overall, Flat 2A at Number Twenty Paragon Square could swallow up the Milligan house in Marksbury Road.

Bridget mused on her own wedding cake, a confection thick with fruit and covered in icing and just enough for the close friends they'd been able to invite to the celebration. She still regretted not being able to invite the whole family, but they'd made a quick deci-sion, one loosely based on who knows what might happen tomorrow.

The superb little cake had given rise to an obvious question. 'How did you do it?'

'Always keep on the right side of the guys in the cookhouse. I greased palms,' Lyndon had stated with some pride.

She smiled as the sight of him, the sound of his voice and the simple things he did came and went in her mind. It had been two months since she'd seen him. Autumn was long gone and winter was closing in. In these past two months she'd thrown herself into the work at the hospital, applying for any course as part of her studies, including the one in East Grinstead. Keeping busy had kept her mind off things. One thing she was certain of was that if Lyndon hadn't trained to be air crew she wouldn't be feeling so anxious. He'd laughed when she'd expressed her fears. 'I'm just the guy that cranks the handle that lowers the wheels or greases the gun turret.'

She'd pretended to believe him but knew he did more than that. Just the fact that he was flying put him in danger. If only he'd stuck to giving lectures to green recruits newly arrived in Britain. The single flight he'd sneaked aboard some time back had convinced him that he was cowardly in being just a 'back room boy'.

'All those young faces,' he'd said, a faraway and slightly awestruck look in his eyes. 'I felt so responsible for them, felt I had to swallow my fear and do it anyway.'

The sound of whistling accompanied his appearance from the end of the street. Her heart skipped a beat at the sight of his long stride coming closer and closer. She spun away from the window, checked the flowers in the centre of the dining table – a terrible extravagance she'd thought, but this was a special occasion.

For what must have been the tenth time, she straightened the knives and forks then patted her hair, pinching her cheeks and pouting her lips at the hallway mirror.

Before he had chance to ring the bell, she flung open the door and there he was standing with his back to her.

For one dreadful moment, she wondered why he had his back turned. Was he hurt? Had he crashed, had he...

The dreadful fears so lately acquired slipped in, then swiftly out again as he turned round, as handsome as ever and smiling from ear to ear.

\* \* \*

The evening was even more than she expected it to be. Bed came before dinner simply because their only hunger was for each other.

The sheets were cool, the curtains were drawn and the candles she'd set on the table fluttered an amber glow round the bedroom.

Just as she'd anticipated, their lovemaking was urgent and passionate, and even once replete, they still touched, making the most of the precious moments as they would each and every night and day until they parted once again.

He stroked strands of her silky brown hair over the white pillows, concentrating on smoothing them flat until they were like sun rays round her head.

Neither of them mentioned feeling hungry until it was almost ten o'clock at night.

'It just needs warming up,' she said to him.

'I've got wine.'

'I've got cheese.'

'And bread straight from the cook house.'

She laughed. 'Your friend again.'

\* \* \*

The three days of leave Bridget thought the most wonderful days of her life. Sometimes they reminisced on the time when they'd met, her pretending to be a patient in the W. D. & H. O. Wills clinic, and him visiting with his father. She mentioned her old friends in the factory, Maisie who had been slightly reticent when first joining the firm and now filling Aggie's shoes. They raised a glass to Aggie and also to Phyllis with the hope she would soon return home.

'To everyone. May they keep safe and to those who are no longer with us, may they rest in peace.'

It was halfway through the final evening when they'd exhausted conversation that didn't involve the word 'war' that Bridget sensed Lyndon's mood had changed. She put it down to the fact they were parting though wasn't entirely convinced.

After they'd finished supper and he was packing his bag, she went into the bedroom and stood watching him. His bag was still on the bed, clothes, books and other kit spread round untouched. Lyndon had his back to her, was smoking a Wills' Whiff, a small cigar, staring out of the window, just as she'd stared whilst waiting for him to come home.

'Lyndon.'

He spun round quickly. His jaw was taut and there was no trace of a smile.

They were parting. He would be going soon. That's what this was all about, she told herself.

In an act of reassurance, she went to him and gently placed her hands on his shoulders, caressing muscles that had grown noticeably harder since he'd swapped an administrative job for active service. 'I don't want you to go.'

He put his arms round her. 'Duty calls.'

'For me too.' She lay her head on his shoulder. During these glorious three days, she'd maintained silence regarding her two

weeks in the plastic surgery unit. She'd kept the war and its consequences at bay; had Lyndon done the same?

Fear as chill as particles of ice flowed with her blood.

'Lyndon.' She looked up at him, raised her hands and lovingly
cupped his face. 'Tell me.'

He blinked. His expression was impassive and she knew then,
the words faltering and fearful on her breath.

'You're being made operational.'

He said nothing. Made no movement. His eyes looked deeply
into hers.

'When?'

'About a day, perhaps two, after I get back to base.'

There was a lump in her throat as she buried her head against
his chest and murmured, 'Stay safe, darling. Please stay safe.'

# 33

## MAISIE

The big shock of January 1944 was the news that Miss Cayford was getting married and there were many comments as to why. Miss Cayford was the woman in charge of hiring new factory girls. It was her who had inspired confidence in Maisie and had torn a strip off Phyllis when she insisted on wearing lipstick at work.

Middle-aged, dark haired, small and rounded like a robin, she had always seemed the eternal spinster, staying at home, looking after her mother.

'Her mother's died at long last.'

'That's not a very nice thing to say.'

'Mrs Cayford, the old lady, wasn't very nice. Over eighty and kept her daughter on a tight leash.'

'Fast work though.'

'I hear he's a Yank.'

'He's black.'

'He's still a Yank. Lucky her. She'll be off to America. Wish it was me.'

Too busy supervising the induction of two new girls who had been refugees, one from Belgium and one from France, Maisie didn't comment. It was lunchtime and she was perusing Sid's latest card whilst eating some kind of fish which she guessed was the oddly named one that came from South Africa. There were fewer words now and his drawings were no more than matchstick men with no flesh on them whatsoever. The message was clear and tugged at her heartstrings. He was too weak to write and so thin he did indeed resemble a matchstick man, the kind a child would draw with no body, just a rudimentary frame.

Once she'd eaten as much fish as she was able and swamped the taste left in her mouth with a portion of jam roly-poly, she gathered her report on Francine and Arlette and made her way to Miss Cayford's office.

Thoughts of Sid occupied her mind as she walked along the corridor. Just as she reached the door, a few papers slid from her folder and floated to the ground. As she stooped to pick them up, a muffled sobbing came from the other side of the door.

Once she'd straightened, she counted to ten before tapping on it lightly

'Who is it?'

'Maisie Miles. You wanted to see me about the two new girls.'

'Oh yes. Come in. Please come in.'

The plants Miss Cayford grew in her office had once been ordinary house plants. They now mostly consisted of tomatoes and lettuce, depending on the time of year.

Miss Cayford herself was sitting red-faced behind her desk; it was obvious to Maisie that she'd been crying.

'Right,' Maisie said, determined the old Miss Cayford needed reassurance. 'Have you had lunch?'

Miss Cayford resumed her sobbing as she shook her head.

'Shall I get you something, though I must warn you it's only snook. The roly-poly's good though and it helps take the taste away.'

'No.' Again the shaking of head, the smallness of voice.

'A cup of tea?'

She didn't wait for a reply but after checking there was enough methylated spirit, lit the small camping stove and put on the kettle.

It wasn't easy to make small talk as she waited for the kettle to boil, so instead she talked about the two foreign girls who had lately joined the workforce.

'Arlette, the Belgian girl, is married. She speaks good English. Francine is single but doesn't know where her family is. I wonder at how hard they work, whether it's because they're trying to immerse themselves in something to take their mind off their troubles. It seems quite likely.'

Miss Cayford's sobs had subsided by the time the tea was poured. Maisie couldn't find any milk or sugar, so there was no other option but to drink it black.

'I think you'll agree that these girls are doing a good job and deserve to be kept on. Am I right?'

Miss Cayford nodded and even managed a weak smile. 'You're always right, Maisie. And you're strong. I think you're the strongest person I've ever known.'

Maisie looked at the finely chiselled face, the smart clothes, the bejewelled fingers, a sure sign that she was from quite a well-off family. Following on from what she had overheard back in the stripping room, she decided to be blunt and force the conversation.

'I heard you're engaged to be married. Where and when is it happening?'

Fresh tears dripped from Miss Cayford's overlong eyelashes. 'It isn't happening.'

Maisie took a sip of tea, more easily to moisten her mouth. Anyone else might have refrained from probing, but Maisie didn't do things that way.

'He's broken it off? Why is that?'

Miss Cayford shook her head. 'He didn't. It's the law. We're not allowed to marry because he's black and I'm white.' She gulped. 'That's United States law.'

Maisie was appalled. 'But we're not in the United States. We're in the United Kingdom.'

'It makes no difference. It's not allowed. Now, if you'll excuse me.'

Despair was replaced by dignity. Maisie left her there, respecting her privacy and in sympathy with her predicament. It just didn't seem fair. Lots of women had married their American sweethearts, but none, she realised – at least as far as she knew – had married black Americans. She recalled Jonah informing her that as twenty-six of the states forbade mixed marriages, then it was forbidden for all US states presently serving in Europe.

So much for fighting for justice, she thought to herself.

Somebody asked her about Carole being ill and giving in her notice.

'She needs an operation,' Maisie informed them – an outright lie, but the fact was Carole was getting too big to hide her pregnancy and the corset was no longer doing its job.

'Is she 'aving a leaving do?'

The questioner was nothing if not persistent.

'No. There won't be time. She's on about moving up north to be with 'er mother – at least for a time.'

'Thought she lived with you.'

'Well I ain't 'er bloody mother am I.'

Unwilling to answer any more awkward questions, she stalked off, her face slowly turning pink.

'Excuse me.'

She turned to face a fresh-faced girl who obviously worked in the office, judging by the simple blouse and skirt she was wearing. Maisie frowned. The girl's features were vaguely familiar.

'Do I know you?'

The girl's smile lit up her face as she extended her hand. 'I'm Sarah, Sid's sister. He tells me you're his sweetheart.'

'He did?' Maisie's eyebrows rose.

'I'm so glad of that. He needed someone to care, given where he is at the moment. Can't wait to see you both reunited. If the chance arises, and if it's not too cheeky of me, can I be a bridesmaid?'

Maisie wanted to laugh and say wherever did she get that idea? There was a hesitant pain behind Sarah's happy smile and it touched her that Sid attached such importance to her short letters. How could she let the girl down?

'If there's enough parachute silk to make a dress, you're on. But you might have to wait a while, until the war is over.'

'Wonderful!' said Sarah, clapping her hands together. 'I'll start looking for some right now.'

Out in the privacy of the ladies' cloakroom, alone in the pristine whiteness, Maisie broke into sobs. So much had happened over these last few years, so many people in dire circumstances when all they wanted was to be happy and live an ordinary life. For the life of her, she couldn't deny Sid that or Sarah too, for that matter, and there, mopping at her tear-filled eyes, she prayed for Sid and for everyone who had yet to come home. How would he be in a future that even now seemed so far off? She'd heard war did terrible things to people because they'd experienced such terrible things.

# 34

## PHYLLIS

The battlefield that was the heart of the Mediterranean was winding down and there was the prospect of being reassigned to a more active theatre of war.

It was a lot to hope that they would be assigned in the same theatre, but with a bit of plotting and planning, they worked something out – or thought they had. Their objective had been Europe where the Allies were riding roughshod over the enemy army which was in full retreat.

For a while they were on tenterhooks when Mick was offered a posting in the Far East where the Japanese were not making victory look easy.

He went as high as he could to achieve what he and they both wanted. At last he achieved success.

'I'm scheduled to fly reconnaissance over Europe, mainly concentrating on Normandy..'

Phyllis was offered a posting at RAF Duxford, a fighter base in the east of England. Mick was being posted to a lately established dedicated reconnaissance base close to Dover.

'We'll get leave.'

She felt his concern. 'Before it all happens,' she said quietly.

He said nothing but just stared into the distance. No date had been set for the invasion of Europe, but the scent of it was in the air.

They agreed that it was the best they could do. Under the circumstances, Phyllis decided that she had to give him enough slack to opt out of their affair, what with distance and other circumstances.

It was difficult, but she decided only fair that she confess to her relationship with Tom. Over a glass of mediocre wine, she told him all there was to know, how she'd felt, how healing it had been to share her sadness with Tom.

'He was in UXB. He died one day thanks to a booby-trapped mechanism. Gone forever,' she said softly, looking down into her glass of blood-red wine.

Mick didn't hesitate. His hand covered hers. 'Look, Phyl. I'm not blaming you. You thought I was dead. How else could I expect you to react? You're hardly committing adultery. It happens.'

His smile made her knees go weak and she felt the warmth of his hands through her cotton sleeves as he cradled her in his arms.

'Yes.' She nodded vigorously enough to shake her thoughts into some kind of order. She had so wanted to explain, to apologise that she'd had a relationship – a very short one as it turned out – with another man. 'You were away and he was so...'

'On the edge of his seat.'

She looked up at him, not quite understanding what he meant.

'Anyone dealing with unexploded bombs must feel they're on borrowed time. I felt it myself a few times, but the odds for blokes like him are pretty dire. Glad I learned how to fly.'

There was humour in the way he said it, yet she couldn't quite get away from this oppressive feeling of guilt.

'He's dead, but I think you should know that we were pretty close for a little while.'

'You're trying to tell me that you went the whole way with him.'

She caught her breath as though she were drowning, slipping into the deep and unable to thrash her way back up to the sunlight.

'Yes,' she said, the one word sticking like glue in her throat. 'Mick, I'm so sorry.'

He gave her a gentle shake. 'Don't be so bloody stupid!'

Her eyes filled with tears as she breathed back a sob. 'It's you that I loved – love,' she corrected herself.

He took her face between his calloused hands, the hands of a man who had always laboured hard for a living. 'Darling, darling, darling. Stop that right now. He's gone and we're still here.'

'You still want to marry me?'

He threw back his head, exposing the strong tendons lacing his neck. 'Phyllis, our emotions, our lives, have been thrown up in the air, along with the old rules we used to swear by. You sought solace, he sought solace and you sought solace from each other. Is that such a bad thing?'

She hung her head, eyes hidden behind a honey red tress. 'I shouldn't have.'

'I did.'

'What?' The stab of jealousy was sudden and short, replaced by outright curiosity.

Mick read her mind and smiled. 'Her name was Natalia and she showed me round the vineyards.'

'Did she now?' Just a little indignant.

His hair flicked over his eyes and he made a little clicking noise as he cocked the corner of his mouth. Then he threw back his head and burst out laughing. 'I took advantage of her. There was nothing she didn't know about vines. We'll be needing that knowledge when we establish our vineyard. And we're still doing that, Phyllis.

I'm holding you to it. Just you, me and row upon row of grape vines. The future is ours, yours, mine and a premier wine. And kids of course. I reckon we'll also have kids.'

Somehow she knew he was speaking the truth. That was the way it would be.

# HISTORICAL NOTES

Malta is a place I know very well. We used to keep our first sailing yacht in Grand Harbour and saw first-hand the wartime damage still showing on buildings in existence back then. Just up from there, I visited the underground shelters carved out of sheer rock centuries earlier, alcoves where people lived during the frequent air raids, some never venturing to the surface for close on two years.

Each summer for five years after that, my late husband and I sailed our second sailing yacht, Sarabande, from her winter base in Sicily down to Malta, mooring in Marsamxett Harbour. From there, we could gaze up on the splendid buildings termed 'Whitehall Mansions' where nurses and other female personnel were billeted. Just below there is a plaque commemorating the departure of the invasion force for Sicily.

For further reading, try *The White Ensign*, an account of Operation Pedestal, the tanker Ohio, and the final lifting of the Axis siege.

You might also try *The Kapillan of Malta* by Nicholas Montsarrat, which gently takes you through the history of Malta from its first flowering of civilisation.

Many people from all over the world visit the church in Mosta where the interior of the dome, hastily repaired and repainted, is still visible. So is a replica of the bomb that fell through the roof but failed to explode. A miracle indeed!

The heart of Bristol, an area of medieval buildings, their upper floors jutting out over their lover floor, constituted much of the old city centre. Destroyed in the air raid of November 1941, it was not rebuilt until after the war – and not nearly as attractive as it had been. Castle Street and its shopping thoroughfare is now Castle Green, a pleasant riverside walk dominated by the tower and fabric of St Peter's Church – all that remains of the city that Robert Louis Stevenson and Jonathan Swift would have known.

# MORE FROM LIZZIE LANE

We hope you enjoyed reading *Heaven and Hell for the Tobacco Girls*. If you did, please leave a review.

If you'd like to gift a copy, this book is also available as an ebook, digital audio download and audiobook CD.

Sign up to Lizzie Lane's mailing list for news, competitions and updates on future books:

http://bit.ly/LizzieLaneNewsletter

If you haven't yet why not discover the first in the series, *The Tobacco Girls*.

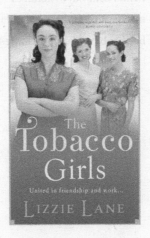

# ABOUT THE AUTHOR

**Lizzie Lane** is the author of over 50 books, a number of which have been bestsellers. She was born and bred in Bristol where many of her family worked in the cigarette and cigar factories. This has inspired her new saga series for Boldwood *The Tobacco Girls*.

Follow Lizzie on social media:

[f] facebook.com/jean.goodhind
[t] twitter.com/baywriterallat1
[IG] instagram.com/baywriterallatsea
[BB] bookbub.com/authors/lizzie-lane

# ABOUT BOLDWOOD BOOKS

Boldwood Books is a fiction publishing company seeking out the best stories from around the world.

Find out more at www.boldwoodbooks.com

Sign up to the Book and Tonic newsletter for news, offers and competitions from Boldwood Books!

http://www.bit.ly/bookandtonic

We'd love to hear from you, follow us on social media:

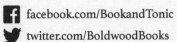

facebook.com/BookandTonic

twitter.com/BoldwoodBooks

instagram.com/BookandTonic

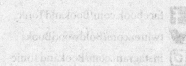